CURSE OF THE
JADE LILY

CURSE OF THE
JADE LILY

David
Housewright

MINOTAUR BOOKS
NEW YORK

CURSE OF THE JADE LILY. Copyright © 2012 by David Housewright. All rights reserved. Printed in the United States of America. For information, address St. Martin's Press, 175 Fifth Avenue, New York, N.Y. 10010.

www.minotaurbooks.com

Library of Congress Cataloging-in-Publication Data

Housewright, David, 1955–
    Curse of the Jade Lily : a McKenzie novel / David Housewright.–1st ed.
        p. cm.
    ISBN 978-0-312-64231-0 (hardcover)
    ISBN 978-1-4668-0262-9 (e-book)
    1. McKenzie, Mac (Fictitious character)—Fiction.
    2. Private investigators—Minnesota—Fiction. I. Title.
    PS3558.O8668C87 2012
    813'.54—dc23
                                                            2012005490

First Edition: June 2012

10 9 8 7 6 5 4 3 2 1

For Renée
always and forever

ACKNOWLEDGMENTS

I wish to acknowledge my debt to Tom Combs, M.D., India Cooper, Tammi Fredrickson, Keith Kahla, Alison J. Picard, Lisa Vecoli of the Minneapolis Institute of Arts, and Renée Valois.

CURSE OF THE
JADE LILY

ONE

The last time I saw Vincent Donatucci, he handed me a check for $3,128,584.50. My first thought when I found him standing outside my front door—I ain't giving it back!

"Hello, McKenzie," he said when I opened the door.

"Mr. Donatucci," I replied. A man makes you an instant millionaire, you call him mister. I opened the door wide enough to give him room to pass. "Come in."

He crossed the threshold and stamped the cold from his feet. He unbuttoned his gray trench coat but did not take it off. He looked around. All he saw was a painting I had bought at the Lowertown Arts Festival hanging on the near wall and a lot of empty carpet.

"How long have you lived here?" he asked.

"I moved in not long after I collected the reward on Teachwell."

Donatucci nodded meaningfully.

"Beer?" I asked. "Coffee?"

He glanced at his watch. It was eleven twenty in the A.M.

"Coffee," he said.

I led him to the kitchen, deliberately taking the route through the dining room so he could see that I had a table, chairs, and matching buffet. It was a large house and expensive. I bought it for my father and me, but he died soon after we moved in, and I hadn't done much with it since. Five of the rooms were still empty, although the master bedroom and bath were fully and, I like to think, tastefully decorated. So was what Dad called the family room, a large hall filled with a big-screen HDTV, Blu-ray DVD player, computer, CD stereo, plenty of chairs and sofas, including a two-hundred-year-old rocking chair, a large desk, floor lamps, and shelves filled with music, movies, and books. I was particularly fond of the kitchen where I stored all manner of culinary gadgets—mini-doughnut, sno-cone, and popcorn machines, iced tea maker, ice cream churn, pizza oven, pasta maker, a miniature guillotine used to halve bagels, a couple of toasters, and a $1,300 Jura-Capresso coffee and espresso maker that I snapped up for seven-fifty.

I poured Donatucci a mug of coffee, but none for myself. I watched intently while he sipped.

"Mmm, nice," he said.

I don't know why it was important that he be impressed. I guess I didn't want him to think I squandered the money.

Donatucci settled at the kitchen table, grunting and sighing as if every movement were an effort for him. He was old, with a face so deeply wrinkled that I wondered how he shaved; more wrinkles than when I had first met him six years ago. He stared out the kitchen window into my backyard.

"May I take your coat?" I asked. He didn't answer, and I wondered for a moment if he had heard me. "Mr. Donatucci?"

"No, I'm fine."

"Cookie?"

"Hmm?"

"I have a boatload of Girl Scout Cookies—Thin Mints, Samoas . . ."

He shook his head no.

"So tell me," I said. "To what do I owe the pleasure?"

"Hmm?"

"What brings you here?"

"Are those pet turkeys?"

Donatucci was watching the thirteen wild turkeys that gathered around my frozen pond. They were loitering in a large space where I had packed down the snow with a shovel and my boots. In the center of the area was a wooden box. I had piled dry corn and grain on top of the box, and the turkeys were taking turns picking at it.

"No, not pets," I said. "They showed up last year just before it started to snow. They must have liked it, because they came back again this year. I have a pal with the DNR who says they come into the city during the winter to forage for easy meals—I'm not the only one who feeds them. He says they'll return to the wild come spring, although I don't know what he means by the wild. The suburbs, I guess."

Donatucci nodded, sipped his coffee, and watched the turkeys some more. He seemed to be drifting off, and I called his name.

"I'm not deaf, McKenzie," he said.

"Sorry."

"I've been keeping tabs on you."

"Really?"

"People we make big payouts to, I like to keep an eye on them, see how the money changes them."

"Does the money change them?"

"Always. Always it changes them. Sometimes for the better. They become philanthropists, you know? Share the wealth. Most of the others, they become prisoners to their money. Not always their fault, though. Suddenly everyone wants a piece. Friends turn on them, usually out of resentment. Most end up wishing they could go back to the way it was before they were rich. And then there's you. You became Batman."

"Hardly."

Donatucci snorted. "Everything but the cape and the car," he said. "Tearing around, working with the cops; sometimes working against the cops; doing good for goodness' sake. Tell me I'm wrong."

"You're wrong."

He snorted again.

"Mr. Donatucci, exactly what is it that you want?"

"I need a favor," he said. "That's what you do, isn't it, now that you're not with the police anymore? Favors for friends."

"You're not my friend."

Donatucci smiled slightly. "You owe us," he said.

"Us?"

"Midwest Farmers Insurance Group."

"How do you figure that?"

"Three million one hundred and twenty-eight thousand—"

"That was a business deal, pure and simple," I said.

"—five hundred and eighty-four dollars and fifty cents."

"And if you could have avoided paying it, you would have."

Donatucci groaned slightly as he adjusted his position in the chair. He was a big man, someone you would have stepped aside from when he was young and limber. Not so much now.

"No insurance company pays off on a claim if it doesn't have to," he said.

"Then let's not talk about owing favors, all right?"

Donatucci took a long swallow of his coffee and then fixed his eyes on me. "Have you ever heard of the Jade Lily?" he asked.

"No."

"Are you sure? It's been advertised pretty heavily."

"Wait," I said. "Wait, wait, wait. Okay. There's a museum in Minneapolis that's been sending flyers. It even called a couple of times looking for donations. It has an art exhibit— the Jade Lily. Apparently there's a curse attached to it like King Tut's tomb. Something terrible is supposed to happen to whoever possesses it."

"Exactly right."

"What about it?"

Donatucci handed his empty mug to me. I asked if he would like a refill and he said yes. While I was pouring the coffee he answered my question. He spoke abruptly as if he wanted to see if my hand shook.

"It was stolen last night," Donatucci said.

I finished filling the mug and gave it to him. "So?"

"We want it back."

"We?"

"Midwest Farmers insured it for three-point-eight million."

"Why come to me? Call the cops. Call the FBI." I gestured toward Donatucci like a host welcoming a contestant to a game show. "I remember you were a fair investigator once."

"Still am."

"Well, then?"

"Where were you last night, McKenzie?"

"Are you asking if I have an alibi, Mr. Donatucci? Why would you ask?"

I had one. I was at the Minnesota Wild hockey game with Bobby Dunston, who coincidentally held the rank of commander in the Major Crimes and Investigations Division of the St. Paul Police Department. Yet I had no intention of telling Donatucci that. Come into my house and demand an alibi—screw that. I crossed my arms over my chest and leaned back against my kitchen counter.

"Any other favors you want?" I asked.

Donatucci waved his mug at me. "This is good coffee," he said.

"Yes, it is."

"You're upset."

"Not particularly. Just impatient."

"I didn't want to come here, McKenzie. I think it's unethical."

"Then why are you here?"

"I need a favor."

"We're back to that, are we?"

"The Jade Lily was stolen from the City of Lakes Art Museum last night. At eight o'clock this morning, the artnappers placed a call to the museum's executive director, a woman named Perrin Stewart."

"Artnappers?" I said.

"What else would you call them?"

"You tell me."

"The artnappers told Ms. Stewart that they were willing to sell the Lily back to the museum for a third of its insured value. It goes against my better judgment, but we agreed—my company and the museum agreed. We have a couple of days to get the cash together, and then the artnappers will contact us with instructions."

"I can appreciate why it pisses you off, Mr. Donatucci. Yet this sort of thing happens all the time, am I right?"

"Not all the time, but yeah, it happens. That's pretty much how you got your money, if memory serves."

"So why are you here against your better judgment?"

"We want to hire you to act as go-between—deliver the money, retrieve the Lily. We'll pay you ten percent of the ransom."

"You must be kidding."

"No, I'm not."

I started laughing just the same. "No, no, no," I said.

"McKenzie . . ."

"Not a chance."

"One hundred and twenty-five thousand dollars."

"I don't care if it's a million. A guy could get killed doing that sort of thing, and luckily for me—thanks to the Midwest Farmers Insurance Group—I don't need the money."

"That's what I told them you'd say."

"Them?"

"The museum board and my boss."

"Wait a minute. Coming to me, that wasn't your idea?"

"Of course not."

"Well, whose idea was it?"

"The thieves."

"What?"

"They asked for you. They said, 'Send McKenzie with the money or it's no deal.' "

That threw me. I turned my back on Donatucci and took a long time filling a mug with coffee for myself. I slowly sat at the table across from Donatucci and stared at the turkeys.

They asked for me, my inner voice said. *Me? Why would they do that?*

Donatucci watched and waited.

"Who are those guys?" I asked.

"Have you ever done this sort of thing before?"

"Act as a go-between?"

Donatucci nodded.

I explained that there had been two occasions. The first was when I delivered the ransom after Bobby Dunston's daughter was kidnapped, but all the people involved in that incident were either dead or in prison. The only other time was when I helped out a woman named Jenny, an acquaintance from the old neighborhood who had married really, really well—at least that's what I thought at the time. Unfortunately, her husband cared more about making money than he did about her, and Jenny drifted into an affair with a man she had met on the Internet. They arranged to meet at a hotel. When she woke the next morning, he was gone and so were the jewels her husband had given her—matching necklace, earrings, and brooch. The thief offered to sell the jewels back before Jenny's husband missed them—sell them for more than they were worth—and she agreed. I handled the exchange. I went to a motel and waited in the room the thief had designated. When he called, I left the money in the room and went to a second room that he specified. That's where I found the jewelry. I packed it up, and after a few minutes I went home. I never saw the thief.

"He was penny ante," I said. "I doubt he could manage a caper like this. Besides, he didn't know my name."

"The thieves know you from somewhere," Donatucci said.

"Just because they know me doesn't mean I know them."

"That's true. The thieves could have heard your name

somewhere. Where would they have heard your name, Mc-Kenzie?"

I shook my head slowly even as I wondered the same thing myself.

"You keep saying thieves," I said.

"There are at least two," Donatucci said. "Unfortunately, we can only ID the man who walked out of the museum with the Lily tucked under his arm."

"Who was that?"

Donatucci smiled. There was this girl in high school; because of her I joined the chess club. The president of the chess club was a good guy, backed up the starting point guard on the school basketball team. He would smile just like Donatucci when I fell into one of his traps, which was just about every time we played.

"C'mon," I said. "Don't do this to me."

Donatucci smiled some more. "Do what, Batman?" he said.

"Give me a break."

"My advice, McKenzie? Forget the whole thing."

I knew what Donatucci was trying to do, and I wasn't going for it.

"You know what?" I said. "That's exactly what I'm going to do—forget the whole thing."

"What difference does it make if the artnappers asked for you? You don't know who they are. It has nothing to do with you."

"Besides, you don't need me."

"Don't need you, don't want you."

"If I don't act as go-between, the thief, the thieves, they'll find someone else."

"For one-point-three mill, you know they will." Donatucci stood up and started buttoning his coat. "Just go about your business, McKenzie. Tend your turkeys. Forget about the Jade Lily. Forget I was even here."

I stared out the window, watching the turkeys peck at the food on top of the box.

Batman was a vigilante nut job, my inner voice said. *That's not me. It's not! Still, he was my favorite superhero when I was a kid. Him and Spider-Man, who was a bit of a vigilante, too.* I took a deep breath. *Damn the Lily. Damn the thieves. Damn Mr. Donatucci, that old man. He should have retired years ago.*

Donatucci made his way as noisily as possible to the arch between the kitchen and the dining room. I turned toward him just as he knew I would. He was smiling again.

"Do you play chess, Mr. Donatucci?"

"Yes. Do you?"

"Yeah, but apparently not very well."

"We should play sometime."

"I think we already have. One hundred twenty-seven thousand."

"Excuse me?"

"You said ten percent of the ransom. That's a hundred and twenty-seven thousand."

"So it is."

"Plus expenses."

"In that case, you can buy lunch."

Dammit.

Besides Mr. Donatucci and myself, there were six men and one woman gathered around a long table in a windowless conference room. Three of the men looked as if they wished they were somewhere else doing something far more important. From the expressions on the faces of the other three, this was as much fun as they'd had in quite a while. The woman, on the other hand, was visibly agitated. She was one of those ultra-chic plus-size gals that gave you the impression she could have been Heidi Klum if only she dropped a hundred pounds.

"This is an emergency meeting of the executive board of trustees," she said.

"Hey, Perrin. Who are you talking to?" asked one of the happier board members. "We all know why we're here, Madam President."

"Ms. Stewart is not the president," said the man next to him. "She's the executive director. We don't have a president, remember?"

"Whose idea was that?"

"It was yours, Mr. Anderson," Perrin said. She folded her hands on top of a manila folder that lay on the table directly in front of her. She tried to appear calm but didn't quite manage it.

"Since when did you start listening to me?" Anderson said.

From the spelling of his name, I knew Anderson was Norwegian, which made him part of a dwindling minority. Used to be you couldn't swing a dead cat without hitting a Norwegian around here. Not so much anymore. While Minnesota's population is still essentially white and Northern European, the number of our Asian, Hispanic, and African residents is increasing steadily. That has annoyed some people, mostly politicians, who have demanded that the cops conduct "immigration stops" to make sure they're all here legally, Minnesota Nice be damned. On the other hand, the food is better.

"Can we get on with it, please?" asked one of the more serious members.

"For the benefit of Mr. McKenzie," Perrin said, "I will introduce each member of the board."

She went around the room. Everyone was a mister, everyone was a prominent something or other. When she reached Anderson, he said, "Geezuz, Stewart," and made a big production out of looking at his watch. "I need to get back to the office."

Finally Perrin reached the sixth man.

"Mr. Randolph Fiegen," she said.

Fiegen was in his late fifties and elegantly dressed. He reminded me of Donald Trump in that he sported the most elaborate and artful comb-over that I had ever seen. Certainly he had that look of contempt on his face that some people get when they've been ordering people around for a long time. He didn't give Perrin a chance to add any accolades.

"I think I speak for all of us when I thank you for agreeing to help us, Mr. McKenzie," he said.

"I didn't agree to anything yet."

"Oh?" Fiegen's sad, cold eyes regarded me carefully. "I was under the impression that you had. You see, the future of this fine museum may very well hang in the balance."

"How so?" I asked.

Fiegen spread his hands wide. "For a young institution like ours," he said, "reputation is everything."

"How does this work?" I asked. "Who owns the museum?"

"City of Lakes is a nonprofit organization," Perrin said. "By definition, we do not have private owners, and while we are able to earn a profit, or, more accurately, a surplus, none of the moneys are paid out to shareholders. Instead, such earnings are retained by the museum for our self-preservation."

"Bullshit," Anderson said. "We own it. When I say we, I mean the board of trustees, because we're the ones that'll be picking up the tab should this place fail. Right now there are forty-seven members on the board. You become a trustee when you contribute half of seven figures or better to the museum, except for the mayor of Minneapolis, two state senators, and a couple members of the state house who are honorary members. The trustees elected the six of us to serve three-year terms on the executive board. I should point out that we all ran unopposed. No one else wanted the job. Madam Executive Director here was hired by the executive board to oversee the day-to-day operation of the museum. She serves at our pleasure. How's that working out, by the way?"

Perrin didn't reply, although, from the look she gave Anderson, I thought it fortunate that the formidable conference table lay between them.

"Calm yourself, Derek," Fiegen said. To me he added, "Derek enjoys comporting himself in an insouciant manner. Clearly it is a facade."

Anderson smirked. I might have, too, if only I had known what "insouciant" meant.

"Tell me how the Lily was stolen," I said.

"Is that necessary?" Perrin said.

"It'll give me an idea of who I am dealing with," I said.

Anderson rubbed his hands together. "This is my favorite part," he said.

Perrin scrunched up her face, and for a moment she looked less like Heidi Klum and more like Margaret Hamilton, who played the Wicked Witch of the West in *The Wizard of Oz*. She unscrunched and started speaking slowly and carefully, as if she were afraid I might ask her to repeat something. She started by saying that the City of Lakes Art Museum had the most sophisticated electronic security system available; that it had been thoroughly vetted and updated just six months earlier. Anderson had a nice laugh at that, but Perrin continued.

"A forced-entry theft or a smash and grab, I believe that is what it is called, is virtually impossible now," she said. "The crime was an inside job."

"They usually are," I said.

I glanced at Donatucci for confirmation, but he sat quietly, his hands folded on the table in front of him, his half-closed eyes staring at a painting on the conference room wall. I don't know why. The painting consisted solely of primary colors that looked like they had been splashed on the canvas by a frustrated third grader.

"We have a rear entrance," Perrin said. "It consists of a series of small rooms. It is impossible to unlock and open the street door leading to the first room without first closing and locking the interior door. You cannot unlock and open the interior door without first securing the next door. And so on. A door that is left open for more than twenty seconds will activate an alarm. Also, digital cameras cover each room. Guards monitoring the cameras can electronically seal all the doors if they see anything amiss."

"Bandit traps," I said.

"Just so," Fiegen said, to prove that he was listening.

"Here," Perrin said. She opened the folder in front of her and slipped a half-dozen photographs off the top and pushed them before me. The photos had the muddy feel of stills taken from a videotape. They showed a figure dressed in black with a black ski mask hiding his face working a keypad, opening a door, moving through a room, and then heading outside.

"At two o'clock last night," Perrin said, "or this morning if you prefer, our deputy director in charge of security, a man named Patrick Tarpley, carrying a package under his arm that we now believe contained the Jade Lily, walked through the bandit traps. Cameras show that he opened the doors using codes that he punched into the keypads and strolled—he wasn't hurrying at all—to an unidentified red SUV that pulled up just as he was leaving the building. He handed the package to someone sitting in the passenger seat of the SUV. The SUV drove off. Tarpley then went into the parking ramp adjacent to the museum, got into his own car, and drove away."

Two thoughts piled on top of each other. The first—three thieves, the man dressed in black, the driver of the SUV, and the passenger. *Donatucci must have lost a step*, my inner voice said. *He said earlier that he didn't know if there were more than two thieves.* The second thought I spoke out loud—"How do you know it was Tarpley?"

"He checked in at 4:00 P.M, but there is no evidence of him checking out," Donatucci said. "Only two other people knew the security codes, and they were both accounted for. No one has seen him since the theft was committed. Also, he knew the schedule of the guards. He made his move at the exact moment of a shift change. That's why the guards that were supposed to be watching the monitors didn't override the codes."

Why bother with a mask, then? my inner voice asked.

"Had he ever conducted security drills similar to this?" I asked.

"No," Perrin said, "but our director of security had."

"Where is the director of security?"

"On vacation in Africa."

"Did you contact him?"

"Why?" Anderson said. "What can he do about it?"

"Have you contacted the police?"

"We are hoping that will be unnecessary," Perrin said.

"The Lily was stolen last night, but you didn't get a ransom call until eight this morning. You waited six hours without reporting the theft because you expected a call, didn't you? Why were you expecting a call? Anybody?"

Fiegen shifted uncomfortably in his chair. "That was my decision," he said.

"This has happened before, hasn't it?"

Neither Fiegen nor anyone else said yes. They didn't say no, either.

I said, "The cops don't like it when you neglect to report a major crime. They especially frown on it when you arrange to buy back stolen property."

"Yet it's done all the time," Donatucci said softly, as if he didn't care whether he was heard or not. "You said so yourself."

"We prefer to deal with this quietly if at all possible," Fiegen said.

"Trying to protect your reputation," I said, repeating what he mentioned earlier.

Fiegen gently tugged at his hair just behind his right ear as if he were fingering an heirloom. "Some of the artwork we exhibit is on loan to the museum, like the Jade Lily," he said. "In addition, there are the numerous traveling exhibits that we compete for. If word should leak that we are unreliable custodians . . ."

"City of Lakes doesn't own the Lily?" I asked.

"No," Perrin said. "The owner of the Lily lives in Chicago.

He was good enough to loan the piece to us. He has not yet been informed of the theft."

"Who is on the hook for the insurance, you or him?"

"We are. The lending agreement clearly states that the borrower—City of Lakes—is responsible for the loss or damage to the artwork while the art is on our premises, in the amount of the stated value of the art."

"Who decides what the stated value—"

"We agreed to insure the Lily for the same amount that his insurance company had insured it for," Fiegen said. "Is this important?"

"How valuable is the Lily? I mean compared to the rest of your exhibits."

"Top twenty," Donatucci said.

That made me pause for a few beats.

"How long did Tarpley work for you?" I asked.

"He was hired three months before the museum opened," Perrin said. "We will celebrate our second anniversary a week from Saturday. May I add, his credentials were impeccable and thoroughly vetted. He had worked at several other museums without as much as a whisper of improper behavior. We also investigated his wife, Von. She was the soul of propriety as well."

"Do you have a photograph?"

Perrin found two colored glossies in the file in front of her and passed them across the table. The first was a head shot of Tarpley, like the kind used for identification badges. He was an older man, at least fifty, with features that suggested he might have been handsome once. His eyes seemed flat, though, as if all the energy had been drained out of them. It could have been a trick of the photographer, but the picture gave him all the vitality of a paper bag. The woman in the second photograph, however, seemed full of life. She was perhaps twenty years younger and had a quizzical smile on her lips and dancing lights in her brown eyes, as if she considered her good looks to be a lucky accident, like finding a 1943 copper penny in the street.

"It doesn't make sense," I said. "Forget asking why this seemingly honest man turned thief or why he waited twenty-seven months before making his move. He could have taken many items, yet he didn't. Instead, he took only one piece, and the piece he took didn't even rank in the top ten in value. What's wrong with this picture?"

"If he wished to harm the museum, he couldn't have done better than taking the Lily," Perrin said. "It was the cornerstone of our year-two celebration. We are a young museum, as Mr. Fiegen stated. It was hoped that the publicity and attention garnered by the exhibit would help us gain the same respect and prominence currently enjoyed by the Minneapolis Institute of Arts and the Walker Art Center."

"If Tarpley was looking to hurt the museum, why would he offer to sell the Lily back?" I asked.

"Who gives a shit?" Anderson said.

"Derek, please," Fiegen said.

"C'mon. We've already had this discussion." Anderson gestured toward Donatucci, who continued to stare at the painting. "McKenzie, we're not asking you to solve the crime or catch the thieves. As far as we know, you might be in on it."

"Is that what you think?"

Anderson raised the palms of his hands toward heaven. "The thieves asked for you," he said. "Why is that?"

I didn't know, and not knowing was the only reason I

didn't get up and walk out of the room; maybe slap Anderson a time or two before I left.

"Well?" Anderson said.

"Kiss my ass," I told him.

"Whoa," he said. He pointed at me even as he turned to the man sitting next to him. "I like this guy."

Perrin set her large hand on my wrist.

Fiegen leaned toward me. "Mr. McKenzie," he said, "I hope you will forgive Derek's outburst."

"No, I won't," I said. "On the other hand, it is a question that needs asking, isn't it? Look, this go-between business is all a matter of trust. You're trusting me with one-point-three million bucks because Mr. Donatucci convinced you that I won't take it to the nearest Indian casino and bet it on red; that I'll use it to get the Lily back. I'm guessing that for some reason the artnappers trust that I'll give them the ransom with no tricks; that they won't end up with a suitcase filled with old telephone books and a face-to-face with a SWAT team. As for me, I have to trust that the artnappers won't take the money and the Lily and leave me with a bullet in my back."

"Isn't that why we're paying you a hundred and twenty-five grand?" Anderson asked, "To take that risk?"

"It's a hundred and twenty-seven, and while I expect to be paid, if I do this thing it won't be for the money."

"What would trigger your participation?" Fiegen asked.

I shook my head slowly because I didn't have a satisfactory answer for him. So far, I had been motivated by curiosity—but as the proverb says, curiosity killed the cat.

Satisfaction brought it back, my inner voice said.

Cats have nine lives, I told myself. I have only the one.

"No hard feelings, McKenzie, huh?" Anderson said. "We just need to know—will you help us get the Lily back?"

The timing of the question couldn't have been better, because a few seconds after Anderson asked it, the cell phone in Donatucci's pocket rang. He answered it and listened for a moment.

"Ask him yourself," he said. "He's sitting right here."

Donatucci set the cell on top of the conference room table and slid it toward me.

"It's the thieves," he said.

TWO

Lake Calhoun is the biggest of the twenty-two lakes found within the City of Minneapolis. When TV networks come to town to broadcast live sporting events, they usually set their cameras on the southwestern shore of the lake because it gives them a gorgeous establishing shot of the city skyline reflected in the water. That's where I had parked, on the southwest shore, as the thieves had instructed. Now I was walking along the 3.1 miles of plowed jogging trail that circled the lake with a red rose in my hand—also as I had been instructed. The sky was brilliant blue and the sun was dazzling, but that was just for show. It was so damn cold that the petals of the rose froze solid a few moments after I left my Jeep Cherokee. My hands and feet nearly froze, too. I was dressed to endure the chill that I expected to encounter dashing between warm buildings and warm cars, not for the numbing cold that blew off a frozen lake in Minnesota in January.

The rose was for identification purposes. It meant that

while the artnappers knew my name, they didn't actually know me or what I looked like. Demanding that I carry it around the lake gave them a chance to get a good look at me. Meanwhile, I wouldn't be able to distinguish them from all the other men and women who nodded and smiled as we passed on the trail. Or maybe they were hiding in a snow-drift or camped out on one of the countless benches taking my photograph. It was unlikely that Tarpley would have risked being discovered—he had to know that I would have seen his photograph by now. Of course, it could have been just a test designed to see how well I followed instructions. They demanded that I give them the number of my cell phone when we spoke. Maybe they'd call and tell me to drive to the Mall of America. Maybe they'd tell me to jump in the lake. The only thing I knew for certain was that everything they'd done so far, including involving me in their affairs, smacked of deliberation.

I had been circling counterclockwise around the lake, walking at a brisk pace for no better reason than to keep warm. I hoped Donatucci wasn't following me. The artnappers demanded that I come alone, and I said I would. I made Donatucci promise that there would be no surveillance of any kind, either at the lake or later when I delivered the money; nothing that would make the thieves twitchy. It might seem counterintuitive, but I felt I would be much safer without backup than with it. 'Course, I've been wrong before.

I passed the Thirty-second Street Beach and the sailing school, making my way toward West Lake Street and the edge of Uptown, an eclectic neighborhood of bars, clubs, restaurants, cafés, coffeehouses, retail shops, movie theaters, and one decent blues joint. I thought about the blues joint and the bars and restaurants as I made my turn around the top of the lake, telling myself how well a warm beverage would go down right about then. Like I said, though, the artnappers might have been testing to see how well I followed instructions, so I kept walking, moving past the North Beach and following the trail until I was heading south.

I was at about the 2.5-mile mark when they made their move, two men coming up fast behind me. I heard their footsteps and turned my head just as the larger of the men knocked me to the asphalt. The trail was icy and I skidded a few feet—I dropped the rose. The large man put a knee against my spine, pinning me down while he cuffed my hands behind my back. The smaller man pulled a black hood over my head. I protested.

"This isn't necessary," I said.

They didn't care. They yanked me to my feet and half carried, half dragged me through the snow. A woman screamed. A man shouted, "What's going on?" The two men paused. I heard the sound of a door being pulled back on rollers. A van, I guessed. I was shoved into the vehicle. The door was slammed shut. The vehicle started moving, picked up speed. There were a lot of sharp turns taken too fast. The van hit a patch of ice and fishtailed dangerously after one turn before the driver brought it under control.

"Anyone ever teach you how to drive in the winter?" I asked.

The driver didn't respond. Perhaps he didn't hear me through the hood.

Minutes seem like hours in a situation like that, so I couldn't tell you how long we drove. I tried to remain calm. I reminded myself that the thieves needed me to get their money. They might try to frighten me to death, but they weren't going to kill me. There was no profit in it.

I wasn't kicked or punched or slapped around, although rolling about the van floor with my hands cuffed behind my back was hardly the most comfortable I've been. The kidnappers didn't threaten or curse me, and I didn't threaten or curse them. Nor I did I demand that they tell me who they were or where we were going or what they wanted. There didn't seem to be much point. I just tried to maintain my balance and concentrate while we whipped around corner after corner.

Sharp corners meant city driving, my inner voice told me. *No freeways; no long country roads.*

Eventually the van slowed to a stop. The door slid open again. I felt the frigid wind blow into the cargo area. A woman said, "Are you sure you weren't followed?"

A man answered, "I'm sure."

"Did you search him?" the woman asked. "Did you check for a wire, for a GPS transmitter?"

"Oh shit," the man said.

Suddenly there were hands patting me down, checking my pockets.

"I'm not wired, and I don't have a tracking device," I said. "I don't have your money, either, so what the hell, guys?"

"I'm not interested in money, McKenzie," the woman said. "I'm interested in the Jade Lily."

A pair of hands pulled me off the floor and sat me upright so my back was resting against the wall of the van. Someone yanked off the hood. I blinked against the light. When my eyes focused, I found myself staring into the face of one of the loveliest women I had ever known—and the most treacherous.

"Heavenly Petryk," I said.

She smiled her dazzling smile, opened her arms, the palms of her hands facing upward, and said, "Ta da."

The door was closed and the van's heater was working. Heavenly pulled off a knit hat, allowing her golden hair to flow over her neck and shoulders, and opened her coat to reveal a black turtleneck sweater that seemed awfully tight and not because she had put on weight recently. Her shimmering blue eyes reminded me of a half-wild feline; the kind that was well fed by doting owners who nevertheless allowed it to roam unrestricted at night. She knelt next to me on the floor of the van.

"Kidnapping, Heavenly?" I said. "Really? You couldn't just pick up a phone and call?"

"I need you to know that I mean business," she said. "The last time our paths crossed, I don't think you took me seriously."

"I took you very seriously, especially after your friends threatened to shoot me."

"Oh, they were just fooling."

I glanced at the three men in the van with us. None of them were holdovers from Heavenly's previous band of miscreants, yet they all matched her criteria—they were young, good-looking, and well-muscled and watched her every move as if she were Aphrodite in earthly form. I doubted that the three of them together could have removed the childproof cap from a bottle of aspirin.

"Are you fooling now?" I asked.

Heavenly smiled and patted my knee. "It's good to see you again, McKenzie," she said.

"Gosh, Heavenly. It's good to see you, too. How long has it been?"

I already knew the answer—twenty-six months. I reminded her that she and I and a fairly motley group of scoundrels had rummaged through much of St. Paul in search of gold bullion hidden decades earlier by the notorious bank robber Frank "Jelly" Nash.

"That was fun," Heavenly said. "We made a lot of money. Not as much as we were hoping, but still . . ."

"What are you doing?" I asked. "Why am I here?"

"To hear my pitch."

"Pitch?"

"I know the thieves want to sell the Jade Lily back to the museum. I knew they would pick a go-between to handle the transaction. I honestly didn't know it would be you until early this morning."

Early this morning? my inner voice said. *She knew before I did.*

"Are you saying you didn't steal the Lily?" I asked.

"Of course not."

"You're not the one who sent me around Lake Calhoun with a red rose in my hand?"

"Why would I do that?"

Why, indeed? Heavenly wouldn't need a rose to identify me. She already knew what I looked like, knew where I lived; she probably still had my cell phone number.

"Besides," Heavenly said, "if I had stolen the Jade Lily, I sure as hell wouldn't have involved you. You're a dangerous man, McKenzie."

I didn't know if that was a compliment or not.

"Since we're all friends here, why don't you uncuff me?" I said.

Heavenly laughed at the suggestion. "Oh, you," she said and patted my knee again. She gestured at her three thugs. "This is the famous Rushmore McKenzie I told you about. Do you think we should take off his handcuffs?"

The one nearest her said, "Yeah, go 'head. He doesn't look like much."

"Tommy, Tommy." Heavenly shook her head at the insult and gave him a maternal smile; the kind mothers give their children when they say something foolish. "I think we'll keep the cuffs on."

"So, Hep, are you going to talk to me, what?" I said.

"You remembered my nickname."

"Heavenly Elizabeth Petryk. Who could forget?"

She gave my knee another playful pat. "You're sweet," she said. "Okay, where should we begin? What do you know about the Lily?"

"Very little, I'm afraid," I said. "Truth is, I haven't even seen what it looks like."

"It's beautiful, McKenzie. Exquisite. It's fourteen inches long, nine inches wide, six inches deep, and it's carved from a single block of imperial jade mined in Burma, or whatever they call that country these days. That's the good stuff, imperial jade—intense emerald green color and semitransparent. It was stolen from a Burmese artisan by a Chinese warlord around 1800. Now I admit that part of the story is a little murky. However, we do know for historic fact that the Lily was presented to Jaiqing Emperor, the sixth emperor of the Qing Dynasty, in China in August of 1820, although we don't know who gave it to him or why. On September second of that year, Jaiqing was struck by lightning and died. They say that's when the curse began—the curse of the Jade Lily."

I had to smile, not at the curse but at the obvious joy it gave Heavenly to tell me about it. The first time I met Heavenly, she was in the Minnesota History Center Research Library investigating everything she could find about Jelly

Nash and the gangsters that resided in St. Paul when it was an "open city." She lived for this sort of thing.

"Eventually, the Lily became the property of Empress Dowager Cixi," Heavenly said. "It didn't do her any good, either. The Empress Dowager ruled China during the Boxer Rebellion. The Boxers were simple peasants who resisted the Western powers that wanted to carve China into colonies—France, Germany, Austria-Hungary, Spain, Belgium, Russia, Japan, the Netherlands. The only countries that didn't want to colonize China were the United States and Great Britain, although the British were intent on milking her for everything they could get.

"At first the Empress Dowager attempted to suppress the Boxers in order to appease the Europeans. When the German envoy was murdered on June 20, 1900, she realized that there was going to be hell to pay anyway, so she went all in. She committed the imperial troops to battle and declared war on all the Western powers. The foreign delegations that were in Beijing at the time—back then it was called Peking—took refuge in a fortified compound. They held out for fifty-five days under relentless assault and artillery bombardment until an army consisting of troops from eight different nations relieved them.

"That's when things got really ugly. The Europeans literally raped China. Stole everything that wasn't nailed down and a lot that was. Great Britain held loot auctions every afternoon because it wanted to make sure that 'looting on the part of British troops be carried out in the most orderly manner.' That's an actual quote. It was through a loot auction that the Jade Lily fell into the hands of Colonel G. Nicholas Chaffee, a British serving officer.

"Chaffee was one of those *'Take up the White Man's bur-*

den' kind of guys. Once the Chinese were subjugated, he volunteered for duty in India—apparently he wanted to help keep the natives in check following the Indian Famine. But while on his way to Bombay, Chaffee's ship sank—no one has ever been able to figure out how or why—and Chaffee drowned. Chaffee's widow quickly sold the Lily to the ninth Earl of Huntington for the princely sum of one hundred and fifty pounds. He was killed when the British captured Baghdad from the Ottoman Turks in March 1917 during the First World War. He was run over by General Sir Frederick Stanley Maude's command car—I am not making this up. The Lily then became the property of his brother, the tenth Earl of Huntington, who was military attaché to the British Embassy in what was then called the State of Serbs, Croats, and Slovenes but we know as Yugoslavia. His wife prominently displayed the Lily at social functions and delighted in telling guests about the curse until she died of an undiagnosed ailment. Soon after, the earl gave the Lily to his daughter Lady Julia as a wedding present when she married a Serb politician. A week later, Yugoslavia was invaded by the Nazis. Are you following me?"

"You make the Lily sound like one of the Four Horsemen of the Apocalypse," I said.

"I'm just saying, bad luck follows the Lily," Heavenly said. "For example, Lady Julia and her husband fought with Tito's partisans against the Nazis—apparently she was one helluva girl. However, they protested when Tito took control of the country after the war and established a constitution patterned after the Soviet Union's. They were both shot. The Lily then fell into the hands of the politician's sister, who had no idea what it was. She packed it up in a box and stored it in a bank vault in Sarajevo, where it was forgotten until her daughter,

Tatjana Durakovic, rediscovered it following her mother's death in 1992. Unfortunately, before Tatjana had a chance to cash in on her find, the Yugoslav Wars broke out, and what a happy little bloodbath that was."

"How many dead?" I asked. "One hundred thousand?"

"Twice that. Most of Tatjana's family was among them. Eventually, the war ended, Yugoslavia was divvied up along ethnic lines, and Tatjana's little part of the world became Bosnia and Herzegovina. Unfortunately, by then the bank in Sarajevo had been looted and the Lily stolen. Tatjana immigrated to the United States, met a nice guy, married, became a U.S. citizen, and now is running a resort on the south shore of Lake Superior in Ontonagon, a small village in the Upper Peninsula of Michigan. But the story doesn't end there."

"I didn't think it would."

"Somehow—I don't have the details—the Lily fell into the hands of Dr. Arnaud Fornier, a French oncologist who dabbled in Asian art. Dr. Fornier sold the Lily at auction to Leo Gillard, an American. The publicity and money the good doctor earned from the sale convinced him to retire from medicine and open a gallery specializing in jade. However, he didn't have the resources necessary to acquire true jade artifacts for his many newfound customers, so he resorted to forgery. Dr. Fornier is now doing time in La Santé Prison in Paris for art fraud. He represented himself at trial, never a good idea."

"No, never," I agreed.

"Meanwhile, the man who bought the Lily from him, who lived in Chicago, by the way—"

"Lived?" I said.

"Leo Gillard died last summer," Heavenly said. "He took part in a yacht race that starts at Navy Pier in downtown

Chicago and ends at Mackinac Island. The race had been run for over a hundred years without a single fatality until he fell off his boat and drowned. The weather was perfect, too. People were so shocked, they thought his crew must have mutinied and made him walk the plank, but there was no evidence of such."

"And so," I said.

"And so the Lily became the property of Gillard's son, Jeremy, who apparently believed enough of the curse that he loaned the Jade Lily to the City of Lakes Art Museum. The museum is using the Lily to promote its anniversary. There was also talk of making it part of a traveling exhibit that could be displayed by other museums, for a price of course."

"Until it was stolen."

"Until it was stolen," Heavenly repeated.

"Which you had nothing to do with."

"Nothing at all."

"Then why are you here? Better yet, why am I here?"

"Because you're going after the Lily. It is your intention to buy it back from the artnappers and return it to the museum."

"If you say so."

"I do say so, but here's the thing, McKenzie—the Lily belongs to Tatjana Durakovic. She had pretty much forgotten about it until she saw all the publicity that the City of Lakes generated. Now she wants it back."

"Ahh," I said. Suddenly it all made sense to me. "You represent Tatjana."

"Yes."

"Did she come to you or did you contact her?"

Heavenly shrugged. "Does it matter?" she said.

"How much is Tatjana paying you?"

"Twenty-five percent of whatever the Lily realizes at auction. We believe it will sell for a lot more than the insured value. The other day a two-hundred-and-fifty-year-old jade water buffalo sold for over four million pounds."

"How much is that in real money?"

"Six-point-six million dollars."

"A tidy sum," I said. "What do you want from me?"

"You understand that the Jade Lily is Tatjana's property. It was stolen from her."

"That's not my concern."

"McKenzie, I'm asking you to do the right thing."

"What's the right thing?"

"After you make the exchange, after you buy the Lily from the artnappers, bring it to me. I'll give it to Tatjana."

"No."

"No? Just like that, no?"

"If Tatjana wants the Lily, tell her to hire a lawyer."

"C'mon, McKenzie. Think about it."

"Nothing to think about. I'm not going to break my word to the museum."

"I'll give you ten percent of my end."

Instead of answering, I just smiled at the suggestion.

"That's what I thought you'd say." Heavenly's lovely face became very sad, very serious. "But I had to ask."

"Where does that leave us?"

Heavenly patted my knee again. "Don't worry, McKenzie. We're still friends."

"Uh-huh."

"If you won't help me, I'll get the Lily from the thieves myself." Heavenly's smile suddenly became as luminous as ever. "Failing that, I'll just have to steal it from you."

"Do you know who has the Lily?"

Heavenly leaned in close. "Do you know the secret to a successful relationship?" she asked. "Secrets."

Heavenly kissed me full on the mouth. I might have resisted except, well, my hands were cuffed behind me.

"See you around, McKenzie," she said. Heavenly slid open the door to the van and stepped out. "Tommy, take McKenzie back to Lake Calhoun. Don't be foolish enough to give him the keys to the handcuffs until you're safely driving out of the parking lot."

Heavenly's thugs—they were far too pretty to be called that, but still—did exactly as she told them, the one named Tommy handing me the key through the window of the van before driving off. I unwound the cuffs and dropped them into the pocket of my coat—you never know when they might come in handy. I walked through the cold toward the South Beach. It was nearly 5:00 P.M. and already dark; the lights of the city's skyline glistened like stars against the snow and ice. My cell phone played the Ella Fitzgerald–Louis Armstrong cover of "Summertime" just as I reached the Jeep Cherokee. I answered the way I always did.

"McKenzie," I said.

"What the hell is going on?" a voice asked. It was a young man's voice—he made no attempt to disguise it electronically or otherwise.

"Did you get a good look at me walking around the lake with the rose?"

"We got a good look at the people who jumped you and dragged you off. What was that about?"

We, my inner voice said.

"It would seem someone else wants the Jade Lily," I said.

The caller paused. While he thought it over, I climbed inside the Cherokee and fired it up.

"Who?" he asked.

"I don't know," I said. "Names were not exchanged."

I can't say why I lied, but the caller seemed to believe me. After another pause, he said, "It doesn't matter. Once you pay for the Lily, we don't care what happens to it. Just don't fuck with us."

"Who? Me?"

"You think this is funny? You think this is a game?"

I pivoted in a slow circle in my seat, looking through the SUV's windows, trying to take in everyone around me, looking for someone, anyone, who was speaking into a cell phone. I saw nothing to arouse my suspicion.

"No," I said. "I really don't."

"We'll call again when the money is ready. Make sure they get it right. One million two hundred and seventy thousand dollars, half in twenties, half in fifties. Nonsequential bills."

"Do you have any idea how much cash that is?" I said. "Do you know how much it weighs? Ninety-five pounds give or take."

"Exactly ninety-seven pounds fourteen-point-four ounces," he said. "Have them divide the money into three bags, the same amount and the same weight in each bag."

"You've done this before," I said.

"Have you?"

"No."

That caused him to pause.

"Yes, yes you have," he insisted. "Otherwise how would you have known about the money?"

"Just a lucky guess."

He paused again.

"I told you, McKenzie," he said. "This isn't a game. You know what will happen if you try to play us."

"No. What?"

He hung up without responding.

As soon as the conversation ended, I called Mr. Donatucci.

"What happened?" he asked.

I told him that the artnappers made contact. I didn't speak of Heavenly. I wanted to see if Donatucci mentioned her first, see if he had kept me under surveillance despite his promise not to. At least that's what I told myself.

I explained about the money.

"Three bags suggest three partners," Donatucci said.

"These guys seem to know what they're doing," I said. "But . . ."

"But what?"

"They don't know who I am."

"We guessed that when they demanded you walk around the lake with a rose in your hand."

"I don't mean they don't know what I look like," I said. "I mean they have no idea who I am. They know nothing about my background. To them I'm just a name."

"I don't know if that's good or bad."

"Me neither."

"What next?" Donatucci asked.

"Follow their instructions, I guess. Also, I need to speak with someone who can give me a crash course in analyzing ancient jade artifacts so I can identify the Lily, make sure it's not a fake before I give up the money."

"Then you're going to go through with it?" Donatucci asked.

"Why not?"

THREE

I've known Nina Truhler for four years, three months, and eleven days—yes, I've kept track. We had talked seriously about marriage, although not since year three. I thought that might change when Nina's daughter, Erica, went off to Tulane University in New Orleans, but it hadn't. I also thought we might move in together, she with me or me with her, at least until Erica came back for the summer or holidays, yet that didn't happen, either. I loved her desperately and told her so many times; she said the same to me, and I believed her. "So what's the problem?" our friend Shelby Dunston asked often and with increasing frustration—like many married people she didn't think it was possible for us to be truly happy unless we were also married. The truth was we were both very contented in our relationship and both very afraid of somehow screwing it up. Nina had been married before, and the experience soured her on the institution. As for me, my mother died when I was in the sixth grade, and although I was well raised by my father, I was pretty much left to my own devices.

After so many years living a solitary if not downright selfish life, I didn't know if it was possible to live hand in hand with someone else. So we just kept living the way we always had, her on one side of the city, me on the other, together yet apart. It wasn't perfect. On the other hand, I always knew where I could get a free meal.

Rickie's, the jazz-club-slash-restaurant-slash-neighborhood-tavern that Nina had built and named after her daughter, was crowded. It was pushing six, and the quick-drink-after-work crowd was overlapping the early-dinner-before-the-movie/theater/ballet gang. It was Monday night, so the upstairs performance and dining area was closed, a red sash fixed across the staircase. That meant all of Nina's customers were gathered downstairs. Nearly all of the tables, booths, and comfy chairs and sofas were filled, as I knew they would be. What I didn't expect was the lights and cameras. A film crew had set up in the far corner near the staircase, and a young man dressed in a black sweater with a white ghost stitched over his breast was interviewing—Erica?

"What's going on?" I asked no one in particular. I received an answer just the same.

"It's a cable TV show," a young voice said.

I turned to find Victoria, Bobby and Shelby Dunston's fourteen-year-old daughter, sitting alone in a booth and nursing an IBC root beer.

"Vic?" I said.

"Hi, McKenzie."

I slid into the booth across from her. "What are you doing here?" I said.

"I was interviewed, too."

"For what?"

"The ghost show."

"You have to help me out here, sweetie."

"There's this cable TV show that goes around investigating paranormal activities in, I don't know, haunted houses, I guess."

"What are they doing here?"

"Rickie called them. Said the club was haunted. Which it is, by the way."

"I can't believe Nina went along with this."

"I guess she didn't know until Rickie told her this morning."

I started laughing. "I would love to have heard that conversation," I said.

"It was tense," Victoria said.

I laughed some more.

"Rickie said the publicity would be good for business," she added.

"What did Nina say to that?"

"You know how sometimes her face gets really kinda hard and her hands just kinda quiver like this?" Victoria held her hands out, fingers spread like she was about to claw something savagely. "And then she turns around and walks away without saying anything?"

I did know—it was not a pretty sight.

"Scared me more than the ghosts," Victoria said.

"What ghosts? There aren't any ghosts."

"Sure there are."

"Vic, please."

"I'm just saying."

"Where are your parents?"

"Dad's working—when isn't he?"

"Cops," I said.

"Mom left a few minutes ago. She had to take Katie to her piano lesson."

"They left you alone?"

"I'm with friends," she insisted. "Rickie is going to take me home. Besides, I'm not a little girl anymore."

"You'll always be a little girl to me."

"Are you going to buy me a car when I get my driver's license?"

"Hell no."

"Why not?"

"Because your father carries a gun and he's a good shot. Besides, what part of 'you'll always be a little girl to me' did you miss?"

"You're my godfather."

"So?"

"So you've been doing a pretty good job of spoiling me up till now. If you stop, I might suffer emotional trauma."

"Not as much trauma as your parents will make me suffer if I buy you a car."

"You can just say that since I'm your heir I'm going to inherit your money anyway."

"Your sister is also my heir. You'll have to split it."

"So buy her a car, too. I don't mind."

"Ahh, no."

A moment later, Jenness Crawford, Nina's assistant manager, appeared and asked if I wanted the usual—that would be a Summit Ale. I said I did.

"Where's Nina?" I asked.

"She's hiding in her office," Jenness said.

"Wow."

"Want another root beer, hon?" she asked Victoria.

"That depends. Are you buying, McKenzie?"

"Yes, I'm buying."

Victoria ordered another bottle of root beer.

"I am so getting a car," she said when Jenness left.

"Don't hold your breath," I said.

A few moments later, Jenness returned with my Summit and the root beer and then went back to the bar. Erica suddenly appeared. I gave her a hug.

Nearly everyone called her Rickie, yet I vowed when I started spending time with her mother that I wouldn't use her nickname unless she gave me permission. She never did. Later, I learned she was grateful that I called her Erica, that she had dismissed Rickie as a child's name, and since she was no longer a child, only those people who knew her as a child would be allowed to call her that. Apparently everyone she knew in New Orleans called her Erica.

"How come you're not at Tulane?" I asked.

"I changed my flight to tomorrow morning," she said. "I wanted to be here for this."

She sat next to Victoria on the other side of the booth, giving the younger girl a playful push to make room. Victoria immediately wrapped her arm around Erica's. Erica had become Victoria's big sister at about the same time she got *her* driver's license.

"Ghosts, Erica," I said. "Really?"

"There are ghosts here."

"No, there aren't."

"Sure there are. Last year, after closing, I was helping out, trying to make some spending money for college. I was cleaning the shelves below the bar. I took all the glasses out and set them on top of the bar and cleaned the shelf. When I looked up"—she paused dramatically—"all of the glasses were stacked like a pyramid. Explain that, huh? Then, later, I was vacuuming. Suddenly I felt this hand and it was brushing up and down my arm like this." Erica leaned across the table and started moving her hand across my arm from my shoulder to my elbow. "McKenzie, there was no one there. This happened three times while I was vacuuming and there was no one there."

The skepticism must have shown in my face, because Erica quickly turned to the girl next to her.

"Vicky, Vicky," she said. "Tell him what happened to you."

"It was the same thing with me," Victoria said. "I was broke because some people aren't as generous as they could be and Nina gave me a job cleaning up the basement. Last summer, remember? I was in the basement, moving stuff around, and the lights went off. You know how dark it is in the basement? Scary. I mean, it was really scary. I felt along the wall till I reached the door. Once I found the door, I was able to find the light switch. It was in the off position. No fuse blew, no light burned out. Someone turned off the lights? How was that possible? I turned the lights back on. This time I propped the basement door open with a chair, okay, so I had the hall lights working for me. I went back to work, and the lights, the overhead lights, went off a second time. I went back to the switch; it was in the off position again. I turned the light back on, and then whoosh—the chair went flying across the basement like someone threw it and the door slammed shut. I pushed the door open—and it was hard, it was like someone was leaning against it—and the lights went off again. That was enough for me."

"Okay," I said.

"Okay?" Erica repeated. "Did you hear what happened to the singer?"

"What singer?"

"The jazz singer that you like so much. She's onstage with her trio doing a sound check, and all of a sudden she hears glass like people are mixing drinks and the sound of laughter and she doesn't know where it's coming from because the upstairs performance area is closed. There's no one there, right; it's not open yet. But the noise is getting louder and louder, and she asked her guys if they could hear it and they couldn't. They couldn't hear a thing? Huh? Huh?"

"What happened?"

"What do you mean what happened?"

"Did she do the show?"

"Of course she did," Erica said. "The show always goes on."

"Did she keep hearing the noise?"

"I don't think so. I think it went away."

I looked at Victoria. "What happened to the basement?"

"After a little while, I went back down and cleaned it up."

"Did the lights go off again? Did the door slam?"

"No."

"That doesn't mean anything," Erica said.

"Ladies, have you ever read Sherlock Holmes?"

Victoria's hand went up as if she were answering a question in class. "I have," she said.

"There's a line in one of the stories, maybe more than one: After you eliminate the impossible, whatever remains, no matter how improbable, must be the truth—something like that. You can't explain what happened to you, so you assume it was ghosts, but you can't do that unless you eliminate all the other possibilities first. That's how I look at it."

"That's how we look at it as well," a voice said. I looked up to see the young man who had been interviewing Erica earlier. "We don't believe in ghosts, either—until there is no other possibility."

I gave him room to sit, and he began talking about his work as a paranormal investigator. He was an earnest young man and made a rapt audience of Erica and Victoria. He explained how he and his crew would spend the evening in Rickie's armed with equipment that measured electrostatic fields, cameras, sound equipment, and a K2 meter, whatever that was. Both Erica and Victoria wanted to hang out with him, but he refused the offer. After all, he and his crew were the stars of the show, I thought but didn't say.

"What do you know about curses?" I asked.

"I don't believe in them," he said.

"No?"

"How can a nonliving, non-energy-producing object affect the world around it?"

"Good question."

"I do believe, however, that sometimes spirits will attach themselves to an object," he said. "It could be a favorite chair, a photograph—something the spirit cherished in life." He gestured at his surroundings. "It could be a house or a jazz club."

"How 'bout a centuries-old art object?"

"Yes. Certainly. Why do you ask?"

"Just curious," I said.

The ghost hunter excused himself and returned to his crew. Perhaps he saw Nina approaching out of the corner of his eye and wanted to avoid her for now.

Nina's movements were smooth and effortless—a trained dancer who knew all the steps. She had cut her jet black hair short again, and the style seemed to set off her eyes even more than usual—the most startling silver-blue eyes I had ever seen. She spoke with a clear, unaffected voice in a way that suggested she was in the habit of speaking up for herself. She possessed high cheekbones, a narrow nose, and a generous mouth that required little makeup; her figure was well set off by a rose-colored sweater dress; her athletic legs—look, I know I'm being fanciful when I describe her. But then, I love Nina. I love everything about her.

When she reached the booth I gave her a hug and a short kiss.

"Do you believe this?" she said. She was looking directly at Erica when she spoke. "I'd throw them out except apparently I'm contractually obligated."

"This is fun," I said. "It probably will increase business, too. Why not?"

Nina sat next to me in the booth. "So you're taking Erica's side."

I leaned away. I had learned long ago, never takes sides between mother and daughter.

"Ghosts," Nina said. "I don't have ghosts."

She could have substituted the word "rats" and it would have sounded the same.

"Speaking of ghosts, guess who I met today," I said. "Heavenly Petryk."

"That slut?"

"Whoa, Mom," Erica said. "You don't usually use language like that unless you're talking about my father." She tilted her head toward Victoria. "Exes."

"Mmmm," Victoria intoned.

"The two of you, out of here. Victoria, your mother is going to kill me as it is. And, Rickie, don't forget you have a plane to catch at six fifteen tomorrow morning."

"I won't."

Erica and Victoria slid out of the booth, grabbed their coats, and bundled up for the cold. As they moved to the door, Nina called to them. "Hey."

Erica turned to look at her mother.

"I miss you already," Nina said.

Erica smiled and said she would see her later.

"So what are you up to now?" Nina asked. "If Heavenly's involved, it can't be good."

I explained about the Jade Lily. I didn't tell her I was speaking in strict confidentiality and needed her to keep my secrets. Why insult the woman? When I finished, she shook her head and smiled ruefully the way she does whenever I embark on one of my adventures—that's the word *she* uses, not me.

"You do get involved in the weirdest stuff," she said.

"Me?" I waved at the ghost hunters.

"They're going to stay here all night, too," Nina said. "I can't believe Rickie set this up."

"Maybe they'll find some real ghosts. You could become a tourist attraction."

"Stop it."

"Well, I'm out of here."

"What? No, no, no, no, McKenzie, c'mon. Stay with me."

"I'm going to get some takeout and watch the hockey game."

"You said this could be fun. What if they really do find a ghost?"

"That's why I'm leaving."

"Scaredy cat."

The Minnesota Wild had just taken a 3–1 lead over the Detroit Red Wings deep in the third period when my front doorbell rang. I opened the door. I half expected to see Nina—she had a key yet never used it. Instead, I found a Minneapolis police officer standing there and looking as if he wished he were somewhere else. It was the worst job there was for a cop, knocking on a door at night. I had done it many times when I was in harness. Not once did I have good news to report.

"Mr. McKenzie?" the cop asked.

I nodded. My mouth was too dry to speak, although I could hear my inner voice screaming *tell me quickly*.

"I need you to come with me," the officer said.

"Why?"

"Lieutenant Rask wants to speak with you immediately."

"What about?"

"I wasn't informed, sir, but since Lieutenant Rask is head of the Homicide Unit, I expect it has to do with someone's murder."

We drove west through Minneapolis until we found the winding parkway that cut through Theodore Wirth Park. The officer slowed his vehicle as if he were a sightseer afraid of missing something. Cars backed up behind him; no doubt they would have given him the horn if not for the light bar and the words MINNEAPOLIS POLICE TO PROTECT WITH COURAGE TO SERVE WITH COMPASSION printed on the side of the vehicle.

Theodore Wirth was the largest regional park in the Minneapolis Park System, even though it was actually located in the City of Golden Valley, go figure. I had no idea what we were doing there. The officer wouldn't answer any of my questions, so after a while I stopped asking. Eventually we came to what a sign called Quaking Bog Parking Lot and pulled in, nestling among a dozen other assorted City of Minneapolis vehicles. Directly across the parkway was an area known as

Wedding Hill. The hill overlooked Birch Pond, and a lot of nature lovers thought it was an idyllic spot to take their marriage vows—a couple of friends of mine married there fifteen years ago, and I knew it to be green and gorgeous in the summer. In the dead of winter with cops and medical personnel milling about under a dozen or so bright lights, not so much.

The area was surprisingly undisturbed despite the number of crime scene professionals who were present, including a couple of park patrol officers who looked as if they were seriously considering a different line of work. The investigators were trying to keep the scene intact for a more thorough search in the daylight. I followed the officer along a short, narrow path of packed snow to a small clearing. Lieutenant Clayton Rask was standing more or less in the center of it, directing traffic. There was something crisp and efficient about the way he barked out instructions, and I wondered if it was something some people were born to do or if it required practice. The officer led me to his side.

"Here he is, LT," the officer said.

Rask nodded without looking. A tech holding a small digital camera turned it on me. It was his job to film the crime scene as well as articles of evidence as they were discovered, record the observations of the investigators, and generally keep a time-sensitive log of the proceedings. In the old days they called him the "master note taker." Nowadays he's the "photographic log recorder," not to be confused with the "crime scene photographer," who was busy taking photos with a 35 mm camera mounted on a tripod. Film might seem old-fashioned, but digital photographs are easy to alter—can you say "Photoshop"?—and rarely are used as evidence in court.

"Name, please," the recorder said.

"Rushmore McKenzie," I said. "I'm here at Lieutenant Rask's insistence."

Rask pretended not to hear. I wasn't surprised. I'd had dealings with the lieutenant in the past. We were not friends.

"McKenzie," someone said.

I turned toward the voice. A man extended his hand. He was tall and good-looking, not unlike Robert Redford in his *Great Gatsby* days, with wisps of blond hair peeking out from under a gray all-wool fedora. He was also wearing a charcoal Westbury overcoat from Brooks Brothers, Italian ankle boots, lambskin gloves, and a white cashmere scarf that nearly covered a tie that looked like it was made of blue silk. All in all, he was the best-dressed cop I had ever seen.

"Lieutenant Scott Noehring," he said. I shook his hand. "I'm with Forgery Fraud."

"Hey," I said.

"Sorry to drag you out on a night as cold as this." His words rose as a puff of steam and were quickly snatched away by the wind.

"What's it about?" I asked.

Rask gestured with his chin at a body bag lying in the snow. "Take a look," he said. There was distrust in his voice, but I didn't take it personally. That was how he always talked.

I knelt and unzipped the black vinyl bag and peeled back the sides, all my actions duly chronicled by the recorder's camera. The arch light reflected off the dead man's pale, frozen face. It was Patrick Tarpley. He was dressed pretty much as he was in his photograph. There was a bullet hole in his throat, and blood had saturated his shirt, tie, suit jacket, and overcoat before his heart had stopped pumping. I pulled the zipper all the way to the end of the bag to get a look at Tarpley's feet. He was wearing dress shoes.

A dozen thoughts crowded into my brain at once. I'm ashamed to say that none of them had anything to do with Tarpley as a man whose cherished life had been violently ripped away, none had to do with his wife, none asked about his children if he had any, his family, or his friends.

"Do you have a time of death?" I asked.

"Do you?" Rask replied.

What's that supposed to mean? my inner voice asked.

I carefully zipped the bag closed and stood facing the lieutenant. I had dressed for the weather—Sorel boots, thick leather coat and hat, warm gloves. Just the same, I said, "Awfully cold to be playing games, LT."

The recorder stepped back a few feet so he could get both of us in the same shot.

"ME won't even guess until he gets the body on the table," Noehring said. "Given the temperature and the vic's clothing, it'll take some doing to get a precise time."

I was astonished to hear someone—anyone—answer for Rask. As it was, Rask gave Noehring a look that could have melted glaciers. If Noehring noticed, he chose to ignore it, another astonishment. I kept pressing to see how much I could get away with.

"Did he return fire?" I asked.

"He had a piece in his inside suit pocket," Noehring said. "Nine-millimeter S&W. His overcoat was buttoned over it."

"Any witnesses?"

"None so far."

"Who discovered the body?"

"Cross-country skier. He deviated from the usual path; otherwise we might not have found him till spring."

"Any indication that the body was dumped here?"

"No. We have two sets of footprints coming from the direction of the parking lot and one set going back. We'll know better when we conduct a daylight search in the morning."

"Vehicles?"

"The parking lot was empty."

"Someone drove him here, killed him, and drove away," I said. "Someone he wasn't afraid of. He didn't know he was going for a walk in the snow; otherwise he would have dressed for it. Did he have a cell phone?"

"Yes," Noehring said. "We checked the call log. We're running the numbers now."

"Is mine among them?"

The two cops looked at each other and then back at me.

"Should it be?" Rask said.

That made me step backward. Up until that moment, I thought they had dragged Tarpley's call log, discovered that he had spoken to me earlier, and summoned me to the crime scene to explain myself. Now I wasn't sure.

"Why am I here?" I asked.

Rask gestured at the body bag again.

"Do you know this man?" he asked.

"We've never met."

"That doesn't answer my question."

"You haven't answered mine yet, either."

"Should we take this conversation downtown?"

C'mon, my inner voice said. *Take me downtown? Did you really say that?*

"At least we'll be warmer," I said. The log recorder was still photographing me. "Would you get that damn camera out of my face?"

"McKenzie . . ." Rask said.

"Don't try to intimidate me, Lieutenant."

"Do you want to see intimidation?" He took a menacing step toward me. "I'll show you intimidation."

Noehring cut him off, moving quickly between us, and flashed a full-mouth smile. The light reflecting off his perfect teeth damn near blinded me.

"Can't we all just get along?" he said.

Let me guess—you're the good cop.

"Come to think of it," I said. "Why is the Forgery Fraud Unit involved in a homicide investigation?"

"Lieutenant Rask contacted me."

"Why?"

"Tarpley was my CI."

"CI?"

"Confidential informant."

"I know what it means," I said. Most CIs are criminals who trade their knowledge of the streets—and their friends—for cash or favors. The French police rely heavily on informants and always have. The Brits do not. U.S. cops used to follow the English system. Now when it comes to criminal investigations, as with most of our problems, we tend to throw money at it. Still, "What would make a guy like Tarpley turn informant?" I asked. "What would he inform on?"

"He was very good at his job," Noehring said. "He knew as much about what was going on in the art world as anyone who lived between Chicago and the West Coast."

"You're telling me he was smarter than the average door shaker."

"Yes, I am."

"That still doesn't answer my question." I pause for a moment. When no one spoke, I said, "Anyone?"

"He liked girls," Noehring said.

"Don't we all?"

"Little girls, preferably between the ages of seven and nine."

Then I'll stop feeling sorry for him, my inner voice said.

Out loud, I said, "You were blackmailing him into giving information."

"That's one way of looking at it," Noehring said.

"Talk to us," Rask said.

"I don't know what to say," I said. "I don't even know why I'm here yet."

"You're here because of this."

Rask produced a clear plastic bag. Inside the bag was a small sheet of wrinkled paper ripped from a pocket notebook. Written on the sheet was the name McKenzie.

"We found it stuffed in the outside pocket of his overcoat. Notice the ink?"

The first two letters were printed in vibrant blue, but the ink soon began to fade—the *e* was barely readable.

"You know what it tells me? It tells me it was written by a pen whose ink had frozen. Officer Thoreson? What's the current temperature?"

"Minus nine, LT," the log recorder said. 'The wind chill is around minus twenty."

"So, McKenzie, no bullshit," Rask said. "Who would want to kill a man and then stuff your name in his pocket?"

"I don't know."

"You said you never met Tarpley, but you knew who he was, didn't you?"

"Yes."

"Well?"

"It's kind of a long story. Sure you don't want to go someplace warm?"

Noehring smiled his movie-star smile. Rask folded his arms across his chest. "Out with it," he said.

I flashed on what the City of Lakes Art Museum executive board of trustees had said earlier about keeping news of the theft secret in order to protect the museum's reputation. That made me hesitate, but only for a moment.

"Gentlemen," I said, "have you ever heard of the curse of the Jade Lily?"

FOUR

The room was silent except for the monotonous drumming of Fiegen's fingers on the tabletop. He and the other members of the museum's executive board were seated in the same chairs in the museum's conference room as the day before. This time no one looked happy to be there. Perrin leaned back in her chair, her eyes closed, her head tilted so that her chin was pointed at the ceiling. She looked as if she had aged a decade since I had seen her last. Mr. Donatucci, on the other hand, hadn't changed at all. He still sat quietly, although this time his gaze was fixed on a large oil painting of what appeared to be Split Rock Lighthouse. A seventeenth-century sailing ship lay just off the shore, and hordes of savage-looking Indians were attacking or greeting it—take your pick—from a dozen canoes. It was impossible, of course, for the lighthouse, ship, and Native Americans to be in the same place on Lake Superior at the same time, but as it had often been pointed out to me, I know nothing about art.

"Mr. McKenzie, I thought we had an understanding," Fiegen said. "This matter was to be kept strictly confidential."

"What can I tell you?" I said. "I see a dead body in the snow, I become a regular blabbermouth."

"Are we facing any liability issues?" asked a member of the board whose name I forgot.

Perrin raised her hand a few inches and then let it drop as if the effort had been too great. "I didn't get any sleep at all," she said. "First the police, that rude Lieutenant Rask, then the lawyers, then the police and the lawyers, and then the lawyers again. I asked for discretion. Lieutenant Rask made it clear that the museum's reputation is the least of his concerns. The police confiscated all of our security footage. They started interviewing our employees this morning."

"Do the police have any suspects, McKenzie?" Fiegen asked.

"Tarpley's partners," I said. "That's merely speculation on my part, though. Lieutenant Rask does not confide in me."

"It's only a matter of time before news of the theft gets out," Perrin said. "I'll be sitting down with our PR director following this meeting. The question is, do we want to get out in front of this, make an announcement to the trustees, our membership, the press, or wait until reporters start calling?"

"Wait," the unidentified trustee said. He spread his hands wide, the palms facing upward. "Who knows? We might get lucky."

"Define lucky," Fiegen said.

The trustee shrugged and leaned back in his chair. "We might still recover the Jade Lily," he said.

Fiegen nodded his head slightly. "That would mollify the situation somewhat," he said softly. "In fact, news of a major art theft would elevate the museum's profile, probably even attendance, if"—he emphasized the word—"the Lily is recovered." In a louder voice he added, "We should hold off on any public announcement. Should members criticize us later, we'll tell them that we remained silent at the behest of—what was his name, Lieutenant Rask? We'll insist he asked us to keep quiet about the theft so as not to compromise his investigation."

I had to smirk at that. The police get blamed for so much bullshit.

"In the meantime, Mr. Gillard must be informed. That cannot wait."

"I'll see to it," Perrin said.

Throughout the conversation, Anderson had been staring at me, a snarl on his lips.

"McKenzie." He said the word like it was an obscenity.

"Derek." I tried to match his inflection but failed.

"If you had kept your mouth shut—"

"It's murder," I said.

"The whole point of involving you in this matter was to protect the museum from—"

"It's murder," I repeated. I thought that should have been enough to explain my actions, only Anderson wasn't buying it.

"Adverse publicity," he continued. "Now, thanks to you, we'll be the laughingstock of the industry."

I hadn't thought of art museums and galleries as being "an industry," yet what else would you call it?

"Don't blame me, pal," I said. "I didn't steal the Lily. I didn't kill Tarpley."

"You can fix it."

"Fix it, how?"

"We must retrieve the Lily. We must."

"We?"

Perrin opened her eyes and leaned forward. "Mr. McKenzie, we are relying on you," she said.

"Forget it."

"McKenzie," Fiegen said.

"It's murder, boys and girls, and that's where I draw the line. I'm not going to get shot for a glorified centerpiece."

"We need you," Perrin said.

"No, you don't. I have no idea why the artnappers picked me, but if I'm not available, they'll find someone else. That's assuming they call back. They might not. Hell, if I were them, I'd be on the first stage out of Dodge."

"You're a coward," Anderson said.

Some men, if they called me that, I'd be hurt or angry to the point of reprisal. Anderson wasn't one of them. I smiled.

"You should see me do the chicken dance," I said.

"Coward," he repeated.

Fiegen leaned forward in his seat, effectively inserting himself between Anderson and me. "Do you really believe the thieves will abandon their plan now?" he asked.

"Depends on how greedy they are. Originally, they knew they could depend on your"—I glanced at Perrin—"what did you ask for? Discretion? The thieves were reasonably sure there would be no police involvement, which meant they were relatively safe. The murder of Tarpley brings the cops into it. Possibly they didn't mean to kill Tarpley. Or maybe they thought his body wouldn't be discovered until after they completed their business. I can't say. I can say, however, that suddenly trading the Lily for cash has become a dangerous thing to do—for them and for me. They'd be silly to try it. I'd be even sillier."

"Still, they might call."

"They might. Like I said, it depends on how greedy they are."

"Mr. Donatucci," Fiegen said. "What is your opinion?"

Donatucci tore his gaze from the painting that had so mesmerized him for the length of the meeting. "They'll go forward with the exchange," he said.

"What makes you think so?" I asked.

"It's what they do for a living."

I hadn't thought of it that way, although he was probably right. This was their job.

"I bet they have more guts than you do, McKenzie," Anderson said.

"In that case, you're all set," I said. "If the thieves, the killers, call back asking for their money, you can deliver it. Whaddaya say, Derek?"

Derek didn't say.

I was sitting at the bar at Rickie's. Nina was sitting next to me. She was drinking coffee, so I did, too.

"How did it go last night?" I asked.

Nina yawned. When she finished, she said, "They said they saw and felt spiritual energy. Whether or not they captured any of that energy on camera or their audio files remains to be seen. They also claim there were noises and objects moving on the stage upstairs."

"Did they get that on film?"

"Who knows?" Nina started to laugh. "It's all so silly." She rested her head on the bar top.

"At least these guys seemed to be serious ghost hunters, if there is such a thing," I said. "Not like those nitwits on the Travel Channel that mock the ghosts, call them names, and then squeal like little girls on a backyard sleepover whenever anything happens."

Nina's head came up in a hurry. "You watch these shows?" she said.

"I might have caught an episode or two."

Nina whacked me in the arm. "You watch this stuff, you like this stuff, and you left me alone with those lunatics?" She whacked me again. "What kind of boyfriend are you?"

"The hockey game was on."

She whacked me again.

"I don't believe it," she said.

"I could come over tonight . . ."

"Forget it. Between these people and getting Rickie off, I've had like an hour's sleep. Besides, what about your Jade Lily?"

"I decided not to get involved in that mess."

"You're not going after it?"

I explained about seeing Tarpley's body in the snow.

"The Lily can curse somebody else," I said. "I wash my hands of it."

"Good for you, McKenzie." She whacked me again, only this time not so hard. "My little boy is growing up."

"Speaking of growing up. About tonight . . ."

"I am going home. Alone. I'm sure you can find a hockey or basketball game that'll amuse you."

I tried to explain to Nina that I hadn't had much sleep the previous night either, but she wasn't buying it. So I drove home wondering if there was indeed a hockey game on that night.

I live in Falcon Heights, a first ring suburb of St. Paul, my hometown. My house is located on Hoyt Avenue, a long pass from the St. Paul campus of the University of Minnesota. There is always traffic on Cleveland Avenue, the street that borders the campus, so I didn't notice the police car that followed me off Cleveland onto Hoyt until its lights started flashing. My first impulse was to ask myself what I had done wrong—was I speeding, did I turn without signaling? Then I noticed that it was a Minneapolis police car far out of its jurisdiction. Whatever way I was driving was none of his damn business, so instead of stopping like a good and proper citizen, I continued along the avenue until I reached my driveway and pulled in. The squad car parked at the mouth of the driveway, blocking my escape. I shut down the Jeep Cherokee and stepped out while the cop left his car. It was the same police officer who had fetched me the night before. He called my name.

"Ahh, c'mon," I said.

"Lieutenant Rask wants to see you."

"Again?"

"Again."

"What now?"

"He didn't say."

"The sonuvabitch could have called. He has my phone number."

"He wanted to make sure you accepted his invitation."

Oh God, my inner voice said. *Now what?*

This time the officer let me drive myself—but only after I promised I wouldn't try to flee to Canada. I met him at the Fifth Street entrance of the Minneapolis City Hall, hoping the meeting wouldn't take longer than the one hour the parking meter allowed. The cop led me down a long marble corridor to room 108, which was actually a suite of offices that served the police department's Forgery Fraud and Homicide units, among others. The cop opened the door for us. When he did, a woman stepped past him into the corridor. I recognized her instantly.

"Mrs. Tarpley," I said.

The smile was gone, but her eyes still sparkled as they had in the photograph I saw despite the red, puffy flesh around them. She brought a knuckle to her eye as if to brush away a tear. Her voice was soft and anxious.

"Do I know you?" she asked.

"My name is McKenzie. I work with the museum. I just wanted to say that I'm terribly sorry for your loss."

"They say he stole the Jade Lily from the museum. They say he was murdered for it." She reached out a hand and rested it on my arm. "Do you believe Patrick stole the Jade Lily?"

Actually, I did. There was no reason to tell the woman that, though, so I hedged my bet.

"It doesn't make a lot of sense to me," I said.

She patted my arm, apparently thankful to have an ally.

"They think—the police, they think I had something to do with it, I know," she told me. "That man, that awful foreigner—he threatened me. Called me names. Said I had the Lily and I should return it to him or he would hurt me."

"What foreigner?"

"In there." She gestured with her head toward the office suite. "McKenzie, I don't know anything about it."

"I'm sorry."

I didn't know what else to say.

The woman nodded and continued down the corridor. I wanted to offer her some comfort. Or at least a ride. *She should have someone to drive her home,* my inner voice said. And she did. Before I could finish my thought, a man with dark hair and a dark complexion—he could have been Hispanic, I decided—rushed to Mrs. Tarpley's side. He put a comforting arm around her shoulder and led her away. At the same time, Rask's flunky yanked on my own arm.

I was ushered into a small meeting room that also served as an interrogation room. Lieutenant Rask sat at the head of the table looking angrier than I had ever seen him, which is saying a lot.

"LT," the officer said, and Rask nodded at him. The officer took that as a sign to depart. As he was leaving the room, shutting the door behind him, Rask said, "This is McKenzie."

There were two other men in the room, one sitting, one standing, both dressed in suits. The man who was standing was about thirty, with a smooth face and lively eyes. He spoke with a smile in his voice that most men have when talking to attractive women. I found it disconcerting.

"Mr. McKenzie," he said as he extended his hand. "Thank you for coming. My name is Jonathan Hemsted. I'm with the U.S. State Department."

The words "State Department" caused me to glance at Rask. He was staring at Hemsted as if he were trying to bend a spoon. After he finished shaking my hand, Hemsted directed me toward the man who was sitting.

"This is Branko Pozderac," he said. "Mr. Pozderac is a representative of the government of Bosnia and Herzegovina. He is, in fact, a member of the House of Peoples in the Parliamentary Assembly."

Pozderac was twice as old as Hemsted. The lines across

his forehead and around his mouth suggested that he was easily irritated, and I wondered how many flight attendants, hotel clerks, and waiters he'd tried to get fired over the years. I offered him my hand. He glanced at it, then looked away. I didn't know if it was because I was an American or a commoner, but plainly he was afraid it might be catching.

"Is this the man who threatens grieving widows?" I asked.

Hot rage infused his eyes. He stood up blinking, and for a moment I was sure he would take a swing at me. However, the rage quickly gave way to contempt, and he returned to his seat with a dismissive grunt.

Yeah, that's him, my inner voice said.

"Mr. McKenzie, please," Hemsted said. "We wish to speak to you of a matter of utmost importance to our government and the government of Bosnia and Herzegovina."

The entire scene made me nervous, so I did what I always did when I was out of my comfort zone—I shifted into smart-ass mode.

"Do I have time to go out for popcorn?" I asked.

Pozderac gave me a quick glance before finding something else more interesting to stare at. Hemsted continued as if I hadn't spoken at all.

"I should point out," he said, "that we have already discussed this matter with your mayor, the chief of police, and Lieutenant Rask."

I sat next to Rask. I swear to God I could hear him growling. I didn't think he was growling at me, though, so I ignored him.

"Okay, Jon," I said. "I'm officially intimidated. What's going on?"

I spoke to him as if we were equals, two guys chatting in the locker room, taking my time, grinning like I had seen him in the shower and was less than impressed. It was a style of conversation guaranteed to drive self-important people like Hemsted and Pozderac up the wall.

"This is not a matter to be taken lightly, Mr. McKenzie," Hemsted said.

"I didn't think it was, especially after you started dropping names and such."

"McKenzie," Rask said.

I tilted my head toward him. "Yeah?" I said.

"Listen to the man."

Oh boy, my inner voice warned me. *If Rask is intimidated— you are in so much trouble.*

I gestured at Hemsted to continue.

He took a deep breath. "It is our understanding that you are currently employed by the City of Lakes Art Museum," he said. "That you were retained to recover the Jade Lily, which was stolen from the museum two days ago."

"I was," I said. "Not anymore."

"No?"

"The discovery of Patrick Tarpley's corpse last night soured me on the job."

Pozderac spoke for the first time. He had an East European accent, a lot of rolling *R*s, a lot of *W*s pronounced as *V*s, and a few missing articles. Yet he had no problem making himself understood.

"You let death of this man frighten you?" he asked. "Are you coward?"

He was the second man who'd questioned my courage that morning, yet I was no more affected by Pozderac's opinion of me than I had been by Derek Anderson's.

"Sure, why not?" I said.

"That is, is . . ."

Pozderac couldn't think of an English word to describe my crime, so he resorted to a string of adjectives spoken in the Bosnian language—at least I think they were adjectives.

"Mr. McKenzie," Hemsted said. "You have informed the museum that you will not attempt to recover the Jade Lily from the thieves, is that what you are saying?"

"That is exactly what I am saying."

"We want you to reconsider your position."

"Why would I do that?"

"Recovery of the Lily is essential to the continued good relations between the United States and Bosnia and Herze-govina."

"I have no idea why that would be true," I said. "Even so, what does it have to do with me?"

"The thieves requested that you act as go-between, is that not correct?"

I turned to look at Rask.

He shook his head slowly. "I didn't tell them anything," he said. "They came to me with a complete report and several threats."

"Threats?" I said.

"Mr. McKenzie," Hemsted said. "Is it not true that the thieves asked for you?"

"They did."

"Why?"

"I don't know."

"It does not matter," Pozderac said. "You will recover Lily."

He waved his hand in a way that both announced leadership and dismissed argument. The fact that I continued to argue annoyed him greatly.

"I will?" I said.

"You will recover. You will give to me. It is decided."

"Wait a minute. Give the Lily to you?"

"Yes," Hemsted said.

"Let me see if I got this straight. The insurance company is paying approximately one-point-three million for the safe return of the Jade Lily. But you guys, after I make the exchange, you guys expect me to steal the Lily from the insurance company and the museum and give it to you instead. Does that pretty much cover it?"

"The Lily belongs to Bosnia and Herzegovina," Pozderac said. "It belongs to me."

"I heard that it rightfully belongs to Tatjana Durakovic; that it was stolen from her during the Yugoslav Wars."

Pozderac was on his feet in a hurry. He was not quite as enraged as before. Still . . .

"That is lie," he said. "That is damnable lie. You will not repeat such lies. Do you understand?

"Kiss my—"

"McKenzie," Rask shouted. In a lower voice, he said, "McKenzie."

"Here's the thing, pal." I was speaking directly to Pozderac. "I don't work for the government. I don't work for the mayor of Minneapolis or the chief of police or Lieutenant Rask. I certainly don't work for you. So, if you want something from me, ask politely."

"Mr. McKenzie," Hemsted said. "There is no need for hostility."

Yeah, right, my inner voice said.

"Look, fellas," I said aloud. "As far as I am concerned, this is a moot point, anyway, for the simple reason that if I do what you request"—I nodded at Lieutenant Rask—"the police are going to lock me up and throw away the key. Isn't that right, LT?"

He didn't answer, but I was sure I heard him growl again.

"Arrangements have already been made, Mr. McKenzie," Hemsted said. "There will be no arrests. As for the insurance company, we will guarantee that it is compensated for its loss."

"One million two hundred and seventy thousand dollars?" I said. "Can I have that in writing?"

"You'll need to take my word for it. McKenzie, this conversation never took place."

"C'mon. If the Lily is so important, why don't you just go to the museum and collect it; go to whatsisname Gillard and confiscate it, or whatever the hell it is you do when the government wants something that doesn't belong to it?"

"If we could, we would. Unfortunately, the Lily is in the wind—isn't that the criminal vernacular for an item that is missing?"

"I wouldn't know."

Pozderac slowly edged to where I was sitting and looked down at me. "Lily must be returned," he said. "Immediately. See to it." He moved to the door, opened it, and stepped out. "See to it," he repeated over his shoulder.

I guessed that he was speaking to Hemsted, because the man pulled out a chair and sat at the table directly across from me.

"McKenzie," he said. "It greatly distresses me to be forced to speak to you in this manner. I had hoped you would embrace our cause out of a sense of . . ."

"Patriotism?"

"To be blunt, Branko Pozderac is not the first asshole that our government has had to appease in order to keep the peace. I cannot go into details. I can tell you that Bosnia and Herzegovina is made up of three ethnic groups, constituent people they're called—Bosniaks, Serbs, and Croats—that were happily slaughtering each other not so very long ago. Each group has an equal share in governing the country. As you can imagine, the government is a fragile enterprise at best. So far it works. To keep it working, at least in the short term, means catering to Pozderac. He wants the Lily. He claims it's a national treasure. We're going to get it for him."

"You mean I'm going to get it for him."

"I'm not very good at threatening people," Hemsted said, "but I can arrange an audit of your tax returns for each of the past seven years and every year from now until you die, at which time I'll have your estate audited. I can arrange to have your name placed on the Do Not Fly list. I can arrange for you to have problems with your passport, your Social Security, your Medicaid, with any federal program. I can have men dressed in black interview every person you have ever met about your character, your love of country, threats you might have made against the government. I can have you detained and released over and over again as a person of interest in whatever interests Homeland Security at the moment. That's what I can do legally. Give me time and I'll think of a lot more."

"I get it."

"Illegally, well . . ."

"I get it."

"I can make your life miserable."

"You're mistaken, Jon," I said. "You are very good at threatening people."

"Will you retrieve the Lily for us?"

"I'll think about it."

"Please do."

He smiled then, but there was no joy in it. In fact, I could detect a measure of pain in that smile, the kind of pain that comes from self-knowledge gained at a heavy price, and it occurred to me that Hemsted might have become a prick against his will.

"I'll be in touch, McKenzie," he said.

He stood and nodded at Rask. "I am sorry about all of this, Lieutenant," he said. "I truly am."

He left the room a moment later. Rask got up and carefully closed the door as if he were fighting the impulse to slam it.

"Our federal tax dollars at work," I said.

Rask turned slowly toward me. The scowl on his face reminded me of the Tiger tanks that chewed up Tom Hanks and his men in *Saving Private Ryan*.

"Tell me about Tatjana Durakovic," he said.

"Didn't I mention her last night?"

"It must have slipped your mind. 'Course, you have a history of withholding vital information from the police, don't you?"

"I never actually met the woman."

"Tell me."

I did, giving up Heavenly's name along the way, recalling our conversation without explaining the details of how we came to have it.

"You're saying that this Tatjana is in Ontonagon, Michigan?" Rask said.

"I'm saying that's where I was told she was from. I have no idea where she is now or where she was last night when Tarpley was killed. What time was that, by the way?"

Rask paused for a moment as if he were weighing the consequences of his next statement before he made it.

"I need a favor," he said.

"A favor? From me?"

"That's right."

"Well, I'm not promising anything, but you can always ask, LT."

"Call me Clay."

That made me pause. I've known the man for half a dozen years, and we've never had what you might call a warm relationship. Usually it was downright frosty. In any case, he's never called me by my first name and I've never used his.

"No, LT, I don't think I can do that."

Rask nodded as if I had passed a test. He sat next to me and leaned in. His speech started slow and calm but increased in ferocity toward the end.

"It took a lot to just sit here and listen to those sonsabitches talk, pushing people around, making demands. Who the hell do they think they are? They come into my house and tell me which homicides I can investigate and which homicides I can't? In my house? I don't give a shit what the mayor says. I don't give a shit what that politician he appointed chief of police says, either. Cooperate with federal authorities? If I don't bend over and kiss my own ass for the FBI or the DEA or those incompetents at Homeland Security, I sure as hell am not going to do it for these miserable bastards. No, no, no." He held the third "no" like it was the final note in a trumpet concerto. "You know what I'm going to do? I'm going to investigate this homicide. I'm not going to redline it just because these bastards find it inconvenient. I'm going to discover who killed Patrick Tarpley and why. You're going to help."

"I am?"

"You're damn right you are."

"Why would I?"

"Because you used to be a cop, McKenzie. Here's your chance to be a cop again."

"Don't do this to me, LT."

"You're going through with the exchange. If the thieves call back, you make the deal."

"You want me to steal the Lily?"

"What? What are you talking about? Did I say that? Did I say steal the Lily and give it to those assholes? I did not. Give the Lily to the insurance company like you're supposed to. If those assholes want the whajamacallit so bad, they can go to court like civilized people. But, McKenzie, listen. When you make contact with the artnappers, you need to give me every scrap of information about them that you can. You know what to look for, what to listen for. You know people, too. Don't look at me like that. The people you know, you can get information that I can't. You do this for me, McKenzie. Meanwhile, I'll pursue the investigation on the down low. When I get anything, I'll tell you. You do the same."

Like you would do that, my inner voice said.

"In that case, when was Tarpley killed?" I asked aloud.

"The ME fixed the time of death at between one and four A.M. Monday," Rask said. "He couldn't narrow it down further because of the extreme cold."

"The Lily was stolen at two . . ."

"Tarpley was probably clipped between, say, two thirty and four, then."

"The artnappers first contacted the museum at eight. According to the museum's security footage, Tarpley handed off the Lily to at least two accomplices inside an SUV. Maybe they clipped him later for his trouble. That would sever any identifiable connection between them and the heist and leave them with one less partner to share the ransom with."

"Always an incentive."

"But, LT—"

"What was he doing in Wirth Park, in the middle of the night, in the cold, in the snow?" Rask said, finishing my thought. "We spoke to his wife. Her name is Yvonne Tarpley, called Von. Twenty-two years younger than her husband. Pretty. At least she was pretty before we told her we found her husband—you know how grief can, what it does to some people."

"Yeah, I know."

"She claimed she hadn't seen or heard from her husband since he left for work Sunday afternoon. She said he hadn't answered his cell phone and she was starting to get anxious. She said she called the museum, but there was no answer. She refused to believe Tarpley had anything to do with the theft."

"What about the murder weapon?"

"A 25."

Despite what you might see on TV and in the movies, only amateurs use guns the size of howitzers. Professionals prefer small-caliber weapons, get in close, aim for vital organs. I didn't express that theory out loud, of course. It would be like telling a landscaper that grass was green. Instead, I said, "I don't suppose you were allowed to ask Hemsted and Pozderac where they were between two thirty and four yesterday morning."

"No, I wasn't."

"It would be fun to put them at the scene, wouldn't it?"

"It would make my day."

"I appreciate that. They hurt your pride."

"Yeah, they hurt my pride. Coming in here and telling me *not* to be a cop, *Not* to do my job. Threatening me if I do.

They threatened you, too, McKenzie. Are you going to let them get away with that?"

"I don't know what I'm going to do yet. I'll tell you this much, LT. If I do what you ask—you follow baseball, right? When they list transactions, do you know what it means when Team A trades a guy to Team B for a player to be named later?"

"It means the quality of the player Team A gets in return will depend on how well the deal works out for Team B. You're saying that the more you do for me, the more I'm going to owe you."

"You might want to think about that before we become co-conspirators. I'm high maintenance."

I stepped out of the front door of the Minneapolis City Hall and got slapped in the face by a hard, cold wind for my trouble. I pulled my scarf tight and zipped my leather jacket closer to my throat as I made my way to the Jeep Cherokee. The time on the parking meter had expired. Fortunately, there was no ticket under my windshield. I unlocked the vehicle, slid inside, and started it. I pulled my cell from my pocket and made a call while the engine warmed up. The phone was answered by Special Agent Brian Wilson of the Federal Bureau of Investigation.

"Hi, Harry," I said. I had given him the nickname when we first met because he reminded me of the character actor Harry Dean Stanton. As far as I knew, I was the only one who called him that. "How are things?"

"Hey, McKenzie. What's going on?"

"Same-old, same-old."

"That bad, huh?"

"Just another day in paradise. So, Harry—how's my credit?"

"I think you might be one or two favors ahead," Wilson said. "Why?"

"I need information."

"You are so high maintenance, McKenzie. What kind of information? Tell me it's not confidential."

"I don't know if it is or it isn't. I need to find out as much as I can about a State Department wonk named Jonathan Hemsted."

"The State Department? Getting a little ambitious, aren't you, McKenzie?"

"Just a few minutes ago, Hemsted asked me to do something that I'm pretty sure is illegal."

"How illegal?"

"If I did it, you would throw me in the can without a moment's hesitation."

"Hell, McKenzie, I'd do that if I caught you littering. What exactly do you want to know?"

"How much trouble I'd be in if I told Hemsted to stick it where the sun doesn't shine."

"Anything else?"

"Well, if you can get me anything on a politician from Bosnia and Herzegovina named Branko Pozderac, that would be helpful, too."

"This doesn't sound like one of your usual gigs. What's going on?"

"I'll be happy to tell you everything, Harry, once I find out how dangerous Hemsted is. After that, you might not want to know."

FIVE

Chopper's wheelchair was parked behind a small table in the center of the restaurant by the time I arrived, and a pretty waitress dressed in black was fussing over him. It wasn't the let-me-help-you-because-you're-handicapped sort of fussing, either. It was the kind that accompanied the question "Your legs don't work, but what about the rest of you?"

I paused inside the front door to give him time to make his play. Even from his wheelchair, which Chopper operated with the fearlessness of a dirt-track biker, thus the nickname, he managed to have more fun—and pick up more girls—than anyone else I knew. I had known him since I found him lying in a parking lot in St. Paul with two slugs in his spine—this was back when I was a cop and he was a robber. He had insisted that I saved his life and therefore was responsible for it, although it seems like he has always done more for me than I ever have for him. Over the years he slowly but surely gave up the business of thievery for the far more lucrative and entirely legal occupation of ticket scalper.

That's what he insisted on calling it, "scalping," although by act of the state legislature he was now a taxpaying "ticket broker." What other enterprises he continued to involve himself in were kept secret—"the less you know, the more you'll like me," he once said.

After a few moments, an attractive hostess carrying menus as if they were stone tablets asked if I wanted a table.

I pointed at Chopper. "I'm with him," I said.

"Oh, you're Mr. Coleman's guest," she said. "Please come this way."

Mr. Coleman? my inner voice asked.

By the time we reached Chopper's table, he had transcribed the waitress's name and phone number into his iPhone and had even taken her photo. The waitress became flustered when the hostess approached, and I wondered if the restaurant had a nonfraternization policy.

"I'll return with your bread in a moment, Mr. Coleman," she said before hurrying away.

Mr. Coleman? my inner voice asked again.

The hostess seated me and wished us both bon appétit. When she departed, I asked, "Mr. Coleman?"

" 'At's my name, don' wear it out," Chopper said.

"When I invited you to an early dinner an hour ago, you said you never heard of this place, and now it's Mr. Coleman?"

"I told 'em to call me Thaddeus, but they said oh, no, they couldn't, although . . ." He gazed at the waitress and raised and lowered his eyebrows Groucho Marx–style a couple of times.

"How do you do it?" I asked. "I've been in this restaurant a dozen times and they never called me Mr. McKenzie. They don't even know my name."

"When you friendly t' everybody, everybody be friendly t' you. You such a morose fellow, McKenzie. Gots t' lighten up."

The waitress returned with a basket of garlic bread and a small plate that she filled with extra-virgin olive oil and pepper for dipping. She asked for drink preferences, and I ordered a winter ale brewed in Duluth. Chopper said he was in the mood for a well-rounded red wine, supple and spicy, yet not too intense, and asked the waitress to select it for him. She chose a zinfandel, and after he sampled it, Chopper announced that the waitress was not only beautiful, she had exquisite taste. All in all, I thought she took the compliment very well. After she left with our orders, Chopper leaned across the table.

"She has a roommate," he said.

"Lucky you."

"Naw, man. Lucky you. Whaddaya say? T'morrow night. We meet ahh, ahh . . ." Chopper waved his hand in small circles as if he were trying to hurry someone up. "I forgit 'er name."

"Oh, for God's sake."

"I gots it written down." Chopper fumbled with his cell phone. "Emma. Em-ma. Roommate is named Ali. Whaddaya say?"

"I'm already spoken for."

"Still seein' the honey what owns the jazz joint, ain'tcha?"

"I am."

"Been a while now."

"It has."

Chopper sighed deeply. "I gots t' do that," he said. "Find a good-lookin' woman can support me in my old age."

"It's what I recommend."

The waitress soon returned with our lunch orders. After

much flirting, Chopper labeled his pappardelle with duck ragu, red peppers, and tomato the best he ever tasted. Emma was thrilled to hear it. On the other hand, she couldn't have cared less what I thought of my Dijon pork tenderloin.

We talked about this, that, and the other thing until the meal was nearly finished, at which point Chopper said, "I suppose we ought t' git down to biz-ness."

"Business?"

"You buyin' for a reason, ain'tcha?"

"As a matter of fact . . ."

"Uh-huh."

"I was wondering if you heard anything about a crew taking down the City of Lakes Art Museum the other night."

"Someone hit City of Lakes? No shit? Whadda they git?"

"A chunk of jade worth three-point-eight million."

"Nice."

"I'm guessing you know nothing about it."

"Nah, man, but why would I? That kind of heist is a little outta my zone, man. You wanna know who's smuggling cigarettes, who's boosting cars, HDTVs, computers, yeah, I can git the four-one-one on that. But art theft? Uh-uh."

"Who would know?"

"In the Cities? Wow. That's a tough question."

"There must be someone. How about a fence?"

"You gots t' know, this kinda thing don' have a lot of buyers. Steal a big-screen TV, people fall all over themselves t' buy it. A paintin', work of art, somethin' famous, somethin' valuable cuz it's famous, that only appeals to what you call a select clientele, high rollers happy t' pay big bucks for somethin' they can't ever show off, you know? What you need is somebody who tied into that, knows the people who knows the people here in the Cities and elsewhere, am I right?"

"There has to be somebody I can talk to."

"Man, I don' know. Let me think . . . Only one comes t' mind is Cid."

"Sid who?"

"No, no. Cid, like in El Cid."

"The Lord?"

"What?"

"El Cid, it means the Lord. It was the title given to Rodrigo Díaz de Vivar, the Spanish knight credited with driving the Moors out of Spain in the eleventh century, supposedly making Europe safe for Christianity."

"Moors? That was like brothers, right? Africans."

"African Muslims. Truth is, the Cid was a glorified mercenary worked for the Christian king, then the Muslims, then the Christians again."

"Huh? I did not know that. How come you know all this shit?"

"I read," I said. Actually, everything I knew about El Cid came from a movie I once saw starring Charlton Heston and Sophia Loren and a documentary on the History Channel, but what the hell?

"I wonder how Cid got the name," Chopper said.

"We could ask. Think you could arrange a meeting with him?"

"Yeah, yeah, I'll git on that."

Chopper took up his cell phone, and for a moment I thought he was calling Cid from the table. I changed my mind when he said, "I'm ready," into the microphone and then closed the phone. A few moments later, a large black man dressed in shiny leather filled the front doorway of the restaurant. The sight of him filled me with dread.

"Herzog," I said.

"Yeah," Chopper said.

"When did he get out of the joint?"

"Six months ago. Spent time in a halfway house—now he works for me."

"Jeezus, Chopper."

"Ain't what you think, McKenzie. I'm legit now. Well, practically. Herzog, all he does is drive and, you know, take care of me."

"Since when do you need to be taken care of?"

"I bought me a van. Gots one of them elevators and shit. I wheel onto this platform and press a button and it hoists me up. Press another one and it slides me into the van. Fuckin' cool."

"What happened to the tricked-out Porsche you used to drive?"

"I still gots it. I be drivin' it 'morrow night." Chopper tilted his head toward the kitchen where Emma had disappeared. "You know, McKenzie, I ain't bankin' as much as you—I'm talkin' taxable shit—but I gots enough I can afford a driver."

"Herzog, though? He's a stone killer. Chopper, Herzog?"

Chopper leaned across the table. When he did, Herzog started moving across the restaurant toward us.

"Don' you go hatin' on Herzog, man. Me and him go back a lot longer than me and you. He's family. If he wasn't in stir that one time, no way those fuckin' Red Dragons got the balls t' pump two in my back. No fuckin' way. Ain't gonna happen."

I held my empty hands away from my body in surrender, just as Herzog arrived.

"Anythin' I can do for you, Chop?" he said. He watched me intently while he spoke.

"You know McKenzie," Chopper said.

"I knows 'im. Cop."

"Ex-cop," I said.

"Fuckin' cop."

"Okay," Chopper said. "McKenzie, I'll be in touch." With that we engaged in a ritual handshake that I messed up, as usual.

"I don' know why I hang wit' you," Chopper said.

"I'm likable," I said.

"Hmmph," Herzog said.

Chopper spun his chair and started rolling it toward the door; Herzog never touched it. As they went, I heard Chopper speaking.

"You know, Herzy, it's like I was tellin' McKenzie. You gots t' learn t' lighten up."

A few moments later, Emma returned to the table with the tab. She expressed her disappointment that Mr. Coleman had left without saying good-bye. I told her that he was sorry he had to rush off, but he was looking forward to seeing her again the next evening and would pick her up in his Porsche, if that was all right.

"He drives a Porsche?" Emma asked.

"Yep."

"What else can he do?"

I considered the question carefully before I answered.

"I've known Mr. Coleman a long time," I said. "I have never heard him admit that there was anything he couldn't do."

Emma seemed to like the answer very much. Certainly she was smiling when she left with my credit card. By the time she returned, Lieutenant Scott Noehring was sitting at my table. I settled the tab before I spoke to him.

"Where did you come from?" I asked. "Are you following me?"

"The company you keep, McKenzie, makes me wonder. I told Rask that I thought you had more to do with the theft of the Jade Lily than you let on, and here you are, breaking bread with one of the worst criminals in Minneapolis."

"When you say worst, do you mean he doesn't do it very well? Because I don't think Mr. Coleman has ever been convicted of a crime."

"He's been into drugs, prostitution, gambling; he ran a shoplifting ring that had more customers than fucking Mall of America. I know for a fact that he's been smuggling cigarettes into the state from Kentucky and North Carolina."

"You should arrest him, then. Put his black ass in jail. If you can."

"You don't think he has it coming?"

"I know a lot of people who have it coming." I reached across the table and caressed the material of his overcoat between my thumb and forefinger. "Cashmere?"

Noehring slapped my hand away. "Italian wool," he said.

"Nice," I said. "On a cop's salary, too."

"Don't get sanctimonious with me, McKenzie. I know you. I know how you made your money. You arrested an embezzler. Instead of bringing him and the stolen money in like you were supposed to, you quit the St. Paul cops and negotiated a reward from the insurance company. You sold your badge."

I didn't see it that way, but I knew a lot of cops that did.

"Well, didn't you?" Noehring asked.

"What do you want?" I asked in reply.

"How about a drink?"

Why not? my inner voice asked. I caught Emma's eye and motioned her back to the table.

"I'd like another winter ale," I told her. I gestured toward Noehring. He asked Emma to recite the restaurant's Scotch list and settled on Glenlivet, double, neat. He smiled as if he expected both Emma and me to be impressed by his selection. It was the same smile that I had seen the night before, but in the harsh light of day it seemed worn-out from overuse. He kept smiling as he watched Emma walk to the bar.

"Nice ass," he said.

The smile flickered slightly when I didn't reply.

The drinks were served, and Noehring drank half of his in one swallow.

"That's good Scotch," he said.

"Finish it," I said. "Have another."

Noehring smiled some more. "One is fine," he said. "I'm working."

"For who exactly?"

Noehring leaned back in his chair and gave me a look as if I had insulted him and he was wondering what to do about it.

"I've been hearing things," he said.

"What things?"

"I heard that you decided not to make the exchange for the Jade Lily. Something about being spooked from seeing Tarpley dead last night."

"Where did you hear that?"

"Is it true?"

"Let's just say that I was reminded that life is short, too short to live it like a character in an S. S. Van Dine novel."

"Uh-huh. Well, I just want you to know you don't have to worry about it. You don't need to be afraid to retrieve the Lily." Noehring tapped his chest. "I'll protect your ass. Unofficially, of course."

"That's awfully considerate of you, Lieutenant."

"I'm a considerate guy."

I bet, my inner voice said.

"What would you ask in return for this service?" I asked.

"Ten percent of your end."

"Twelve thousand seven hundred dollars?"

Noehring grinned. "That's a little less than I figured," he said.

"What would the Minneapolis Police Department say about the arrangement?"

"It doesn't mind if we make a little on the side providing security. I know a lot of guys that work weddings."

"Problem is, Lieutenant, if the artnappers spot you, they just might put a bullet in my head. Unofficially, of course."

"Not if we put them down first."

That made me sit back.

"Sounds to me like you have a plan," I said.

"No plan. I just want to be there in case."

"In case of what?"

"In case," Noehring repeated.

We spent a couple of seconds staring at each other. Finally I had to ask, "What exactly are you proposing?"

"Let's say—we're just talking here, right, McKenzie?"

"Just talking," I said.

"Let's say that after you deliver the money, the artnappers decide that you're a loose end that they don't need. A loose end the way Tarpley was a loose end. They decide to kill you. Except, at that precise moment, one of the thieves seizes the opportunity—there is no honor among thieves, is there? He decides to waste his partners instead and escape with all of the money, leaving you unharmed and in possession of the Lily. Hypothetically, of course."

"Let me guess. The reason he leaves me unharmed amid all that carnage is so I can tell the police what happened."

"Exactly."

"And the money—"

"A million three—"

"What happens to the money?"

"Fifty-fifty split."

"I have a question—where will you be when all this takes place?"

"Oh, I'll be miles away."

"With an airtight alibi, I'll bet."

Noehring took a sip of his Scotch.

"What do you think?" he said.

"I have another question—what do you think the odds are that the thief might shoot me by accident?"

"Almost nonexistent."

"Almost?"

"With you alive and the Lily in your hands, the museum will be happy, the insurance company will be happy, and the police, they're not going to get worked up over a bunch of dead thieves and murderers—they did kill Tarpley, right? With you dead, the investigation expands, and who knows where it'll lead? 'Course, there are always accidents, aren't there?"

"That's what I'm worried about."

"You might want to worry about the alternative."

"That would be . . . ?"

"You used to be police, McKenzie. You know how it works. I put the word out that you need to be taught a lesson, you'll get a lesson. You'll get more than one. The bleeding hearts call it police harassment."

"The right-wing nut jobs call it the same thing."

"I don't think it'll stop, either. A cop who sold his badge—that's how it'll be played, don't think otherwise—you'll have enemies for life. You might even have to move."

"I collected the price on Teachwell over six years ago and no one has cared."

"Till now."

"You have it all figured out, don't you?"

"Including which bank accounts to hide the money in. C'mon, McKenzie. There's no need for this. We both know how things work. You probably never so much as asked for a free taco when you were on the job until one day the guy behind the counter offered you a free taco and you took it. After a while, you expected all the tacos to be free. Then Teachwell falls in your lap. You weren't looking for a score, but there it was. The opportunity of a lifetime. So you took it. Who can blame you? What we're talking about now, it's just another opportunity. Only this time, you don't need to do anything. I'll take care of the heavy lifting."

"There are at least three artnappers," I said.

Noehring scooped up his glass, finished the Scotch, and set the glass back on the table. "So?" he said.

Jeezus, he'd do it, he really would, my inner voice said. *He'd kill them all. And me, too.*

"I'll think about it," I said aloud.

"Yeah, you do that. We'll talk again."

I did indeed think about it as I watched Noehring leave the restaurant. Mostly I thought that I had known an awful lot of cops personally—local, state, feds, you name it. Some were better at their jobs than others; some were assholes, pricks, bullies with a badge. Yet none of them had been crooks. That's not to say that there weren't plenty of cops with their hands out. God knows half of them portrayed on TV and in the movies are on the take. I had just never known one. Until now.

Something else I thought about—how did Noehring know where I was?

I didn't know what to do about Noehring any more than I knew what to do about Hemsted. Both parties wanted me to steal the Lily for them and threatened to make my life miserable if I failed. Then there was Heavenly Petryk. God only knew what she had in mind. Not to mention Lieutenant Rask. There was no way I was going to please all these people. I decided there was only one thing left to do—ignore them and hope they all went away.

I finished the ale, left a generous tip so Emma would have nice things to say about me to Chopper, and made my way to the Jeep Cherokee parked in the restaurant's lot. It was my intention to go home and have plenty more beers. Before I reached the car, however, my cell phone started ringing. A man passing through the lot, his head down, his face averted by the brisk wind, paused for a moment and then nodded and shook his finger at me. I don't know if it was because he liked the artists, the song, or the irony of hearing "Summertime" in subfreezing temperatures.

The electronic display listed no name, just a number with a 312 prefix—Chicago. I had no idea who it could be. For a long time I had zealously protected my cell phone number, bestowing it on only a precious few people. Yet over time I seemed to have lost control of it. I answered just the same.

"Mr. McKenzie," the voice said. "I apologize for calling. I hope I'm not disturbing you."

"That remains to be seen."

The caller thought that was funny.

"Let me introduce myself. I'm Jeremy Gillard."

"Mr. Gillard," I said.

"Jerry, Jerry, Jerry, call me Jerry. The man at the insurance company gave me your number. Again, I hope I'm not disturbing you."

"Not at all. What can I do for you?"

"Well, first I should tell you that I'm calling under false pretenses."

"Oh?"

"The City of Lakes Art Museum, what's 'ername, Perrin Stewart, told me what's going on with the Jade Lily—did you know that I own the Lily?"

"I did."

"Loaned it to the museum. Thought I was doing a good deed. That'll teach me. Anyway, I was told about the Lily. One of the things I was told was that its recovery might very well depend on your involvement."

"Mr. Gillard—"

"Jerry. Mr. Gillard was the old man's name. Listen, McKenzie, I understand your reluctance. I'm on your side in this. Perrin suggested that a personal appeal from me might change your mind and I agreed to give it a go, but the more I thought about it—you'd be nuts to go after the Lily. Hell's bells, I wouldn't do it and it belongs to me, so why should you? Nearly everyone who's touched the damn thing has suffered for it, including my old man."

"I was sorry to hear about your father," I said.

"Thank you for that. In any case, here's the deal—if you decide to go after the Lily, I'll match whatever amount the insurance company is offering you. But I don't want you taking any unnecessary risks."

"I appreciate that."

"You need to know, McKenzie, really, you need to know—at the end of the day it's just a really pretty rock. And it's insured."

At last, my inner voice said. *The voice of reason.*

"I appreciate that," I said again.

"All right. I made the call as promised. My conscience is clear. I'm flying into the Cities tomorrow. Whatever you decide, I'd be honored if you let me buy you a drink or two or three."

"I know just the place."

"Excellent. I have your number. I'll call when I get in."

"Do that."

"Good-bye, McKenzie."

Gillard hung up, and as I put my cell in my pocket, I thought: Now that's how it's done. No threats. No insults. No sob stories. No appeals to the angels of our better nature. Just plain old-fashioned charm and sincerity. Plus a cash bonus. That's how you make friends and influence people.

The sun had already set by the time I reached my home in Falcon Heights. As I turned into my driveway, the Cherokee's headlights swept across the rear bumper of a Nissan Altima parked in front of my house. I didn't recognize the car, and the sight of it started my internal alarm bells ringing. They became louder when I noticed my kitchen light was on. There were logical explanations for both: The car belonged to someone visiting a neighbor; I had forgotten to turn off the light. Yet that didn't quiet my anxiety. I wasn't usually that paranoid, but let's face it—it had been one of those days.

I parked in my garage and made my way to my rear door. It was unlocked, an astonishing thing in itself, but the fact that my security system wasn't screaming intruder alert and that the place wasn't crawling with private cops from my security company or real cops from the City of St. Anthony, was what made me pause. Do I report a burglary and wait for the police to arrive, or do I go inside? The answer came with a lyrical shout.

"McKenzie, is that you?"

I stepped through the door and into the kitchen. Heavenly Petryk was sitting at the table; a white ski jacket with a fur-lined hood was draped over the back of a chair. She was drinking coffee from one of my mugs.

"I hope you don't mind that I let myself in," she said. "It was damn cold outside."

"How did you . . . ?" I completed the question by throwing a thumb at the back door.

"The door was open and the security system was turned off."

"No they weren't."

"That's my story and I'm sticking to it."

"I could shoot you for an intruder."

"Nah, you wouldn't do that."

"Why not?"

"Because you like me. Besides, it would be a tough story to sell. There's no evidence of forced entry."

I glanced at the back door again. I hadn't been surprised by her talents as a researcher. Heavenly had a master's degree in English, after all. But this?

"You've become more resourceful since we last met," I said. "Daring, too."

"Heavenly Petryk, fortune hunter. I'm thinking of having cards made up."

"Fortune hunter. Isn't that the same as gold digger?"

Heavenly spun in her chair and looked up at me. "If you were still a lowly police officer making a lowly police officer's salary, I bet you would have married your rich, club-owning girlfriend a long time ago."

I had nothing to say to that. I went to the coffeemaker and poured out a mug, then sat at the kitchen table across from her.

"So, Heavenly," I said. "Where are your playmates?"

"It wasn't my turn to watch them."

"No?"

"Besides, I needed a break. They're so needy."

"I thought that was one of your requirements."

"Only in accomplices. I demand more from my men."

"How's that going for you? Still seeing Boston Whitlow?"

"That ended a long time ago." Heavenly exhaled loudly when she said it, and I wondered if it was a sigh of regret. "Are you going to invite me to your bedroom?"

"Why would I do that?"

"Geez, McKenzie, if you have to ask . . ."

"Didn't we have this conversation once before? I'm old enough to be your father."

"Only if you knocked up my mother when she was about fourteen."

"Besides . . ."

"Besides, you're still loyal to Nina Truhler, whom you haven't married after—how many years? McKenzie, you can be had."

"I know. Why do you think I refuse to take you seriously?"

"You took me seriously enough to sic Lieutenant Rask on me."

"Oh, that."

"He's not a very nice man, is he?"

"I don't know. His wife and kids adore him. Obviously, he let you go."

"Why not? I haven't done anything illegal."

" 'Course not."

"You told him about Tatjana?"

"Yep."

"But you didn't tell him that I kidnapped you."

I shrugged at that and sipped my coffee.

"See, I knew you liked me," she said.

"What are you doing here, Heavenly?"

"Since we're friends, will you tell me something? Why did you quit the museum? Why have you refused to recover the Lily?"

"That damn museum has more holes than the Vikings' secondary."

"Well?"

"Well, what?"

"I know it's not because you're afraid."

"On the contrary. I'm becoming very cautious as I get older."

Heavenly looked at the corridor leading from the kitchen to the front of the house. "Not going to invite me upstairs, huh?" she said.

"Nope."

"What else can I offer to make you change your mind?"

"About what?"

"About going after the Lily?"

"Not much, although your proposal is a lot more enticing than anything else I've heard today."

"What have you heard?"

"Well, the State Department, for one, has threatened to make my life a living hell unless I steal the Lily and give it to a representative of the government of Bosnia and Herzegovina."

Heavenly was on her feet in a hurry. "That's insane," she said.

"Any more insane than giving it to you?"

"The Bosnians stole the Lily from my client, and somehow Dr. Arnaud Fornier stole it from them, and now Jeremy Gillard has it. The Lily rightfully belongs to Tatjana Durakovic."

"That's not the way Branko Pozderac sees it."

"Pozderac? That bastard?"

"You know him?"

"He's a rapist and a murderer. He and his militia terrorized Sarajevo, terrorized half the country during the war. Do you know how many innocent people he slaughtered?"

"Well, now he's a member of the People's Assembly or House or whatever."

"How is that possible?"

"I don't know. Maybe he had a great campaign manager."

"It changes nothing, McKenzie. The Lily belongs to Tatjana."

"Possession is nine points of the law."

"McKenzie, you and I both know there is no specific legal ruling to support that proverb."

"Maybe not, but time and again the person in actual possession of the property has a clear advantage over the person who doesn't have it. Right now, the artnappers who swiped it from the museum, they own it. After they pay the ransom, the insurance company will own it."

"I'm just asking you to do the right thing."

"You keep saying that. Your client could invest in a good lawyer instead of hiring a couple of thugs to return her property—maybe that's the right thing."

"Did you just call me a thug?"

"Granted you're more beautiful than the image the term usually conjures, still . . ."

"That's a terrible thing to say."

"You should hear what Nina calls you."

"I can imagine. McKenzie, it takes years for a case like this to wind its way through the courts. Decades. You need to help me."

"Heavenly, all day long I've been hearing from people who demand that I get the Lily for them. Your claim might be a little less mercenary than the others, but not by much, and it still doesn't change the simple fact of the matter—the Lily doesn't belong to you. Or to them. It belongs to Gillard. Funny thing is, he's the only one who's not a fanatic about getting it back."

"That's because he doesn't want it back. He wants the insurance money."

"What are you talking about?"

"Gillard is broke, McKenzie. His old man took a huge hit in the housing crisis, and then he lost some more when commercial real estate started going south, too. He was holding his business empire together with smoke and mirrors. All this came out when they audited his estate. Gillard's inheritance amounted to pennies on the dollar. I mean, he's not broke broke like you and me, well, me anyway, but a three-point-eight-million-dollar insurance claim will set him up nicely."

"How do you know this?"

"It's me, remember. I did the research."

"Heavenly, if what you're saying is true, then Gillard would want the Lily back for the same reason that Tatjana wants it—because it would sell for more at auction than the insured value."

"All right, all right." Heavenly held her arms up in mock surrender. "I tried to be nice."

"So now you're going to be not nice? I have that to look forward to?"

She shrugged like she had a secret she had no intention of sharing and pulled her jacket off the chair. When she finished putting it on and zipping it up, she placed a rose-colored business card with her name and cell number—and nothing else—on the kitchen table and slid it toward me.

"I'll be seeing you," she said.

"Heavenly, I'll tell you what the guys I play hockey with would say—keep your head up."

I escorted Heavenly to the front door and watched her drive away before reactivating my security system. I was wondering how much an upgrade would cost when my cell phone rang.

"Harry," I said. "What's going on?"

"I have some background on your target, but I have to make it quick. The wife is waiting downstairs. We're going to dinner."

"Give her a kiss for me."

"Not a chance. Now, McKenzie, I checked a few sources. Your friend Jonathan Hemsted is a Foreign Service specialist attached to the U.S. Commercial Service Office in the Bosnia-Herzegovina Embassy. Before that he was stationed in Haiti."

"What does he specialize in?"

"He's an economics officer working to expand U.S. trade in the region. This guy Branko Pozderac, he's involved with the privatization of state-owned entities. That's probably how they hooked up."

"I didn't know we had any trade in the region."

"About forty million worth."

"You're kidding? The Twins' infield is worth more than that."

"Just telling you what they told me."

"Would Hemsted have anything to do with recovering stolen artifacts—allegedly stolen artifacts?"

"I wouldn't think so," Harry said. "The State Department might file a report or request assistance, but they're not going to investigate or recover."

"Who would?"

"The Federal Bureau of Investigation. McKenzie, we have an Art Crime Team. We have an Art Theft Program. We have special prosecutors assigned by the Department of Justice. We sometimes work with other organizations like Homeland Security, Interpol, or even Immigration and Customs Enforcement. Which raises the question, what the hell?"

I told him that I would explain, but his wife was waiting.

"Make it fast," he said.

I did.

"I have so much work on my desk," Harry said. "I think I'll take a look into this anyway."

"How much juice do you think a Foreign Service specialist working in a shit hole like Bosnia has?"

"That depends on his boss."

"His boss is the secretary of state."

"I'll get back to you."

"You're a peach, Harry. Give your wife my love."

"Hell no."

I returned to the kitchen table and finished my coffee. I liked it so much that I had another mug, this one laced with Irish whiskey. And then another. That and the two ales I had earlier weren't nearly enough to make me drunk, but they did give me an excuse for what I did next. I called Mr. Donatucci.

"Have you heard from the artnappers?" I asked.

"Nothing yet. Why do you ask?"

"You said you could set up a meeting with someone who could give me tips on how to authenticate the Lily. Can you still do that?"

"You're going for the Lily after all," Donatucci said. It wasn't a question.

"Yes."

"What changed your mind?"

"Peer pressure."

SIX

Perrin Stewart punched a code into a keypad and hit ENTER. Nothing happened.

"I hate these things," she said.

"Patrick Tarpley didn't have any trouble," I said.

Perrin gave me a hard look and cursed softly—some people don't appreciate sarcasm. She tried again. This time a tiny green light blinked on top of the keypad, followed by a metallic sound as the door unlocked. She held the door open until I passed through, then closed it tightly behind her. Her heels made a tick-tock sound that echoed off the white walls, white ceiling, and white tile floor of the brightly lit corridor, and I didn't know which I wanted more, earplugs or sunglasses.

"I've seen hospital operating rooms with less light," I said.

"It's all environmentally responsible, too," Perrin said. "We earned a LEED Gold designation for the building design. That was partly my doing. I saw it not only as a matter of reducing our carbon footprint but also of saving money. Our energy bills are a third of a typical building this size."

"I need to ask a question that might offend you."

"All right."

"How sure are you of your people?"

"If you'd asked me last week, I would have vouched for all of them. Now . . . Why do you ask?"

"There's a leak. Maybe more than one. There are people who seem to know my every move in this matter even before I do. I think they're getting intel from someone within your building."

Perrin suddenly stopped walking and leaned back against the wall of the corridor. Her head was bent toward the floor, so I couldn't see her face, but the sound of her voice told me what I could easily have guessed—this had not been the best week of her life, and it was probably going to get worse.

"I no longer trust the people around me," she said.

"I can appreciate that. You look up sometimes and discover that life has you surrounded and there's no way out unless you're willing to accept casualties."

Perrin snickered at that. "Yeah," she said. "Yeah. That's one way of looking at it. McKenzie, I haven't thanked you for changing your mind about the Lily."

"Yes, you did."

Perrin shook her head. "All of my life I wanted to do this, run a truly great art museum," she said. "City of Lakes isn't great. Not yet. If you take a small, unknown museum and make it a bigger, better-known museum, though, the biggest, best-known museums take notice and . . . You know how it works."

"Sure."

"I have a master's degree in art history. I have a bachelor's degree in museum studies. I've studied marketing, public relations, fund-raising, and business administration to get here. I have over a hundred and thirty thousand dollars in student loans to pay off. I don't care. I make only twelve hundred a week. I don't care. I don't care because I love being here. It's the best job—do you know that the average museum director lasts only four years? The pressure from boards of directors, constant fund-raising, and the demands on their personal life eat them alive. Yet it's just the opposite with me. I thrive on this. The Derek Andersons of the world, those pompous, self-aggrandizing men who spend the money and put in the time so they can be seen, so they can pretend they're important, I can play them like a flute. Unfortunately, if the Lily isn't returned . . ."

"The theft isn't your fault."

"I'm afraid Mr. Fiegen doesn't see it that way."

"He seems like a reasonable man."

Perrin shook her head again. "Fiegen's not in it for the attention. He's not pretending to be anything other than what he is. He genuinely wants to build a museum that's equal to the Minneapolis Institute of Arts, that's equal to the Walker, that's equal to the Art Institute of Chicago. If he thinks I'm not the woman for the job . . . You know what my greatest fear is, McKenzie? What keeps me awake at night? That one day I'll end up being just another art major making mochas in a coffeehouse."

It was at that moment that I made a somewhat impulsive decision. I decided I liked Perrin, all two hundred pounds of her.

"Don't worry," I said. "I'll get it back."

Perrin smiled. "Please," she said.

———

Perrin escorted me through an unmarked door into a storage room the size of a high school cafeteria. It, too, was very brightly lit and consisted of many tables, shelves, racks, and drawers filled with works of art—paintings, sculptures, even furniture—that, for some reason, were not exhibited to the public. There was a woman sitting at a workstation and examining a spinach green brooch through a mounted magnifying glass. She smiled when she saw us coming and stood up. At a distance she looked like the standard movie cliché—the sexy female scientist hiding her beauty behind a white lab coat, black-rimmed glasses, and hair that was worn in a ponytail. Unfortunately, I soon discovered that she needed the glasses, her hair was pulled back because she didn't have time to wash it that morning, and the lab coat hid a body that looked like it hadn't consumed a carbohydrate in months. Oh, well.

She and Perrin hugged in a way that was meant to give comfort and not just say hello. While Perrin was large, tall, and fair-skinned, the other woman was thin and short, with a dark complexion. When they hugged they reminded me of a female version of Laurel and Hardy.

"You look like hell, Stewart," the woman said.

In that moment I knew they were the best of friends, because instead of being insulted, Perrin said, "I feel like hell."

"Did you get any sleep at all?"

"Not much."

Perrin directed her friend's attention toward me.

"This is McKenzie," she said. "McKenzie, India Cooper."

We shook hands, and Perrin said, "Cooper is the curator in charge of our Asian Art Collection."

"Stewart is right," India said. "You are cute."

I glanced at Perrin, who quickly turned a light shade of red. She closed her eyes, and I thought I heard her whisper, "C'mon, Cooper, not today."

"I take it you two are BFFs," I said.

"We met in school—Syracuse University," India said. "I'm from Arizona, and she's from Southern California. We shared a blanket at a football game one day when the wind was waffling off Lake Ontario at about a thousand miles an hour. Huddling together to keep warm, neither of us could believe that it could get that cold for that length of time. I've been trying to get her hooked up ever since."

"Cooper," Perrin said. Her face was now scarlet.

She was saved from further embarrassment by the ringing of her cell phone. She answered it, pivoting away from us at the same time. A moment later, she turned back.

"Mr. Gillard is here," Perrin said. "So is Mr. Donatucci. I'll leave you two alone. McKenzie, I'll . . ."

She brought her hand to her temple as if she were suddenly experiencing brain freeze.

"I'll bring him back to your office," India said.

Perrin gave her a waning smile and nodded. She quickly retreated from the room. India watched her go, actually took a couple of steps as if she meant to follow her.

"McKenzie?" India said.

"Yes?"

"Can you help her?"

"I can try to retrieve the Lily. Beyond that . . ."

"Rumor has it that Derek Anderson wants the board to replace Stewart with some blond bimbo he's been seeing. Losing the Lily might be just the excuse he's looking for."

"That's what I heard, but the board can't blame her for the theft, can it?"

"She hired Patrick Tarpley when no one else would, so yeah, I bet they can."

"I thought his credentials were impeccable."

"No one's credentials are impeccable. I would think you of all people would know that."

"I suppose I do."

"Something else—Stewart genuinely cared about Tarpley. The fact he stole from her hurt. The fact he was killed, I think, hurt even more."

"There's nothing we can do about that."

"What can we do?" India turned toward me. "What can I do?"

"Let's say, for argument's sake, that I'm walking down the street and a guy comes up to me and says, 'Psst, buddy? Wanna buy a jade lily?' How can I tell if it's the real thing and not a counterfeit?"

"There are a number of tests we can perform—Mohs Scale of Hardness, microscopic test, density test, calcification test, patina test. We can examine the workmanship such as the carving technique and the depth of incised and relief lines, tools and abrasion signatures, art style—"

"India?"

"Yes?"

"Let's assume I'll have a couple of minutes with it tops. Let's also assume that I'm as dumb as brick."

"Oh, McKenzie." A shy light flickered in her eyes as she gave my wrist a squeeze, and I felt a sudden surge of electricity that traveled up my arm and then down through my legs. "I'm sure you're at least as smart as Carrara marble."

Where did that come from? my inner voice asked. And then, *Maybe if she did take off her glasses and let down her hair . . .*

India's eyes darted across her work area as if she were searching for an answer. She found it in the form of a 10-power magnifying glass.

"Here," she said.

I took the glass. India reached for the spinach green brooch she'd been examining before.

"Here," she said again.

I took the brooch.

"Hold it up to the light and look at it through the magnifier," she said. "Imperial jade is somewhat translucent. See those little veins, almost feltlike fibers that seem intertwined?"

"Yes."

"That's a good sign. If you see anything resembling layers, then you're looking at jadeite that's been doubled or even tripled."

"I don't get—"

"That means the thin layers of jadeite were glued together."

"Okay."

"If you see air bubbles, that means it's counterfeit."

"Okay."

"Something else—notice how the jade feels smooth and soaplike to the touch? That's a good sign, too. What else? True jade will scratch glass, even metal."

"Do you want me to scrape it across a windowpane?"

"God, no! McKenzie. Are you kidding?"

"What, then?"

"It's a frickin' work of art!"

"Sorry."

"Here." India took the jade brooch from my hand, turned it over, and picked up a pair of scissors. "Gently take the blunt end of a scissors or a knife and gently, gently now, draw a line.

Please, McKenzie, at the bottom of the piece, at the base of the Lily. Do it there. You'll get what looks like a scratch, a white line. See?" She showed me the back of the brooch. "Gently wipe it off. It should be—the white line should be residue from the knife. If it comes off, it's real jade. If the scratch remains, it's a fake."

I took the brooch and repeated India's experiment. It worked just as it had with her.

"Cool," I said. "But . . ."

"What?"

"How will I know if it's the actual Lily and not a fake made of real jade?"

"It would cost tens of thousands of dollars to make a fake Lily out of real imperial jade."

"Nonetheless."

India took a deep breath and searched her workstation again. I could see the wheels turning behind her glasses. "Okay," she said, more to herself than to me, and opened a drawer. She thumbed through a few files, grabbed the one she liked, and dropped it on the tabletop.

"This is the Jade Lily," she said.

She opened the file and started spreading out photographs. Heavenly Petryk was right—it was exquisite. The photographs showed two stalks extending from the base. One held eight blossoms with impossibly thin petals and the other had ten. There was a tiny cuplike flower in the center of each blossom.

"Wow," I said.

"It's a carving of a flower called the Chinese Sacred Lily," India said. "Botanical name *Narcissus tazetta v. orientalis*. In real life the stems are green, almost as green as the jade. The blossoms are white, and the flowers in the center are the color of gold."

"Wow," I repeated.

"The odd thing is, it's neither Chinese nor a lily. The flower, I mean. It's actually a daffodil, and it originated in Egypt, of all places. But the Chinese have used it as a part of their New Year's celebrations for God knows how many generations, hence the name."

"I'm impressed."

"Haven't you ever seen the Lily before?"

"No."

"It's more impressive in person."

"I'll bet."

"Anyway, here." India chose a photograph and slid it in front of me. She took the magnifying glass and held it over the photograph where one of the stalks met the base. "Take a look."

I took the glass from her hand and bent to the task.

"See where the stalk sprouts from the ground?" India said. "You'll notice some imperfections from the carving process. There's a tiny nick that resembles the letter *M*. *M* for Mc-Kenzie. I can't imagine anyone carving a reproduction of the Jade Lily—especially out of imperial jade. I certainly can't imagine anyone adding an *M*."

I stared at the *M* for a while and then moved the glass around, looking for other telltale imperfections.

"Did you appraise the Lily?" I asked.

"No. We don't do that here."

"Who did?"

"I have no idea. You'll have to ask Mr. Gillard about that."

"Have you met him?"

"Gillard? No, but I'm sure he can tell you who put a value on the Lily. There are a lot of private companies that do that sort of thing, although usually they get it wrong."

"Value, no, that's not what I meant. I meant, ahh, what's the word?"

"Authenticate?"

"Authenticate. Did you authenticate the Lily?"

"Yes. When it came in. That was two weeks ago. There wasn't much work to do. I didn't need to perform any tests. The provenance was intact. We could follow the chain of custody back far enough that we were sure we were exhibiting what we said we were exhibiting. I spent a lot of time with it, though. God, it's beautiful."

"How did it arrive?"

"A delivery company that specializes in shipping expensive artwork brought it in. Dublin Pack and Ship. We've used them before. They provide what they call 'white glove pickup and delivery.' In this case they went to Gillard's place in Chicago, packed the Lily in cushioning foam and an ISPM-15 certified crate, brought it here, and unpacked it. There were always at least three people with the Lily every step of the process. They charged eleven thousand dollars. Do you believe that? That's a quarter of my yearly salary. I am definitely in the wrong end of this business."

India had plenty more to say about jade in general—"The Chinese word for jade is *yu,* which translates to mean noble, pure, jewel, or treasure, take your pick"—and the Lily in particular—"Breathtakingly exceptional quality. It must have been done by one of the finest craftsmen in history, and we'll never know his name. How sad is that?"—which made me think she didn't mind being in her end of the business at all.

I have to admit that I am one of those guys who knows nothing about art but knows what he likes, and I liked India's enthusiasm for the Jade Lily. It must be saved, I decided.

While I was deciding this, the door opened and Perrin walked in, followed by Mr. Donatucci and a man who was a little over or a little under forty, with hair that was thinning on top and clothes that were too tight. He breathed as if he were asthmatic. Either that or he was so out of shape that the simple act of walking down the corridor was enough to leave him breathless. Being a semiprofessional unlicensed private detective, I deduced that he had put on a lot of weight recently and wasn't used to carrying it around yet.

Perrin introduced us. "Mr. Gillard, this is McKenzie," she said.

"Ahh, the famous Rushmore McKenzie," he said. He shook my hand briskly and smiled. "So they talked you into retrieving the Lily after all. Foolish, foolish man."

"I hope not," I said. "Have you met India Cooper?"

Gillard spun toward her. "Ms. Cooper," he said. "Always a pleasure."

Donatucci spoke up. "I was telling Mr. Gillard—"

"Jerry, Jerry," Gillard said. "Everyone is so formal around here."

"I was telling Jerry that the money is ready," Donatucci said. "It's been gathered, marked, bagged—"

"What does that mean, marked?" Gillard asked. "Do you put a little blue dot in the upper right corner or something?"

"The bills are funneled through a couple of scanners featuring optical character recognition software," I said. "When the process is complete, you'll have an electronic file containing the images of the bills—front and back—as well as all of the serial numbers. That way, if we do catch the artnappers and they do have the money on them, we can prove the bills were part of the ransom."

"Do we really want to catch these guys? Once we pay off

the ransom and get the Lily back, no harm, no foul, am I right?"

"How 'bout that, Mr. Donatucci?" I said. "One-point-three million. No foul?"

"Our primary concern is retrieving the Jade Lily," he said.

"Of course. Anyway . . ." I turned back to Gillard. "The thieves won't get away scot-free. The cops will go after them. Lieutenant Rask will insist on it."

"Sounds like somebody else's problem," Gillard said. "Where's the money now?"

"In a vault in the Midwest Farmers Insurance Group offices in downtown St. Paul," Donatucci said. "Three bags, each weighing exactly thirty-two-point-six pounds as instructed. When the call comes, we'll hand off the bags to Mc-Kenzie in the parking ramp under our building. There will be several armed guards keeping watch."

"Hope they're more reliable than the guards working here," Gillard said. "Ohhh," he added as he spun to face Perrin. She winced as he faked a couple of punches. "Low blow. A foul is called. The ref deducts points. No kidding, Perrin. Don't worry about it. I'm not. So what happens next?"

"We wait until the thieves call," I said.

"Well, we don't have to wait here, do we? McKenzie, what's this bar you were telling me about?"

We decided to drive separately since I might have to abandon him at a moment's notice. I gave Gillard detailed directions on how to reach Rickie's from the museum; he had a navigation system in his rental car, but we both agreed that it couldn't be trusted. I asked Mr. Donatucci if he wanted to join us. He declined, saying that he would return to the office and wait for my call.

Perrin thanked me again for agreeing to recover the Lily,

but I blew her off. I wasn't sure why, but I was having fun again.

As we were leaving the storage area, India called my name. I turned. She tossed the magnifying glass to me. I caught it with both hands and stuffed it in my pocket.

"Good luck," she said.

Gillard was parked illegally in front of the museum. I told him that this wasn't Chicago and that fixing or ignoring parking tickets was not a privilege generally enjoyed by the better-heeled citizenry. He suggested that was just another reason why Minneapolis was considered a backwater burg. I told him to wait for me at the corner while I went to the ramp for my car.

The vehicle was parked on the third floor, but instead of taking the elevator, I jogged up the stairs. Seeing Gillard made me realize that I could afford to lose a few pounds myself. I used to exercise every day, take martial arts training to keep sharp, target practice at the range. Nowadays, I spent too much time puttering around in my kitchen and playing too many rounds of golf from a cart. You could see it on the ice. I'm slower, relying too much on my stick, not taking the body like I used to. I tell myself that I'm getting older, that's why I've lost a step, even as I applaud myself for still playing hockey thirty weeks out of the year. That was just rationalization, though—the last refuge of a loser. The truth is, I was getting lazy. I was starting to enjoy my money too much.

I was breathing hard when I reached my floor, but not too hard. A couple of days in the gym and I'd be as good as new, I told myself. My car, a phantom black (that's the color, honest) Audi S5 coupe with all the bells and whistles that I picked up at the bargain price of $71,000, was parked a half-dozen stalls from the door. I used to drive an Audi TT 225 until it was shot to death by a thug armed with an MP-9 submachine gun. I had been extra careful with this car, storing it in the garage for most of the winter, preferring to let my beaten-up four-wheel-drive Jeep Cherokee do the heavy lifting. However, among other things, the Audi had a splendid security system, and if I was going to schlep around a million-three in cash . . . I used my remote control key chain to disable the alarm and unlock the doors. I was reaching for the door handle when I heard him.

"McKenzie."

He screamed my name loud enough from close enough to make me leap half a foot in the air. I spun around and went into a clumsy karate stance.

God, you're out of shape, my inner voice reminded me.

Lieutenant Noehring was standing in front of me, a brilliant smile on his face. He enjoyed startling me. His hands were inside the pockets of his Italian wool overcoat. I had no idea what was in his hands inside his pockets.

"Jumpy, jumpy," he said.

"Noehring," I said as if pronouncing his name would placate my fear.

"You look like you've seen a ghost," he said.

"This is the third time we've met in the past three days. Once more and I'll have you cited for harassment."

"Not to worry, not to worry." He removed his hands from his pockets, showing me that they were empty. "Just trying to make a point."

"What point is that?"

"I can reach out to you anytime I want."

"Good for you."

"But bad for you." Noehring smiled his Robert Redford smile again. "Just remember what I told you and it'll all work out."

"You must have checked on me. You can't possibly believe I'm going to give you the ransom. You're not that fucking stupid."

"Tsk, tsk, tsk. Such language. You know, you should do a little research of your own before you make such an important decision. Ask for some advice."

"From whom?"

"Nina Truhler. Her daughter, Erica, too. Seems to me you're sweet on both of them."

"Do you want to die, Noehring?"

He smiled again. "All I want is the money," he said. "I'll get it, by hook or by crook. Think about it, McKenzie. Make it easy on yourself. And your friends."

He turned then and walked swiftly to the stairwell. He disappeared behind the door. I didn't know if he went up or down.

I slipped behind the steering wheel of the Audi and gripped it tightly while I fought my anger, telling myself to relax, relax, breathe, breathe. It was difficult. Noehring had threatened Nina and Erica. It was a calculated risk on his part because if he had indeed checked me out, he would know that I would kill for them.

I started the Audi and sat for a moment, listening to the engine purr while I pondered the same question I had asked myself the day before.

"How the hell did he know I was here?"

———

Gillard had no trouble following me to Rickie's, and we entered the club together. I suggested a booth, but he liked the bar, so we pulled up a couple of stools and sat. Jenness Crawford was spelling the regular bartender, and after greeting us, she asked for our drink preferences.

"Let's get this settled right now," Gillard said. He tapped his chest with both hands. "Everything is on me. McKenzie's money is no good here."

"McKenzie's money has never been good here," Jenness said.

"Huh?"

"My girlfriend owns the place," I said.

"That's wonderful," Gillard said. He looked directly into Jenness's eyes. "You are lovely."

Jenness blushed. She knew she was blushing and brought her hands to her cheeks to hide it.

"That may be so," I said, "but Jenness is not my girlfriend."

"Even better," Gillard said. He stood on the rungs of the stool and leaned over the bar, his hand extended.

"Hi, I'm Jeremy Gillard."

Jenness returned the handshake. "I'm Jenness Crawford," she said. "Pleased to meet you."

"The pleasure is all mine," Gillard said.

So the dance began, the two of them taking turns trying to outflirt each other. I might have been amused by the exchange except I kept thinking about Noehring and what he had said. Somehow my Summit Ale was served without my noticing. I took a long pull and wondered, how many times have I put Nina in danger? Just that once, I reminded myself, but that was already once too often, and I had vowed to never do it again. Now this.

My frustration must have shown on my face, because when Nina came out of her office and saw me sitting at the bar she asked, "What's wrong?"

"Oh, that's just my friend McKenzie psyching himself up for the big game like any great athlete," Gillard said. "See the ball, be the ball."

"What big game?" Nina asked. "Who are you? Never mind. McKenzie. McKenzie, you're going after the Lily, aren't you? You said you weren't."

"What do you know about the Jade Lily?" Gillard asked.

"This is my boss, Nina Truhler," Jenness told him.

"Alrighty then," Gillard said. "You're McKenzie's squeeze. I get it now. This is a great joint you have here, Nina."

Nina ignored him. "McKenzie," she said, "I thought you said you were washing your hands of it."

"Some unscrupulous types appealed to his benevolent nature," Gillard said. "They also doubled his fee. Hi, I'm Jerry Gillard. I own the Lily."

"Then you're one of those unscrupulous types."

"Whose guiltlesse hart is free from all dishonest deeds or thought of vanitie." Gillard glanced at Jenness. "Thomas Campion," he said.

"Nice," Jenness said.

"McKenzie?" Nina said.

"It's complicated," I told her.

"It always is."

"Sorry."

"I guess I'll have to go back to worrying again."

"Nina . . ." I let the rest of the sentence hang there. We've had this conversation so many times in the past. I reached out and rested my hand on top of hers. She turned her hand over so she could hold mine.

"That's sweet," Gillard said.

"Does this change of heart have anything to do with Heavenly Petryk?" Nina asked.

"No. Why do you ask?"

Nina released my hand and wagged her finger at the entrance to the club. Gillard and I both turned to look. Heavenly was standing just inside the doorway, unwinding a long muffler from around her neck.

"Who is she?" Gillard asked.

"Oh, perfect," I said. "Just perfect."

"She just might be," Gillard said.

"Oh, puhleez," Jenness said.

Gillard turned just in time to see her sliding down to the end of the bar.

"What did I say?" he said.

Heavenly made her way to where we were sitting. She removed her coat and draped it over the back of a stool. Her smile reminded me of the promise on a package of lightbulbs I had recently purchased—"Lasts up to 10 times longer while using 75% less energy."

"McKenzie, I thought I might find you here," she told me. "Hello, Nina. You look good. Have you had work done?"

"Heavenly," Nina replied. "You cause so much joy whenever you go."

Heavenly smiled at that. "Good one," she said.

"Heavenly," Gillard said. "You just might be the most aptly named woman I have ever met."

"Oh brother," Nina said before she, too, left the area.

"You know something, Jer?" I said. "You deserve this, you really do."

"Deserve what?"

"Heavenly Petryk, this is Jeremy Gillard."

"Call me Jerry," he said.

"Heavenly represents Tatjana Durakovic."

"Where have I heard that name?"

"Tatjana Durakovic claims she is the rightful owner of the Jade Lily."

"That's right," Gillard said. "She sent a letter to the old man a couple years ago. Whatever happened about that?"

"Nothing happened," Heavenly said. "Tatjana's claim was ignored."

"Yeah, that sounds like the old man. So, what can I do for you?"

"Heavenly has assured me that if you do not give up the Lily, she is going to steal it," I said.

"Why not?" Gillard said. "She's already stolen my heart. Can I get you anything? A drink? Dinner? The number of my hotel suite?"

Heavenly took the stool next to him. She drew her hands behind her head and fluffed her golden hair so Gillard could get a lasting impression of what lay beneath her thin blouse.

"Baileys on the rocks," she said.

Gillard conveyed Heavenly's order to Jenness. Jenness served the drink, but she wasn't happy about it.

Gillard smiled pleasantly. "More and more I find that I am spending time with what my father called the wrong element," he said. "This is great."

"Mr. Gillard, McKenzie was not joking earlier," Heavenly said. "I mean to see the Lily returned to its rightful owner."

"Well now, Heavenly. According to my attorneys, who are paid an ungodly amount of money to know these things, the Lily belongs to me. Want to see the bill of sale?"

"You purchased stolen goods," Heavenly said.

"I didn't. The old man did. The bastard. Say it with me—the bastard."

Neither Heavenly nor I joined in.

"Ha," Gillard said. "That's okay. He was actually a pretty good guy, if I do say so myself."

"A poor businessman, though," Heavenly said. "He bankrupted his company."

"Well, it was his to bankrupt."

"Now you're broke."

Gillard thought that was funny. "Depends on how you look at it," he said.

"How many ways are there?"

"When dear old Dad died, I thought I had inherited eighty million. A couple of weeks later, I was informed by a very serious man who spoke in a hushed tone that I had actually inherited only eight million dollars. Poor, poor, pitiful me. I had to give up the company plane. Listen, during the Depression—the old man told me this story. He said during the Great Depression, there was this businessman who was worth ten million bucks. When the market crashed, he lost eight million. The next day he committed suicide. He just couldn't believe it was possible to get by on only two million dollars. And this was back when two million was real money. Kids, I'm not that guy."

"Still," Heavenly said. "If you lose the Lily . . ."

"C'mon, honey, I already told McKenzie. The damn thing's insured. What do I care what happens to it? Listen—I really don't care what happens to it. I'll even make a deal with you right now. This minute. I have a lending agreement with the folks at the museum. They get it for two years. Assuming McKenzie here recovers the Lily, how 'bout this—after the lending agreement expires, we'll sell the Lily at auction. I'll take out what the old man paid for it; Tatjana can have the rest—providing you spend a weekend in Vegas with me. Whaddaya say?"

"Wait a minute."

"Going once, going twice, three times." Gillard slapped the top of the bar with the flat of his hand. "Oh, sorry, time's up. Too bad, so sad."

"Wait a minute," Heavenly said again. "Are you serious?"

"As serious as a nuclear explosion." To prove it, Gillard made a thunder sound from deep in his throat and mimicked an expanding mushroom cloud with his hands.

"Are you insane?" Heavenly said.

Gillard turned to me. "What is your diagnosis, doctor?" he asked.

"Certifiable," I said. "No doubt about it."

"Whaddaya say, Heavenly?" Gillard said. "Do you agree to my terms?"

Heavenly stared at him for a moment and then bent her head so she could look past him at me. "McKenzie?" she said.

"What did that water buffalo you told me about go for?" I asked. "Four million pounds?"

"Yes, but . . . Wait a minute."

Gillard smiled brightly at her while she did.

I was interested in her response as well. Before she could answer, though, I heard Ella singing *"Summertime, and the living is easy"* from my cell phone.

"This is McKenzie," I said into the microphone.

Less than a minute later, I hung up.

Gillard and Heavenly were staring at me.

"Let the games begin," I said.

They both smiled, so I did, too.

SEVEN

Their opening move was the same as before—walk around a park, this time Loring Park on the edge of downtown Minneapolis.

The money had been neatly packed in three medium-sized gym bags that I strapped to a portable dolly, the kind you see travelers pulling behind them at airports, with bungee cords. I had emptied the bags one at a time in the trunk of my Audi when they were first given to me on the bottom floor of the parking ramp that served the Midwest Farmers Insurance Group. I was taken aback by how wide the eyes of the three armed security guards had become when they saw all that cash. Obviously, they had no idea what they had been hired to protect. I carefully searched each bag and the bundles of cash for ink packs and tracers before repacking them, because I knew that's what the artnappers would do. Mr. Donatucci kept telling me that I could trust him. Maybe so, but a lot of hands had handled both the money and the bags besides his, and I vowed I wasn't going to get killed because someone along the line decided to be tough on crime. Besides, Donatucci had missed the third thief, and I was still concerned that he might be too old for this kind of play.

I made my way out of downtown St. Paul to I-94 and drove west, crossing the river into Minneapolis. It was at the peak of rush hour and excruciatingly slow going. It didn't help that the sun had set—only five forty-five and it might as well have been midnight. I watched carefully to see if any cars were following me. I decided they all were.

I could sit almost anywhere and be comfortable with my own thoughts, except in traffic. After a few minutes of going nowhere very slowly, I started fidgeting, started squirming in my seat, started craning my neck this way and that in an attempt to see past the vehicles in front of me and find out what was causing the delay. In moments like that, not even the jazz they played on KBEM or one of my own CDs could soothe me. I understood road rage very well. Why I had never succumbed to it myself was a total mystery. Especially then. What was the matter with these drivers? Didn't they know I was taking $1,270,000 in cash to a godless horde of thieves and killers! Finally the traffic began to loosen and we all started moving forward, picking up speed until we nearly matched the posted limit. I passed no accidents, no road construction zones, no disabled cars on the shoulder; saw nothing to explain the snarl. Which only made it worse.

Then came the Lowry Hill Tunnel where the freeway narrowed. Scores of frustrated drivers were backed up once again, some staying on I-94, some shifting to I-394, and some, like me, carefully picking their way across several lanes of unyielding traffic to reach the exit shared by Hennepin and Lyndale avenues. It was as if the artnappers had deliberately chosen a time and place guaranteed to make sure I was in the best frame of mind for a gunfight, which certainly would have been one-sided since I wasn't carrying a gun as per instructions.

Eventually I parked the Audi on Willow Street in the shadow of a brownstone apartment building on the east edge of the park, not far from a coffeehouse. I left the engine running but turned off the radio. Enter Loring Park at the Willow and Fifteenth Street entrance, they had instructed. Enter at 6:27 P.M. Not 6:15, not 6:30, 6:27, which convinced me that the artnappers were purposely messing with me.

At 6:23, I left the Audi and its warm interior and heated seats. The wind and cold immediately reminded me that it was winter in Minnesota. I felt goose bumps up and down my body—even the most seasoned Minnesotan sometimes needs a moment or two to adjust—but they soon went away.

I stepped behind my car. There was ample space between my bumper and the vehicle parked directly behind me. Because of the heaps of snow and ice thrown up onto the boulevard by the plows, we were both parked several feet away from the curb, which narrowed the roadway and put sideview mirrors in jeopardy. A narrow path through the mound of snow began where the other car's front bumper ended and led to the sidewalk.

There was plenty of traffic, both vehicle and pedestrian, much more than you would expect on what was ostensibly a side street. When I was sure there was none close at hand, I popped the trunk, using the remote control key chain, and muscled the dolly and the gym bags out, and I do mean muscled. The dolly, bags, and money together weighed over a hundred pounds, and as has already been established, I've been letting myself go lately. Looking carefully right and left, wishing I had ignored the instructions about the gun, I grabbed hold of the handle and wheeled the heavy dolly across the street to the entrance of the park.

Instead of shoveling or snowblowing the many trails that circled the small lake and traversed the park, the city had plowed them so they were much wider than they would have been normally and were covered with packed ice. The wheels on the dolly didn't so much spin as they skidded behind me as I followed the trails. Sometimes the wheels found a rut or a chunk of ice and I had to yank the heavy dolly forward with both hands. Walk clockwise around the lake until you reach the Loring Park Community Arts Center, they told me, so I did.

Loring Park was established one hundred thirty years ago. It's bordered on the east and south by expensive condominiums, apartments, office buildings, and that bastion of discontent, the Woman's Club of Minneapolis. On the west, across Lyndale, are the Walker Art Center, the Minneapolis Sculpture Garden, Lowry Hill, and, behind that, the very wealthy, very contented Kenwood neighborhood. On the north you'll find a number of restaurants, art galleries, and clubs housed in a series of buildings that are nearly as old as the park itself, as well as the Minneapolis Community and Technical College. Looming above it all is the mighty century-old dome of the magnificent Basilica of St. Mary's.

Yet despite its high-tone neighbors, Loring Park is more than a little creepy. The lights aren't what they could be, and the shadows they cast hold a menacing quality despite the bright city skyline that hangs above them. Some people call it "whoring park" because of its reputation as a prime site for late-night hookups. When I was a kid, it was also known as a spot where gay men would cruise other gay men, especially after the bars closed. Suburbanites would drive up and down

Willow and Fifteenth, point at a man, any man, and say, "There's one." That was a long time ago, though. The Twin Cities Gay Pride Festival is held in Loring Park now.

I once heard a story that when the city temporarily drained the lake a couple of decades back, they discovered the remains of at least twenty bodies settled in the soft bottom. It was said that most of them were allegedly deposited there by Isadore Blumenfeld, alias Kid Cann, who ran the rackets in Minneapolis until he was arrested for violating the Mann Act and jury tampering in the early sixties. I presume the story was exaggerated. On the other hand, last November they found a human skull in the marshy area around the dock that juts into the lake, and as far as I knew, forensic anthropologists still haven't determined its age, sex, or race, much less who it had belonged to.

In any case, the people I encountered did little to contradict the park's checkered past. I counted at least five meth addicts chilling on the metal benches that faced the lake. One kid strolled by cradling a bottle of Grey Goose vodka. "Time to get my goose on," he said before disappearing up a trail that led to the park's horseshoe pitch. In the distance I heard a flute—there's always a white guy playing the flute, always.

Even the black squirrels in Loring Park are overly aggressive. They're insanely obese because people give them food despite the signs requesting that park visitors please refrain from feeding the animals, and if you don't have a snack to share when they saunter by, they can become downright hostile.

I did as I was told, circling the lake, my feet crunching on the ice beneath them. I passed the horseshoe pitch, crossed the concrete and metal bridge, and skirted the tennis courts, the fountain, and the park's sleeping garden. Somewhere along the way I started to shiver. I had worn my Sorels, a thick leather coat, leather gloves, and a knit hat with the emblem of the John Beargrease Sled Dog Marathon, which I pulled down over my ears. I was still cold. Yet, despite the weather, there were a surprising number of people in the park. Individuals cutting through on their way to or from work. Couples strolling while holding hands. Men and women engaged in a brisk walk. Still others jogging, which always amazed me, people jogging in the cold, although—I patted my stomach—it wouldn't kill me to go for a long run.

Finally I reached the Loring Park Community Arts Center. It was a long snowball's throw from the Willow and Fifteenth Street entrance; I had circled nearly the entire park. I had no doubt the thieves had seen me clearly, although I had not seen them. The arts center was closed. It was only open from 1:00 to 5:00 P.M. in the winter, although its rooms were available to rent anytime. There was a metal bench near the building, where I had been ordered to sit and wait. Fortunately, the bench was empty. I don't know what I would have done if it had been occupied. You do not confront people in Loring Park, and if you witness a confrontation between others, you do not intervene.

I sat with the dolly and the gym bags positioned between my legs. My hand rested on the handle at the top. I did not remove my hand once, not even to flex my frigid fingers. People passed me. I nodded at those who nodded at me first. Most ignored my existence; no one spoke. My head was on a swivel, turning this way and that as I observed the people in the park. Most appeared merely as shapes in the darkness, becoming discernible only when they passed under a light.

No one approached me. An hour passed, by my watch. My toes were becoming numb no matter how much I squished them together inside my boots. I was beginning to think that this was a trial run—the thieves putting me out there and watching to see if I followed directions, to learn if I was working with the cops to set a trap. That's when I saw him.

A man dressed in black had been sitting on a bench about a hundred yards from me. I had noticed him before when he left the bench, walked a quarter way around the lake, and then came back. I thought nothing of it at the time. Now he was doing it again. I watched him intently. Distance and night hid his face from me, yet there was something about the cut of his clothes and the way he moved . . . My hand tightened on the handle.

He returned to the bench, sitting so that he was facing the arts center. I realized then that he was watching me watching him. I forced myself to look away, to keep scanning the park, to study the people who approached on the trail and then moved away. Yet my eyes kept coming back to him. Another half hour passed.

"C'mon, pal," I said aloud. "It's cold out here."

He couldn't possibly have heard, yet he rose just the same and started walking toward me. I forced myself to look away, examining all the approaches to the park bench to make sure he didn't have accomplices closing in at the same time. He seemed to be alone. I looked back. He was eighty yards away and still just a dark form moving. I kept scanning the area. Sixty yards and he crossed a shaft of light that fought its way into the park from the streetlamp on Willow. I saw his face clearly, if only for a moment.

"Sonuvabitch," I said. "What is he doing here?"

I stood up.

Lieutenant Scott Noehring of the Minneapolis Police Department's Forgery Fraud Unit was now fifty yards away and walking purposely toward me. His hands were in his pockets.

"Sonuvabitch," I said again.

Awareness of my vulnerability hit me like a sledgehammer. Noehring told me his plan was to kill the artnappers and steal the ransom, leaving me alive with the Lily. *Dammit, what was stopping him from killing me and stealing the money, blaming it on the thieves, screw the Jade Lily?*

I did a quick three-sixty. No one was approaching my position, yet there were still plenty of people in the park. At least one person was walking close behind Noehring.

Start screaming, my inner voice told me. *Scream Noehring's name, his rank, his position with the cops.*

If enough heads turned, I told myself, maybe Noehring would think twice about taking his hands out of his pockets. In the meantime, running was always a good idea. It's harder to shoot a moving target.

I tightly gripped the handle of the dolly and half-turned toward the trail leading to the exit. Before I could move, before I could scream, Noehring's hands jerked out of his pockets. His arms flew open and his back arched and twisted to his left as if he had been punched in the shoulder. He stumbled a few feet toward me. His head snapped violently forward, his chin bouncing off his chest, and he collapsed to his knees. His body kept twisting to the side as he fell against the ice, sliding a few feet.

The dark shape that had been following close behind Noehring quickly pivoted and went off in the opposite direction, not running, but not strolling either.

I had not heard a sound.

My instinct was to hasten to Noehring's side. I fought against it. I was responsible for the money, and this could have been a diversion in an attempt to take it away from me. Instead, I looked around, never letting go of the dolly's handle. No one was running, no one was behaving oddly; there were no neon arrows pointing at anyone and flashing KILLER. I started jogging toward the park's exit, pulling the dolly and its weighty cargo behind me. I slipped several times going up the hill. I heard a woman make a low scream as if she were loosening up her throat for a much louder one. When it came—and yes, it was loud indeed—I glanced briefly behind me. A small group of people was gathering around Noehring's prone body. I continued climbing the hill.

I paused when I reached the exit. It was much brighter there. Cars cruised through the intersection of Willow and Fifteenth Street. Pedestrians crossed at the stoplight. I glanced behind me. No one seemed to be following, yet that didn't convince me to slow down. I jogged across Willow, dodging traffic. I rolled the dolly to the Audi, maneuvering between my rear bumper and the front bumper of the vehicle parked behind me. Once there, I hit the button on my remote. The trunk popped open; the inside light flared.

I did not realize anyone had been lurking there until a man appeared on the narrow path that cut through the mound of snow pushed up against the boulevard.

"Don't move," he said.

A gloved hand seized the handle of the dolly.

"I'll take that."

I saw the gun first. The trunk light reflected off a lightweight 9 mm manufactured by FN Herstal in the good ol' USA, if that means anything to you. I always thought of it as a girl's gun but kept the opinion to myself. Next I saw the grinning face of Tommy, Heavenly's muscle, the one who had insulted me in the van. Screw it, I thought, the FNP-9 *is* a girl's gun.

Tommy shook the handle of the dolly.

"Let go, McKenzie," he said. "I'll shoot you. I will."

When I didn't release my grip he raised the gun so that it was pointed at my face.

I released the dolly and slapped his hand to the left so the gun was pointing at nothing. I punched him in the throat just as hard as I could. He made a gurgling sound as I followed with an elbow to his mouth. I grabbed his arm and yanked him forward. He fell against the dolly, knocking it over. Dropping his gun, he brought one hand to his throat and tried to punch me with the other. I ducked under the blow, grabbed his upper arm, twisted to my left, and used his momentum to heave him over my hip and throw him into the street.

He never saw the car that hit him, that drove his head against the ice-packed asphalt.

The 911 operator was confused. I tried to explain that I needed both police and an ambulance at Willow Street across from Loring Park. I gave her the address of the brownstone apartment building. I even told her where I was in relation to the coffeehouse. She kept insisting that someone else had already called about the incident in the park and police had been dispatched. I told her that this was a different matter and that it occurred outside the park. She didn't seem to believe me. Possibly she was flustered by the young woman screaming a few feet away from me, the one who kept repeating, "It was an accident. He fell in front of my car." Or perhaps it was the deep baritone of the brother on the sidewalk who was telling the woman—and anyone else who cared to listen—that it wasn't her fault. "He didn't fall. He was pushed."

Finally, "Let's try this," I said into the mic of my cell phone. "An officer is down."

"What?" the operator said.

"The man who was shot in Loring Park was a police officer. The man who shot him is lying in the middle of Willow Street."

"Shit," the operator said, which might not have been a very professional thing to say but hardly something you'd hold against her.

I had learned a long time ago to say as little as possible to as few people as possible in matters involving the police. Actually, I didn't learn it so much as my attorney beat it into me. The people who had gathered around Tommy and the car that killed him were of no such mind, however. They had plenty to say. Some of it was even true.

The young woman who hit Tommy was nearly hysterical with grief. She kept telling the police officers that the accident wasn't her fault, that Tommy had jumped in front of her car. "Maybe it was suicide." I felt terrible about the part I had played in causing her anguish, yet I did not attempt to console her. A witness—the brother who spoke up earlier—testified that he had witnessed Tommy and me struggling after he pulled a gun on me and that I threw him into the street. I had nothing to say to him, either, although I was grateful that he remembered the gun. I ignored the other witnesses who, taking the brother's cue, claimed I had deliberately shoved Tommy in front of a speeding car, even though they were nowhere near when the incident occurred.

The officers who responded to the call kept asking for a statement. I told them they should secure Tommy's gun, which had slid beneath the back bumper of my Audi. Beyond that, I kept my mouth shut. By then, word of a cop killing had electrified the entire police department. To say the officers were angry at my refusal to cooperate would be like saying that the sun rose in the east—it really wasn't open to debate. If there hadn't been so many witnesses, I suspect I would have been "tuned up," as they say. Instead, I was roughly cuffed and shoved in the back of a squad car.

Cops have protocols and procedures when dealing with criminal activities, and few of them are executed in a hurry. Policing is, after all, a civil service job and prone to bureaucracy. More and more officers appeared at the scene. Lights were erected. Measurements were taken. Photographs were snapped. Statements were recorded. All this was made even more cumbersome by the simple fact that the exact same thing was happening in the park around Noehring's body. The ME appeared and then disappeared. Forensic specialists arrived and stayed for a long time. Vans with the call letters from WCCO, KSTP, KARE-11, and FOX-9 blocked traffic, their cameras and lights adding to the chaos. Crowds of bystanders gathered, lingered for a bit, and then scattered when they discovered there was nothing going on that was intriguing enough to keep them standing out in the cold.

Eventually Lieutenant Rask came up from the park and crossed the street. He glared at me for a moment through the passenger window before taking verbal reports from his men. When he finished, he had the officer open the rear door to the squad car. I didn't wait for him to ask questions. Instead, I spoke as succinctly as possible.

"I was going for the Lily—the money is in the trunk of the Audi—the dead man tried to take it from me—he might have been the one who shot Lieutenant Noehring, I don't know."

"Did you witness the shooting?" Rask asked.

"I saw Noehring fall, but I can't identify who shot him. Lieutenant, I need to contact Mr. Donatucci and have him secure the money."

"What was Noehring doing here?"

I looked away and then looked back. Rask saw the answer in my eyes.

"Don't say a word, McKenzie," he said. "Just this once, keep your mouth shut."

I eventually gave a detailed statement to Rask. I then repeated it to Rask, a second investigator, and a video camera. Afterward, I gave it a third time to Rask, a second investigator, a video camera, two prosecutors from the Hennepin County Attorney's Office, the chief of police, and Mr. Donatucci, who confirmed everything up to the moment I drove out of the parking ramp. I found myself sliding into a monotone while I spoke. Trust me when I tell you that I wasn't bored. But I was feeling depressed, deflated. It was the inevitable fall after the adrenaline high, but knowing the cause didn't change it. Several times I was asked to speak up. Nearly everyone had a question about Lieutenant Noehring, and each time I saw a look in Rask's eye that told me to keep my opinions to myself.

"I have no idea why he was at Loring Park," I said. "My guess is that he was there on a different matter and the thieves somehow made him, but I'm only guessing."

Afterward, I was installed in the same interrogation room where I met Hemsted and Pozderac and told to wait. I did so, for nearly four hours. I did not complain. Rask had a cop killing on his hands. Nothing took precedence over that, least of all my comfort and convenience.

When he finally did arrive I was struck by the exhaustion on his face and the look in his eyes that suggested he was silently wishing the goddamned apocalypse would come already.

"Did Mr. Donatucci secure the money?" I asked.

"Yeah," he said. "So your problems are over. Is that what you're telling me?"

"I killed a man last night, LT."

Rask pulled out a chair from under the conference table and sat down.

"One of mine was killed, too," he said.

"So we're both hurting."

"I suppose we are."

Rask leaned back in the chair, his chin pointed at the ceiling, and closed his eyes. "McKenzie," he said, "sometimes I think I spend more time watching the sun go up and watching it go down than a person should, you know."

"Did Tommy kill Noehring?" I asked.

"No," he said without opening his eyes. "There was no gunshot residue on his hands or clothes. Plus, Tommy was carrying a nine-millimeter that hadn't been fired recently. Noehring was shot with a .25."

"The same caliber as the gun that killed Tarpley," I said.

Rask glanced at his watch. "I should be hearing from ballistics at about—at about right now, goddammit."

"Think it's a pro?" I asked.

"No. Tarpley took one round to the throat. That's sloppy work. Noehring was shot in the back of the head; I'll give you that. The first round, though, hit him on the right side just below the shoulder blade. It's possible the second shot— the shooter might have been aiming at his back again and missed."

"Or not," I said.

"Or not. This Tommy, no priors, nothing. What the hell was he doing?"

"I have nothing more to add to what I've already told you. I only knew his first name and that he was involved with Heavenly Petryk."

"There's a piece of work for you."

"Have you interviewed her yet?"

"Briefly. I left her alone in the interrogation room to think about it awhile before I go back down."

"What else do you need from me?"

Rask opened his eyes and lurched forward in the chair. "There are no cameras in this room," he said. "No audio."

"Okay."

"I want you to tell me everything that you left out of your statement."

"Even the stuff you don't want to hear?"

"Everything."

"Clay." I used his first name because I wanted him to know that I was on his side. "Noehring was dirty."

"Tell me."

"I don't know how he knew I was at Loring Park, but he was there to kill the thieves and steal the money or kill me and steal the money, one or the other, maybe both. I'm sorry."

"Don't tell me you're sorry. Tell me how you know this."

I gave Rask a near verbatim account of my conversations with Noehring, first at the restaurant early Tuesday evening and then later at the parking ramp of the museum.

"All right, you told me," Rask said. "You got it off your chest. Now there's no reason for you to tell anyone else."

"LT—"

"Do you understand what I'm saying to you, McKenzie? You don't repeat this story, not to anyone, not ever."

"He was a bad cop."

"I fucking know that. You don't think I know that? He was paying alimony and child support, yet he drove a fucking BMW. He wore Italian overcoats and Armani suits and fucking silk ties. I know he was dirty, but no one else needs to know. Noehring was a hero cop—a hero cop who went down in the line of duty. The governor is going to speak at his goddamn funeral. There's going to be a twenty-one-gun salute, so help me God."

"Okay."

"You know why, don't you, McKenzie? I don't have to explain why."

"You don't have to explain."

Rask reached into his pocket and withdrew a small GPS transmitter that he tossed on the table.

"Department issue," he said. "It was attached to the bumper of your Audi. That's how Noehring knew you were at Loring Park."

I picked it up, glanced at it, and dropped it on the table.

Now, if I only knew how Tommy found me, my inner voice said.

"You probably have one on your Jeep Cherokee, too," Rask said. "If you do, destroy it, just get rid of it."

"Okay."

"I keep thinking, if I was allowed to investigate Tarpley's murder the right way none of this would have happened."

"You might be right."

"This Lily, this fucking Jade Lily—it's not just between the thieves and the museum anymore. Or the state department or that bitch Petryk or anyone else. Right, McKenzie? Right?"

"Right," I said.

"It's about cop killers. So if you get anything—anything at all . . ."

"I'll let you know, LT."

"I spoke to the prosecutors. This thing with Tommy is going into the books as self-defense. The gun plus the witness who saw the gun in Tommy's hand proves he came at you with deadly force, and the law allows you to respond with at least equal force, so no charges will be filed."

"Thank you."

"You're free to go."

"Thank you."

"This thing with the Jade Lily, if you continue to pursue it—I'm not saying you should. It could be dangerous for you, McKenzie, but if you do, don't fuck around. Call me. Give me time and place. I'll do my best to cover your ass."

I held out the pinkie of my right hand. "Best friends forever, Clay?" I said.

"I changed my mind. Don't call me Clay."

I took that as a yes.

EIGHT

The media made it official—Lieutenant Scott Noehring was a hero cop, shot in the back by an unknown assailant. I heard it on the radio while I was driving home Thursday morning. But the sun was rising and the turkeys were pecking at their corn in the backyard, and I didn't really care about Noehring. I didn't rush into the house and turn on the TV to hear what the local stations had to say about him, and I only skimmed the brief article that the St. Paul *Pioneer Press* managed to cobble together before it went to press. Seventeen-year veteran, three commendations early in his career, divorced, two kids, the governor asked that flags be flown at half-mast, yadda, yadda, yadda.

None of it pleased me; none of it made me angry. Truth was, Noehring probably had been a good cop, a very good cop to make lieutenant. He had been smart, he had been resourceful, and he had "protected with courage and served with compassion" like the motto says. Somehow that changed, maybe during his divorce. Maybe when he took that first free taco he spoke about. Before that he had been a real cop, so sing his praises, bury him with honor, why not? Shakespeare wrote, *The evil that men do lives after them; the good is oft interred with their bones.* Well, screw that. Bury the evil, too.

Let Noehring be a hero. The world needed heroes. The Minneapolis Police Department certainly needed heroes. In the recent past, an officer had been accused of planting a gun on a Hmong teenager who was shot and killed by mistake, a SWAT team member was arrested for robbing a Wells Fargo bank, members of the Metro Gang Strike Force were charged with stealing cars, cash, and jewelry from suspects, and a cop was indicted for providing confidential police records to a known gangster. A hero might help the remaining nine hundred very fine and ethical police out there get their due.

In the end, that's what Lieutenant Rask wanted, I decided. Law enforcement is a tight fraternity because the members of that fraternity know that in a life-and-death situation, the only people they can depend on are each other. That's why good cops often turn a blind eye to the bad conduct of their brothers and sisters—Rask knew Noehring was dirty long before he was shot. That didn't mean it didn't hurt, the criminal behavior. When a cop goes bad, good cops suffer, and not only in a loss of reputation and prestige in the neighborhood. It makes them sick at heart. That's not just an ex-cop blowing smoke. I know it to be true personally.

So let's pretend that Noehring was a hero. Build him a fucking statue, what did I care? The only thing that interested me that morning was a tiny story tucked in the newspaper's "Daily Briefing" column.

MINNEAPOLIS MAN HIT BY CAR, KILLED DURING SCUFFLE

Thomas O'Brien, Minneapolis, was killed Wednesday night when he fell in front of a speeding car during a scuffle near Loring Park.

Authorities report that O'Brien, 24, had been fighting with an unidentified man on Willow Street on the east side of the park when he slipped on the ice and fell in front of a car driven by Irene Campbell, 29, of Pequot Lakes. He was pronounced dead at the scene.

Officials said the investigation is ongoing, but the incident appears to be a case of self-defense and no arrests were made.

That was it. Apparently no one was going to build a statue for Tommy.

I had killed men before. Sometimes I felt sick and ashamed afterward, and sometimes I felt relieved if not downright exhilarated. With Tommy I felt—embarrassed. I had not meant to kill Tommy. It was an accident. I had not seen the car coming any more than he did. He had shoved the business end of a 9 mm into my face and threatened my life. Yet I didn't know if he meant to use the gun or if he was merely bluffing. In any case, once I disarmed him, he was no longer a threat to me. If it hadn't been for the car I would have sent him limping back to Heavenly.

I read the article until I had it memorized, then balled up the paper and tossed it into the recycling bin.

This should not have happened, my inner voice told me.

"Damn, Tommy," I said aloud. "I'm sorry. I'm really sorry."

I might have said more, maybe even uttered a prayer or two, but my phone rang. Mr. Donatucci wanted to know what went wrong last night. I reminded him that he was in the room when I made my final statement.

"Did you think I was lying to the cops?" I asked.

"No, it's just—this should have been simple. What the hell happened?"

"Greed happened, Mr. Donatucci. Pure greed."

Mr. Donatucci sighed deeply. Greed, yeah, that's a story he knew very well.

"The question is, what happens next?" I asked.

"The police do not want us to pay a ransom for the Lily. If we decide to go ahead anyway, they want us to include them in the exchange so they can arrest the artnappers. However, we are under no obligation to follow their instructions."

"Do you actually believe the thieves will try again?"

"Yes. No. I don't know. Maybe."

This time it was my turn to sigh dramatically.

"I'm not sure about this, Mr. Donatucci. The artnappers killed at least two guys, and one of them was police. Do we want to reward them for that?"

"Do we know that for sure?"

"What do you mean?"

"Do we know that the artnappers killed Tarpley and Noehring?"

"Who else?"

"That's the question, isn't it? Who else had motive?"

I decided I was too tired to play Mr. Donatucci's mind games and told him so. "Remember at the museum when I was told that it wasn't my job to catch the thieves or to solve the crime?" I said. "I'm holding you to that."

Mr. Donatucci said that he would contact me—and I should contact him—if the thieves called. Then he hung up.

I stood in the empty, silent kitchen for a moment. My entire body longed for sleep. Yet I decided to make breakfast first. It wasn't that I was hungry—although I was—as much as that I felt a need to do something. So I fried up a skillet of scrambled eggs with plenty of hot sausage, jalapeño chilies, green onions, tomato, and cilantro.

I didn't taste any of it.

The phone rang. I rolled across my bed to answer it. It was 10:00 A.M. I had all of four hours of sleep.

"McKenzie," I said.

"What the hell do you think you're doing?" a man's voice asked.

I hung up the phone. I rolled over and shut my eyes. The phone rang again. I gave it six rings before I answered, catching it just before the call rolled over to voice mail.

"McKenzie," I said.

"Don't you dare hang up on me again," the voice said.

I hung up. I stretched, yawned, and waited. Sure enough, the phone rang a third time. This time when I answered it, I said, "Good manners are how we show respect for one another."

There was a long pause.

"Mr. McKenzie," the voice said finally. "This is Jonathan Hemsted of the U.S. State Department." Apparently he needed to remind me of that. "I hope I did not catch you at a bad time."

"It's been a long night," I said.

"Yes, I know. I would like to speak to you about your long night."

"Why?"

"Could you meet us at our hotel suite in, say, an hour's time?"

"Us?"

"Mr. Pozderac will be sitting in."

"Where is the hotel?"

He told me. I hung up without saying good-bye. Like I said, good manners are how we show our respect for one another.

The hotel was located west of Minneapolis on the I-394 strip within easy shuttle distance of Cargill, UnitedHealthcare, Minnesota Disposal and Recycling, General Mills, and a couple of other Fortune 500 companies. I crossed the lobby and caught the attention of a pretty clerk at the front desk. I kept my leather coat closed so she wouldn't see the 9 mm I was wearing behind my right hip. She smiled brightly and asked how she could help me.

"Mr. Hemsted, please," I said.

She accessed her computer. The smile became a frown.

"I'm sorry, sir, we do not have a Mr. Hemsted registered."

"Jonathan Hemsted. H-E-M-S-T-E-D."

"No sir, I'm sorry."

"Perhaps it's under the name Branko Pozderac. Please don't ask me to spell it."

She checked again.

"I'm sorry, sir, there is no Mr. Branko Pozderac registered with us, either."

"Are you sure? I spoke to the man an hour ago. He said he had a suite here."

"A suite—" She checked her computer a third time. "Oh, I

am so sorry, sir. Of course, both Mr. Hemsted and Mr. Pozderac are here. They're staying in the suite owned by MDR.
Please forgive me."

"Think nothing of it."

"A number of companies rent rooms and suites from us
year-round for their business associates. We track their guests
differently."

"I understand."

"Would you like me to call up and announce your arrival,
or would you prefer to use the house phone?"

She pointed at a red telephone on a low round table surrounded by several chairs in the center of the lobby.

"If it's not too much trouble, please call up. Tell whoever
answers the phone that McKenzie will be waiting in the bar."

"No trouble at all, Mr. McKenzie."

"Thank you for your consideration."

I turned away from the desk, reconnoitered my position,
and then headed for the bar just off the lobby. As I did so, I
wondered, MDR? How did Hemsted and Pozderac score a
luxury suite owned by a waste management company?

Pozderac drank whiskey, Hemsted drank wine, and I had a
beer. I was sure that there was something significant about
our individual tastes in alcohol, I just didn't know what.
Pozderac also ordered a plate of buffalo-style chicken wings
because he was hungry and lunch was a good hour away. He
ate them without benefit of a napkin, a transgression that
seemed to offend Hemsted greatly.

"First, allow me to offer you my sincere condolences at
the passing of your friend yesterday," Hemsted said.

"You are referring to Lieutenant Noehring," I said.

"Yes, of course."

"He was not my friend."

"Oh?"

"However, if you wish to contact Lieutenant Rask, I'm sure he'll be happy to commiserate with you. In fact, I know the first thing he'll ask. Where were you last night around 8:00 P.M.? You and your"—I passed up the many adverb-adjective-noun combinations that flashed through my head and settled on "friend."

"We have spoken to your Lieutenant Rask this morning, and I must say he is an exceedingly rude man."

I flashed on what Perrin Stewart said about him two days earlier.

"A lot of people think that," I said. "What did you tell him?"

"I reminded Lieutenant Rask that Mr. Pozderac enjoys diplomatic immunity."

Pozderac smiled around a chicken wing. "Im-mun-i-ty" he pronounced slowly.

"What exactly do you want, Hemsted?" I asked. "Why am I here?"

"Mr. McKenzie . . ."

"Drop the mister. Let's not pretend we're friends."

"McKenzie, we can at least be civil, can we not?"

"I killed a man last night, pal. This is as civil as I'm going to get for a while."

"You shoot police?" Pozderac asked.

"No, I didn't. Did you?"

Instead of answering, Pozderac licked his fingers and picked up another wing.

"McKenzie, I thought we had an understanding," Hemsted said. "You went after the Jade Lily without first contacting us."

"Tell you what. Next time I set out to commit a felony, I'll invite you both. We'll have an outing."

"What is felony?" Pozderac asked.

"A criminal act," Hemsted said.

Pozderac smiled again. There was buffalo sauce at the corners of his mouth and on his chin. "Im-mun-i-ty," he said.

"McKenzie," Hemsted said, "I made our position clear earlier. I see no reason to repeat it now. You must believe, I will do what I said I would do."

"Destroy my life unless I steal for you. Is that why you asked me here, to remind me?"

"Frankly, yes. Going after the Lily the way you did without first contacting us smacked of recklessness. I need ample warning next time so that I might have time to make the necessary preparations to receive it from you and then remove it from the country."

"You can't just shove it into a diplomatic pouch and send it back to Bosnia COD?"

"Hardly."

"Why are you here, Hemsted? In Minnesota? How did you know the Lily was going to be stolen?"

"We didn't know. We came to secure the Lily from the museum. Its theft was a terrible inconvenience to us."

"Is that all it was?"

"I wish you could see this our way. It really is in the national interest."

"It's probably moot, anyway," I said.

"What do you mean?"

"Rask is hungry for an arrest. He has two dead bodies connected to the theft of the Lily, and one of them is a police officer. There's no way you're going to keep him off the case now. That means sooner or later the cops are going to get their hands on the Lily. The only way you'll be able to take it out of the country after that is with lots and lots of publicity, and I have a feeling you don't want any publicity."

Hemsted slipped a cell phone out of his pocket.

"Don't worry about that," he said.

I expected him to make a call right then and there, yet he didn't. Instead, he held on to the phone as if it were Aladdin's magic lamp.

Pozderac tossed down a chicken wing and wiped his fingers on the tablecloth. Hemsted winced and forced himself to look away.

"Enough talk," Pozderac said. "You will return Lily. See to it."

He rose, turned his back to the table, and started walking toward the hotel's elevators. Hemsted gave him a head start before he pushed back his chair and made ready to follow. I called his name. When he turned I told him, "Pozderac might have diplomatic immunity, but you don't. Think about it."

I don't know if he did or didn't.

I stopped at the front desk on my way out, once again catching the eye of the pretty desk clerk. I asked her if it was possible to learn when Hemsted and Pozderac had checked into the hotel. She hesitated for a moment, and I had no doubt that we were both thinking the same thing—it was against hotel policy to reveal information about its guests. She must have felt she owed me a favor after the mix-up earlier, though, because she quickly checked her computer and then leaned across the desk toward me.

"Eleven forty-five A.M. Sunday," she said.

Fourteen and a quarter hours before the Jade Lily was stolen, my inner voice figured.

I thanked her and left the hotel.

I didn't realize I was being followed until I turned into a Holiday gas station a block from the hotel.

The guy on the radio was waxing philosophic about a massive snowstorm that was heading our way—that was his word, massive, not mine. When he said the Cities might get hit with as much as twelve inches of the white stuff, I glanced down at my gas gauge. It's one of the things you learn at a young age when you're from Minnesota—whenever a blizzard or an interval of subzero temperatures is predicted, make sure you have a full tank of gas. I discovered that the tank on my Jeep Cherokee was down by three-quarters just as I was approaching the driveway, so I swung the wheel and drove into the Holiday station without signaling. The action caught the cherry-colored Acura MDX behind me by surprise. The driver hit his brakes, slid well past the driveway, recognized his mistake, and sped up. The SUV continued on to the next intersection, hung a U-turn, and came back. It passed the Holiday station, returned to the hotel lot, turned around again, and headed toward the station, this time parking along the street about a hundred yards away.

I pretended not to notice.

I filled my tank, checked my levels, and used the squeegee to clean my windows, all the while keeping my leather coat open so I could reach the 9 mm Beretta in a hurry. The thieves wouldn't like it if they knew I was carrying, but two men were dead and they had probably killed them. As far as I was concerned, the Beretta was nonnegotiable.

While I was at it, I checked around the front and rear bumpers of the Cherokee. As Rask had predicted, I found a tiny GPS transmitter inside a small magnetic box attached to the car frame. I dropped it into the trash bin. I didn't think the driver in the Acura was using it, otherwise he would have hung farther back, and if he was, tough.

After gassing up, I sat in the Cherokee for a few moments, angling my sideview mirror until I had a clear look at the front bumper of the Acura. It took a minute or so to correctly read the license plate in the mirror and write it down—I didn't want to turn around for fear the driver would know that I made him.

Let him think you're oblivious to his presence, at least until you decide what to do with him, my inner voice said.

The Acura stayed close as I maneuvered onto I-394 and headed east into Minneapolis—way too close. By the time we were crossing the river into St. Paul, I decided the driver was a rank amateur. He did very little to disguise his presence, and I don't think it was because he wanted me to know that he was there. Also, the vehicle itself—cherry red? Really? Could you be more obvious? The question was, who did he work for? I was guessing Jonathan Hemsted. That was the reason he summoned me to the hotel, so the tail could pick me up. After all, Hemsted could have just as easily threatened me over the phone.

I let the Acura follow me to the parking lot next to Rickie's. This time he was a little more clever, passing the lot and pulling into an empty space on the street a half block down. He put the luxury SUV in PARK yet kept the engine running. I did the same thing while I fished my cell phone from my pocket, found a familiar name in my list of contacts, and hit CALL.

"Major Crimes," a voice said. "Commander Dunston."

"I remember when you used to answer the phone with just your last name."

"That was before I was promoted to upper management," Bobby said. "What's going on, McKenzie?"

"Same-old, same-old. Did Victoria tell you about her adventures in cable TV?"

"She did. Ghosts at Rickie's? When did that happen?"

"I don't know. I think Erica is messing with her mother."

"Speaking of which, what's this nonsense about you buying Victoria a car?"

"What? No, no. I'm not buying her a car."

"She said you would when she got her driver's license. I don't mind an MP3 player, McKenzie. But a car?"

"I am not buying Vic a car. She's just trying to manipulate me. I mean, buying a car, that's way over the line, don't you think?"

"Yes, I do."

"That girl is so spoiled."

"Whose fault is that?"

"I blame her parents."

"I'm sorry. Aren't you the one who bought eighty-seven boxes of Girl Scout Cookies so Victoria could win a contest?"

"I like Girl Scout Cookies. Especially the Samoas. I have about seventy boxes left if you want any."

"No cars, McKenzie."

"No cars, I promise."

"Are you playing hockey tomorrow tonight?"

"I am unless the snow gets too deep."

"Snow shmow. Don't be a wimp."

"I'll be there if you're going to be there."

"I'll be there."

"I'm going to hold you to that."

"Is that why you called?"

"Bobby, I need a favor."

"I knew it."

"It's a small one."

"I thought we had an understanding. I don't do favors for you. I especially don't use St. Paul Police Department resources to do favors for you."

"Why not? I'm doing you a favor."

"Such as?"

"I'm not buying Victoria a car."

Bobby paused for a moment.

"Does this have anything to do with what happened in Minneapolis last night?" he asked.

"You know about that?"

"Of course I do. McKenzie, what have you got yourself into this time?"

I explained while I watched the cherry red Acura. When I finished, the only question Bobby asked was "Heavenly Petryk is back in town?" When I confirmed that she had indeed returned, he said, "Better Rask's problem than mine. Although . . ."

"Although what?"

"She is a fetching lass."

"Are you going to help me or what?"

"What do you want, McKenzie?"

I recited the license plate number of the SUV that was tailing me and asked for the owner's name.

"Do you need this in a hurry?"

"No."

"I didn't think so; otherwise you wouldn't be gabbing this long on the phone. I swear, McKenzie, you don't get out enough."

The first thing I saw when I walked through Rickie's front door was Nina Truhler standing behind the stick, one end of a bar towel draped over her shoulder while she polished the inside of a glass with the other end. She could have been a stereotypical bartender from an old Western movie—"Hiya, Kid, what'll ya have?"—except, had any bartender ever looked that good, ever?

I slipped off my coat—I had locked the Beretta in my Jeep Cherokee because Nina didn't like guns in her place—and went directly to the bar. I pounded the top of it with the flat of my hand and said, "Barkeep, I want whiskey and fresh horses for me and my men."

Nina smiled a sad sort of smile and covered my hand with hers.

"What?" I said.

"McKenzie, are you okay?"

I was surprised by her concern.

"I'm fine," I said.

"What happened last night?"

"Just the usual confusion and chaos, why do you ask?"

Nina looked toward the far corner of the club. I followed her gaze over the heads of the large crowd eating lunch at the club's small tables to where Heavenly Petryk was sitting. She was alone in the booth nearest the staircase. The expression on her face suggested that she didn't have a friend in the world.

"How long has she been here?" I asked.

"I don't know. She was here when I arrived."

"Has she been drinking?"

"She was until we cut her off. I've been making her drink coffee for the past hour. I tried to get her to eat something, but she won't have it. She's hurting, McKenzie."

"Did she tell you that?"

"I've owned a bar for a long time."

"What did she tell you?"

"She said a friend of hers was killed last night. She said it was her fault."

"Yeah, well, there's plenty of blame to go around."

"What happened?"

I explained, leaving nothing out.

"You killed Tommy?" Nina said.

"I threw him into the street and he was hit by a car. The car killed him. Technically, you could blame the driver. In Minnesota, the law demands that you have complete control of your vehicle at all times."

"McKenzie."

"Yeah, I killed him."

Not once during our conversation did Nina remove her hand from mine. Now she squeezed it tight.

"I'm sorry," she said.

"It shouldn't have happened. I didn't mean for it to happen. That stupid kid, trying to act tough . . ."

"It's okay."

"No, Nina, it isn't. The things I've done—this is the life I chose, and mostly I'm happy with it, mostly I sleep pretty well at night. Yet this was so senseless, so unnecessary."

"Tommy made a choice, too, didn't he?"

"Yeah, he made a choice."

I brought my free hand up and set it on top of Nina's hand on top of my hand.

"Do you want something to eat before you talk to her or after?" Nina asked.

"Why should I talk to her?"

"Go now. We'll have lunch later."

"What's this sudden concern with Heavenly Petryk's welfare?"

Nina shrugged.

"You like her, don't you?" I said.

"I hate to see anyone suffer."

I gave her hand a hard squeeze. "You have the kindest heart," I said. "No wonder ghosts like to hang out here."

Heavenly's eyes told me everything I needed to know. Normally, they sparkled like liquid azurite, yet now they were dull and bloodshot and took a moment to focus when I sat in the booth across from her.

"McKenzie," she said. "I knew you'd come by sooner or later."

"Where are your boys?"

"They have lost their enthusiasm for the task at hand."

"They left you?"

"Sooner or later men always leave me."

"Give me your keys."

"Huh?"

I reached across the table with an open hand.

"The keys to your car," I said. "Give them to me."

"I'm fine."

"Give me the keys to your car or I'm leaving. You came here to talk to me, right?"

"McKenzie . . ."

"Heavenly."

She rummaged through her bag; I thought I saw the butt of a small handgun when her hand emerged with the keys dangling from her fingers. While she was doing that I pried a wad of bills from the front left pocket of my jeans and peeled off a fifty. I took the keys and set the fifty in front of her.

"I'll leave your keys with Nina," I said. "You can take a cab home."

Heavenly didn't touch the bill. Instead, she took a long sip from her coffee mug and made a face like it didn't agree with her. The flesh around her bloodshot eyes was swollen and puffy. What was left of her makeup looked like it had been applied yesterday.

"Have you slept at all?" I asked.

"Did you need to kill him, McKenzie?"

"It was an accident."

"An accident," she repeated slowly.

"He fell into the street . . ."

"No one was supposed to get hurt. Take the Lily and off we go to Ontonagon, Michigan. No one was supposed to get killed."

"How did Tommy know I was at Loring Park?"

"We followed you."

"No," I said, shaking my head. "You're not that good. I would have noticed."

"We used a three-car team, rotating in and out. We also sprayed your rear bumper with liquid glass so we could identify your Audi at night and in heavy traffic from a distance."

"I stand corrected," I said.

"Once we got to Loring Park, we had Tommy sit on your

Audi while the rest of us created a perimeter so we could watch you going in or coming out. We never actually entered the park, just observed from a distance."

When did she become so damn smart? my inner voice asked.

"Did you see Noehring get hit?" I asked aloud.

"I didn't know who he was."

"Did you see it?"

"I saw. He was just a dark figure slipping on the ice. I didn't pay any attention."

"Then you can't identify his killer."

"No. I didn't even know he was shot until Lieutenant Rask, until he . . ."

"Did you tell Rask that Tommy worked for you?"

"Tommy moved without instructions, McKenzie. I told him not to go anywhere near you unless you had the Lily. I don't know why—"

"He wanted the money."

"No, no, we talked about that."

"Either the money or he was trying to impress you just like all of the rest of the men you used over the years."

"I never used a man who didn't want to use me."

"Very scrupulous of you."

"Oh, McKenzie, I never meant for any of this to happen."

"What did you think was going to happen?"

"No one was supposed to get hurt."

"You keep saying that."

"I know."

"Why did you come here, Heavenly? What do you want from me?"

"Absolution for my sins, I guess."

I reached across the booth and slapped her hard. The

sound of my hand against her cheek reverberated through the club like a clash of cymbals. Heavenly's head jerked to the side and she made a kind of gasping sound as if she were trying to breathe in all the oxygen there was. She brought her hand up to soothe her cheek; I could see the deep red streaks my fingers had left on her flesh beneath her fingers. Her eyes filled with tears. She did not seem surprised by my action, though. Just the opposite. She looked as if she had been hit by something she saw coming from a long way off yet refused to dodge.

Many heads turned to look at us. A man sitting with his girl a few tables away stood like he wanted to make something of it, but his girl pulled him back down. I reached into my back pocket for a handkerchief and gave it to Heavenly. That gesture seemed to mollify everyone.

Heavenly swabbed her eyes and blew her nose.

"If you weren't in Nina's place I'd beat the hell out of you," I told her.

"That's why I came here."

"It's your fault that Tommy is dead; don't think for a second that it isn't. But I'm the one who killed him. I have to live with that."

"I'm sorry. I really am, McKenzie. I am so, so sorry."

"Being sorry doesn't help much."

"I know."

We sat quietly for a few moments while Heavenly dried her tears. During the lull, Nina appeared with more coffee for Heavenly and a Summit Ale for me. Before she left she gave me a look. I understood it perfectly—*don't hit her again.* Heavenly must have understood it as well.

"How can Nina be so nice to me?" she asked.

"So many gods, so many creeds, so many paths that wind

and wind, while just the art of being kind is all the sad world needs," I said.

"Ella Wheeler Wilcox." I wasn't surprised that Heavenly knew the quote. She was an English major after all. "As I long suspected, McKenzie, you're a romantic."

"Am I?"

"All those times I threw myself at you, I knew you wouldn't catch me. That's why I did it. Most of the men I know, even the ones I've dated, all they wanted was twenty minutes of my time, you know? You never behaved like that. That's why I always tease Nina. I want what she has. If not you, then someone like you."

"A romantic?"

"A man. An honest to God adult man."

I nodded. Somewhere in there was one of the best compliments I had ever received. It wasn't true, of course, what she said about me. If it hadn't been for Nina, I probably would have acted like all the other men in Heavenly's life. She didn't need to know that, though.

"Maybe if you . . ." I said.

"Maybe if I what?"

"My mother was very beautiful. She died when I was just a kid."

"Oh, McKenzie, I'm sorry."

"One of the few things I remember about her, she used to say, 'Pretty is as pretty does.'"

Heavenly snickered at that. "It's easy to have morals when you're rich," she said.

"Do you think people buy them off the shelf at Neiman Marcus? Besides, my mother wasn't rich. She was a middle-class housewife living in Merriam Park."

"Is this a teaching moment, McKenzie?" she asked. "Are you trying to teach me a lesson?"

"You didn't come here just to get slapped, did you?"

"I wanted you to know that I was sorry about what happened last night and that—that I didn't mean you any harm."

"I asked you before if you knew who stole the Jade Lily, when we were in the van, remember?"

"I remember."

"You didn't answer."

"Didn't I?"

"Last night didn't teach you anything, did it, Heavenly?"

"I'm still going after the Lily, McKenzie. Don't try to stop me."

"Heavenly, you're alone."

"The story of my life."

"C'mon, give it up, please."

Heavenly set two fingers on the fifty-dollar bill and slid it across the table to me.

"I can take care of myself," she said.

A few moments later, she was gone.

A few moments after that, Nina joined me in the booth.

"Well?" she said.

"Some people never learn," I told her.

NINE

Lunch was a walleye po' boy for me and a baby beet and apple salad for Nina. Rickie's had one of the best menus in town courtesy of her chef, Monica Meyer, a temperamental young woman who once worked for Wolfgang Puck. I liked to tease her because, well, she was so teaseable. If Monica had been there, I probably would have said something about going to Taco Bell to get some real food, but she wasn't, so I said, "This is fantastic."

"I'll tell Monica you said so."

"If you do, I'll only deny it."

"What is it with you and Monica, anyway?"

"She's incredibly good at what she does."

"So you harass her?"

"Yep."

"Huh?"

"One of the things that I admire most is competence," I said. "I don't care what you do as long as you do it well—you could be an accountant, a janitor, a cook, the guy who sharpens my hockey skates, if you're really good at what you do, you get my admiration and respect."

"You tease Monica because you admire and respect her?"

"You'll notice I never pick on people I don't like."

"McKenzie, if you were a woman you'd be a blonde."

"Are you teasing me, Nina?"

"Never."

"I wonder if I should take a sandwich out to the guy who's following me."

Nina stopped chewing her salad and stared at me from across the booth.

"Someone is following you?" she said at last.

"Cherry red Acura parked up the street."

"Who?"

"I don't know." I was skimming the menu. "What's the least expensive thing you have? Kalua pork quesadilla? That's way too good for him."

"What are you going to do?"

"Think he'd like a turkey meatball sandwich?"

"Who wouldn't? McKenzie?"

"Hmm?"

"What are you going to do?"

"The guy's an amateur. I could lose him in a minute, don't worry about it."

"I meant about everything."

"Honestly, Nina, I don't know. Apparently everybody and his brother want the Jade Lily, and they all expect me to either lead them to it or give it up after I make the exchange with the artnappers. I'd like to blow off the whole thing, only I'm afraid of the State Department. I guess I'll decide what to do with the Lily once I have it."

"You're still going after it despite everything that's happened, that's what you're telling me."

"Yes."

"Dumb blonde. Dumb dishwater blonde."

We went on like that for a while, talking about this and that, none of it worth repeating until my cell phone rang. I was prepared to let the call roll over to voice mail—I was having lunch with Nina, after all—until I saw the name of the caller.

"Hi, Chopper," I said into the microphone.

"McKenzie, you still wantin' t' meet El Cid?"

I decided against buying lunch for my tail. Let the SOB starve.

Instead, I went to my Jeep Cherokee and fired it up. The rear lights of the Acura changed from red to white to red again, telling me that the driver had put his SUV in gear and was ready to follow wherever I went. I knew I could shake him easily enough, only you know what? Screw it.

Bending across the seat, I removed the Beretta from the glove compartment, checked to make sure there was a round in the chamber, and set it on the seat next to me—I was bending down so the tail wouldn't see what I was doing. I looked left then right then left again for traffic. There was a lull, with no vehicles or pedestrians approaching from either direction. I drove out of the parking lot and up the street to where the Acura was parked, abruptly stopping when my rear bumper was parallel with the SUV's front bumper. The driver seemed surprised when I got out of the Cherokee and approached him. He was even more surprised when I raised the Beretta. He brought his hands up and turned his head, not that it would have helped him any.

I put one round into his rear tire. The exploding rubber was louder than the gunshot. The SUV suddenly listed hard to the left. The driver looked at me, an expression of terror on his face. He was wearing a suit and tie; he looked like a middle-management wonk. I didn't know what he actually did for a living, although following an armed and slightly deranged ex-cop apparently wasn't it.

A moment later, I was back in the Jeep Cherokee and maneuvering my way toward Minneapolis.

"Problem solved," I said, except I didn't really believe it.

The Phillips neighborhood is located in the center of Minneapolis and has some of the city's oldest and most historic buildings. It also has a high percentage of crack houses, slum apartments, poverty, and crime—ninety-three rapes, robberies, burglaries, auto thefts, assaults, and homicides had been committed there this month alone. It seemed the entire area was on the skids, with house after house and shop after shop trying to nudge each other into ghetto status. The buildings on the street where I was driving all had closed drapes, bolted doors, bars on the windows, aging vehicles, and no children, yet I knew from experience that invisible eyes were watching every move I made.

I found Chopper's van in the parking lot of a small grocery store. He must have seen me coming, because the door on the side of the van glided open, the platform his wheelchair was on slid forward, and the elevator slowly lowered him to the ground before I even parked my car. Herzog was at his side, helping him off the platform and then retracting the elevator back into the van.

"Chopper, how did it go last night?" I asked.

"Do I look like a cuddler to you?" he said.

"Ahh, no."

"No is fuckin' right. I don't snuggle. I'm a dude, man. Only this Em-ma, she's like stay, stay, stay. Stay the night? Cuddlin'? The whole fuckin' night? What reason have I gots t' stay the night unless we goin' again? Then her roommate shows up and I'm like whoa, cuz she's hot, Ali is, and I'm like, 'kay, I'll stay the night if the roommate joins in, and all of a sudden it's git out, git out, git out." Chopper shook his head, a bewildered expression on his face. "I don' understand women."

"They are a mystery," I said.

"You carryin'?"

"I am."

"That piece o' shit Beretta, I bet."

"She gets the job done."

"There ain't no carryin' in Cid's place. 'At's a rule. You go carryin' in Cid's place they might shoot you walkin' through the door."

"Pussy," Herzog said.

I didn't know if he meant me or the person who might shoot me, and I didn't ask.

"Best leave it here," Chopper said.

He reached out his hand. I set my Beretta in it. Chopper held it up by the barrel. Herzog reached over Chopper's shoulder, took the gun, and tossed it in the back of the van as if it were a flyer distributed on a street corner by one of those Jesus Saves groups. I heard it clatter against the metal frame of Chopper's elevator just before Herzog slammed the door shut.

"You gonna be cool, now, ain'tcha, McKenzie?" Chopper said. "Not gonna do nothin' rash?"

"Who? Me?"

"Yeah you. Fuck."

"I'm just going to ask the man a few questions."

"It's like he says—you can ask. Just don' go pushin' no buttons is what I'm sayin'."

"I promise."

Herzog set his hands on the handles at the back of Chopper's wheelchair and prepared to push Chopper across the parking lot. Chopper turned his head and gave him a look. Herzog's hands came off the handles as if he had touched hot burners on a stove. The expression on his face said, "I can't believe I did that."

Chopper propelled himself to the street, off the curb, across the street, and up the opposite curb quickly, efficiently, and without assistance. Herzog followed dutifully behind. I had the impression that he really wanted to help and was disappointed that Chopper wouldn't allow it. His mood brightened when we reached the front door of a beer joint and Chopper waited for him to open it. I assumed it was a beer joint because of the neon sign in the window flashing the name of one of those crappy pasteurized brews from St. Louis. There was no other means of identification.

I followed Chopper and Herzog inside. It was dark in the bar. The lights were kept low, and a thick curtain had been pulled across the one and only window. Tony Bennett could be heard singing softly from invisible speakers. Two older men were sitting in an old-fashioned wooden booth next to the door, the kind with high backs that you can't see over. They looked like working men having a quick beer before their shifts began. A third man, much younger, sat at a table and read the newspaper. The table was situated so that he had an unobstructed view of both the front and back doors. His winter coat was draped over the back of the chair. His gloves and a knit cap had been set on the table near his right hand. He moved his hand toward the hat when we entered, yet did not touch it. He was not drinking.

"Got him?" I whispered.

"Pussy," Herzog whispered back.

A fourth man was sitting in a booth parallel to the guy with the hat. There was a half-filled glass of beer in front of him, along with two cell phones and an iPad. He was talking on a third cell phone, his voice a soft murmur. I could make out only one word. "No." There was a finality to the word that made my arm hairs stand on end—somehow I had the feeling he wasn't saying no to a slice of French apple pie.

If there was a bartender, he was invisible.

Chopper wheeled his chair right up to the booth.

"Cid, my man," he said.

"Chopper," Cid said. He turned off his cell and set it on the table before slipping out of the booth. He was tall, with angular features, and was deceptively dressed in sweater, jeans, and black cowboy boots. I say deceptively because despite the casual appearance, I had the impression that his clothes cost more than the average new car payment. He bent down and gave Chopper a hug as if they were veterans of the same war.

Chopper waved me over.

"This here is McKenzie I told you 'bout."

Cid did not say hello; he did not offer his hand. Instead, he gave me a perfunctory head nod and slid back into the booth.

"Have a seat," he said.

I sat on the wooden bench across from him. Herzog stood by the door where he could keep a wary eye on the exits as well as the man with the knit hat. All in all, I felt as if I had walked into a Martin Scorsese movie.

"Nice place you have here," I said.

"Did you think I would have a ritzy office with a good-looking receptionist, a mahogany desk, and Queen Anne chairs?" Cid asked

"Something like that."

"Men in my line of work aren't afraid of the police. We can always make deals with the police. Do you know who we're afraid of?"

It wasn't a rhetorical question. Cid expected me to answer it.

"The Internal Revenue Service," I said.

He smiled slightly and nodded his head as if he had just learned something of value.

"You're quick," he said. "Yes, the IRS. In my business it pays to keep your visible assets to a minimum."

"I understand."

Cid stuck his head out of the booth and looked behind him. As if by magic, a bartender appeared.

"What can I get you gents?" the bartender asked.

"I'm good," Chopper said.

"Hey, Chop," Cid said. "This isn't a nonprofit organization."

"Gimme a Miller Genuine Draft," Chopper said.

When the bartender turned his gaze on me I pointed at Cid's glass.

"I'll have what El Cid is having," I said.

Cid smiled as if it were the first time he had ever heard the name.

The bartender gestured with his chin toward Herzog. "What about your friend?" he asked.

"My friend doesn't drink," Chopper answered.

When the bartender scurried away, I said, "How does one get the nickname of an eleventh-century Spanish lord?"

"I don't know," Cid said. "People just started calling me that. Perhaps they were impressed by my regal bearing."

I liked the answer, yet I knew it was a lie. To survive, much less flourish, in his line of work, a fence must be able to negotiate with the most dangerous thieves as well as the least scrupulous customers. The fear of betrayal, of being ripped off, of being arrested, was always present, so it was important to demonstrate a certain amount of fearlessness. "El Cid" was an affectation, just like his barroom "office," just like the barely concealed muscle pretending to read his newspaper while carefully watching us. It was designed to make associates believe that Cid was someone not to be trifled with. From what I'd seen, it certainly got Chopper thinking. Just the same, I said, "I believe it."

Cid must have liked my response, too, because he suddenly extended his hand. "My real name is Dave Wicker," he said.

I shook his hand and said, "Mr. Wicker."

"Cid."

"Cid," I repeated.

The bartender returned with our drinks. "Twenty-two fifty," he said.

Chopper was shocked. "Wha?" he said.

"I got it," I said and handed the bartender the fifty that I had offered Heavenly Petryk earlier. "Keep the change."

Chopper looked at me as if I were insane. Cid smiled some more.

"McKenzie," he said, "you didn't come here to throw around your money. What can I do for you?"

"I have it on excellent authority that if anyone between

Chicago and the West Coast knows what happened to the Jade Lily, it would be you."

"I appreciate the flattery, but why bring Chicago into it?"

I spread my arms wide, the palms of my hands facing upward, as if I couldn't think of a single reason.

"I know that the assistant director of security walked it out of the art museum Sunday night and handed it off to his associates," Cid said. "I know that the next day he turned up dead, call it an occupational hazard. I know the artnappers contacted the museum Monday morning and offered to sell the item back for one-point-three million. I know that you were enlisted to act as go-between. Beyond that . . ."

This time he spread his arms and hands apart.

"Have you ever met the assistant director of security?"

"We don't exactly travel in the same circles."

"Do you have any idea who his associates might be?"

"Why would I?"

"I think it's obvious that they stole the Lily with the intention of selling it back to the museum. However, with two shootings and the heat on, they might now be interested in a fence. Who else would they go to?"

Cid did indeed appreciate the flattery. He smiled and leaned against the wooden wall of the booth.

"There is no one else," he said, "and I prefer the term facilitator. Unfortunately no, McKenzie. I haven't heard anything."

"Would you tell me if you had?"

"Yes, I think I would. I don't appreciate it when out-of-towners piss in my soup without asking permission first. It's a sign of disrespect."

"You're sure they're from out of town?"

"I inquired among the usual suspects when I first learned

of the heist—like I said, I was upset that the job was initiated without my consent."

Good Lord, this guy is full of himself, my inner voice said. *Who does he think he is, Kid Cann?*

"I am now convinced that no local talent was involved," Cid added. "It's an out-of-town crew, all right. Maybe they recruited Tarpley, maybe he hired them, that I can't say."

"It does raise a question—why ask for me?"

"To act as go-between? I don't know. After I spoke to Chopper, I had you checked out as well. You seem capable, but you're inexperienced. You don't have a history of this type of work."

You're telling me, my inner voice said.

"Based on your expertise, what do you think of this crew?" I asked aloud.

"It's hard to say after the fiasco in Loring Park last night."

"You know about that?"

"Of course. Now understand, the park was a good move. It demonstrated care and forethought. It was a test run, you see. That's why they chose such a public place. They wanted to know if you could be trusted to come alone. Probably they hunkered down hours before, watched the exits and watched the traffic, saw how you handled the money, if you were nervous, if you were stand-up. When Noehring appeared, they should have just walked away. I don't know why they didn't. Shooting him was careless. In matters such as this, you invite as little police intervention as possible. Now—a cop killing? Everybody with a badge is looking for these guys. It's bad for them. Bad for me. Bad for business. Bad all around. The police are leaning on anyone they can find."

Cid looked at Chopper. "Have they rousted you yet?"

"No."

"I'm sure they'll get around to it. They've already chewed on my ass a number of times. And, gentlemen, the pressure isn't going to let up until someone takes the fall. It doesn't matter that Noehring was as dirty as they come. You knew that, didn't you, McKenzie, that Noehring was dirty?"

I winced at the question. "What makes you say that?" I asked.

"Me and Noehring, we've had dealings, and they were always to his benefit."

"Why do you think the artnappers killed him?"

"The only way it makes sense to me is if they thought Noehring was there to fuck them over—steal the money, steal the Lily. It puts them in a bad spot, though. Now the Lily is too hot to fence. Before the killing, they had the option of taking the Lily underground, wait a few years, and then find a private buyer. I know a dozen men in the Twin Cities alone who would have paid top dollar for the Jade Lily and then stash it in a vault until the statute of limitations ran out and they were able to establish a phony sales pedigree. Not now, not with a cop killing attached to it. There's no time limit on that. The only thing the thieves can do now is either toss the Lily in a Dumpster or"—Cid wagged his index finger at me—"make the deal as previously agreed upon."

"Then you think they'll try again."

"I know they will. Only next time, McKenzie, they'll put you in a position where they can see trouble coming from a mile away. You'll be isolated. You'll be alone. An empty holster"—he pointed at the spot just behind my right hip where I carried the Beretta before Chopper made me give it up—"won't help you."

"You see a lot," I said.

"It's my business. Now let me ask you a question, Mc-Kenzie. Why did you smoke Heavenly's boy?"

God, he's well informed.

"How did you know about that?"

"Like I said, it's my business. Besides, it isn't the deepest, darkest secret in the world."

"He went for the money," I said.

"Odd."

"In what way?"

"Heavenly doesn't want the ransom. She wants the Lily. She wants to return it to its rightful owner, for which she expects to be handsomely rewarded. Personally, I don't see the difference."

"How do you know Heavenly Petryk?"

"Oh, I don't know her," Cid said. "Never met her. But I keep track of talent. They tell me she's a stone babe. Almost as pretty as Tarpley's wife—I'd have to see her myself to believe it, though."

"Believe it."

"I don't get it, a woman like that. Why knock yourself out chasing a buck when you can marry for it and then divorce if it doesn't work out?"

"Something to do with scruples, I guess."

"In this line of work scruples can be a major hindrance."

"I'm learning that."

"You know, McKenzie, if you do get the Jade Lily back, I'd be happy to take it off your hands."

"You, too?"

"Just putting it out there."

"I thought you said it was too hot to fence."

"In the United States. Europe, the Pacific Rim—who knows?"

"I'll keep it in mind."

I thanked El Cid for his time. I slid out of the booth, and Cid did the same.

"Chopper, good to see you, man," he said.

He and Chopper clasped hands, and then Cid bent down to give him a hug, the hands between them to prove that, despite the show of affection, they were both manly men. At the same time, Herzog stepped forward, his impassive face giving away nothing. At first, I thought he might grab the handles of Chopper's wheelchair again and roll him away. Instead, he stepped to the table where the muscle was pretending to read his newspaper. He yanked the knit hat off the table. Beneath it was a small-caliber semiautomatic handgun—a Ruger, I think. He tossed the hat into the young man's lap and smirked.

"Pussy," he said.

Herzog spun around and headed for the door. Chopper and I followed him out. Neither one of us said a word to him.

It had started to snow while we were cloistered inside the unnamed bar, and the wind was whipping it around. It didn't seem to bother Chopper, though. He tightened his gloves like a race car driver waiting for the starting flag and wheeled his chair forward; his tires seemed to give him plenty of traction. After Chopper cleared the far curb, Herzog aimed his remote control at the van. There was a clicking sound; the door to the van unlocked and slowly rolled open. As he approached the van, Chopper said, "Cid likes t' think he a fuckin' gangster. Likes t' think he's Don Corleone."

"I noticed that," I said.

"He ain't. But he does know everything."

"I noticed that, too."

"He didn' give you much, though, did he?"

"He gave me plenty."

"What?"

"He said an out-of-town crew took down the Lily."

"Yeah? So? I coulda told you that."

"If it was out-of-town talent, how did they know Scott Noehring was a cop? How did they know he was dirty? How did they recognize him in the park—in the dark?"

"You're sayin' Cid was wrong. The crew gots t' be local or out-of-town talent workin' wit' local."

"He was wrong or he was lying."

"Look here, man. I hates t' see what happened to Noehring happen to you. Why not I lend you Herzy to provide air support? You know, watch your back?"

"I ain't workin' for no cop," Herzog said.

"How many times I have to say?" Chopper told him. "McKenzie ain't a cop no more."

"You crazy you think that, Chop. Didn' you see his face when Cid called out the dirty cop? McKenzie always be police."

Herzog looked me directly in the eye.

"Fuckin' cop," he added.

"Just give me back my gun," I said.

I drove straight home. It should have taken about fifteen minutes, only the blowing snow lengthened the trip to nearly thirty. It wasn't particularly deep, just a dusting so far. However, the Minnesota Driver's Manual as produced by the Minnesota Department of Public Safety clearly states you should slow down and increase stopping distance when roads become slippery and visibility is compromised, although the two accidents that I passed suggested that a lot of drivers hadn't read it. All in all, it did not bode well for rush hour traffic—one more reason I was happy not to have a nine-to-five job.

I put the Jeep Cherokee in the garage, went inside the house, made myself a café mocha with my expensive coffee machine, sat in front of my big-screen TV to watch *SportsNation* on ESPN, and promptly fell asleep. (I did mention I had only four hours of sleep, right?) I was awakened abruptly by the sound of my phone ringing. By then the sun had fallen and the only light in my house came from the TV screen. I found the phone on the kitchen wall and answered it without checking the caller ID.

A young man's voice said, "What the hell happened last night, McKenzie?"

I turned on the kitchen light and checked the LED display. It said the name and phone number were being withheld.

"Who is this?" I said.

"This is the guy who's going to throw the fucking Jade Lily into the goddamn Mississippi River, asshole."

"The only way you're going to do that is if you chop a hole. The fucking river is frozen over, numb nuts."

I should confess that I sometimes get cranky when I don't have enough sleep.

"Is that what you want us to do?" the caller asked.

"You killed a cop last night. I don't care what you do."

"We did not kill that cop. We didn't even know he was a cop until we read it in the newspaper."

"You expect me to believe that?"

"Yes." His voice dropped a few octaves and he spoke slowly. "All we're trying to do is make a buck, McKenzie. It would have been insane for us to shoot a cop. What reason would we have? He wasn't interfering with the exchange. Hell, there wasn't going to be an exchange. We just wanted to see if you would follow instructions, if you would come alone."

"Is this your sincere voice?" I asked.

"Dammit, McKenzie, you're the one who brought the fucking cop."

"I didn't, actually."

"Then what was he doing there?"

I could have explained, but I didn't really want to go into it.

"I don't know," I said.

"What are we supposed to think now?"

"What am I supposed to think? The cop is dead and you claim you didn't kill him. What about Patrick Tarpley? He's dead, too."

"We don't know what happened to Pat," the voice said. "He handed off the Lily just like clockwork. We were supposed to meet up later, after we were sure we were okay, before we made the call to the museum. He didn't show. We thought he might have lost his nerve and gone on the run. We didn't know he had been shot until Tuesday."

"If you didn't kill him, who did?"

"We don't know."

"Uh-huh."

"We had no reason to kill Patrick."

"You had plenty of reasons to kill Patrick."

He paused, gave it some thought, sighed. "It doesn't matter," he said.

"Tell that to his wife."

"It doesn't matter to us. We're still willing to make the exchange."

"With a crazed killer on the loose? That's brave."

"Do you want the Jade Lily or not?"

I almost said "not." I came *this*close.

"Talk to me," I said.

"We'll try one more time."

"When?"

"When we're ready."

"I suggest you wait until after the blizzard."

He paused again and said, "Get the money from the insurance company so that you'll have it on hand—using the gym bags and dolly like you did at Loring Park is fine with us. Once we call, you will have exactly as much time as it takes to drive from your home to the exchange point plus five minutes. If you're not there on time, we'll call the whole thing off—fuck the Lily."

"Will you be using MapQuest or Google Maps?" I asked.

"We asked for you, McKenzie, because we were told that you could be trusted. We weren't told that you're a smart-ass."

"Who gave you my name?"

"Make sure the money is ready."

"If you're going to hold me to a timetable, you had better make sure the roads are plowed before you call."

He hung up.

I did the same.

"Well, at least he didn't threaten me," I said.

The phone rang so quickly after I hung up that I thought maybe the artnappers actually had forgotten to threaten me and were calling back to rectify the situation. Instead, a young man's voice said, "What the hell happened last night, McKenzie?"

Didn't I just have this conversation? my inner voice asked.

"Who is this?" I asked.

"Jerry. Jerry Gillard."

"Oh, Jerry."

"Don't be so glad to hear from me," he said.

"Sorry 'bout that. I thought you were one of the bad guys."

"I've always wanted to be one of the bad guys. I've just never had the proper motivation. I blame my sheltered upbringing. So, what's going on?"

"What have you heard?"

"I spent some time with that Donatucci guy and the people at the museum—what a humorless crowd they are. Anyway, he said that very, very, very bad things happened at some park last night."

"Very bad things," I said.

"He said we still don't have the Lily."

"Not yet."

"I'm going to be serious with you for a second, McKenzie. Can I be serious with you?"

I don't know, can you? I thought but didn't say.

"Sure," I told him.

"I want you to walk away. Fuck it, McKenzie. Three people are dead over this piece of crap. It's a green rock. C'mon. Let the assholes keep it. I'll take the damn insurance settlement. So what if I don't get to sleep with Heavenly?"

"Okay, two things, Jerry. First, sleeping with Heavenly could be hazardous to your health. Second, I don't think you understand how this works. Midwest Farmers Insurance Group does not have a policy with you. It has a policy with the City of Lakes Art Museum. I don't know the specific language in your lending agreement, but I'm guessing the museum isn't going to pay you until the insurance company pays them, and the insurance company isn't going to pay the museum until it's convinced the Jade Lily is lost forever. If a car is stolen, most insurance companies will settle within thirty days because they figure if the vehicle hasn't been recovered by then, it never will be. The Jade Lily isn't a Buick that might end up in a chop shop, though. Nor is it a diamond ring or emerald necklace that can be recut and cast into a new setting. It retains its value only as long as it remains intact. The artnappers are not going to damage it. That makes it recoverable. I promise you, both the insurance company and the museum will drag their feet on your claim for a long time while trying to get it back. Hell, Jer, there are organizations out there like the Art Loss Register that exist solely for the purpose of recovering stolen art and antiques. This is big business, man. If we don't recover the Lily from the artnappers, it'll be a year before you get your money, if not longer. In any case, you don't get to decide whether we continue or not. Midwest Farmers is the one that writes the check. They get to decide."

Gillard thought about it for a moment, and then he said, "Do you really think sleeping with Heavenly would be dangerous?"

"Jerry . . ."

"I hear you, I hear you, McKenzie. I just don't want anyone else hurt over this."

"I appreciate that, Jer."

"Okay, okay. I'm going back to my Jacuzzi. I have a Jacuzzi in my hotel suite."

"Good for you."

"I was going out, but this snow—it reminds me of the lake-effect snow we get blowing off Lake Michigan."

"I'm glad you're feeling at home."

"Screw that. I hate Chicago in the winter. Chicago is the best summer city in America. In the winter, no way."

"People say the same thing about the Twin Cities."

"Why do we live in these places, I wonder."

"Just don't know any better, I guess."

Gillard promised that when all this was over he and I were going out and getting smashed—but in a good way. After he hung up, I called Mr. Donatucci. He did not like the idea of stashing $1,270,000 in my house and refused to allow it unless the money was protected by at least two security guards at all times. I gave him an argument, yet he refused to budge. Eventually I gave in. Donatucci said he would bring the money around tomorrow afternoon after the snow stopped and the streets were cleared. He was taking no chances, he said. I told him he was correct, I was the one taking all the chances. He didn't seem to mind that at all.

By then it was seven thirty and I was thinking about dinner. I love to cook and often host dinner parties just so I'll have an excuse to play Iron Chef in my kitchen. I had a great Chinese barbecue chicken recipe that used onions, red bell pepper, ginger, hoisin sauce, orange marmalade, tamari, green onions, and cashews—mmm mmm good. It seemed like an awful lot of work, though. That's the problem—it's no fun to cook just for yourself. I had decided to doctor a frozen pizza with sharp cheddar and pepperoni slices when I was startled by a heavy knock on my back door. I spun toward it, pulling the Beretta from its holster as I turned, cradling it in both hands. I moved sideways to the door, making myself as small a target as possible, and looked through the window. I saw the top of Nina's hat—she wore this broad-brim wool chapeau with a couple of pheasant feathers that she found in a consignment shop—and I quickly retreated back into the kitchen, hiding the gun in my junk drawer where she wouldn't find it.

"Nina," I said when I finally opened the door.

She stepped inside and stamped her feet on the rug, knocking away the snow.

"Baby, it's cold outside," she said.

She had an overnight bag draped over her shoulder. I took that as a good sign.

Hugs and kisses were exchanged, and Nina said, "Five inches of snow have fallen already with no end in sight. Business is almost nonexistent, as you can imagine. I decided to close up and send everyone home."

"Good for you," I said.

I helped her with her coat—and her bag. She rubbed her hands together as if trying to warm them.

"What's for dinner?" she asked.

"Chinese barbecue chicken with onions, red bell pepper, ginger, hoisin sauce, orange marmalade, tamari, green onions, and cashews."

"How long will it take to make?"

"About a half hour."

"Good." Nina came into my arms and kissed me full on the mouth. "I'm going to be hungry later."

TEN

I was sitting up in bed, my back against the headboard. Nina sat between my legs, her back resting against my chest. She was eating French toast sticks—my own recipe—that she dipped in a small bowl of warm maple syrup while I slowly and gently kissed my way from the point of her shoulder to the nape of her neck.

"Mmm," she hummed.

I didn't know if she was reacting to the touch of my lips or the food. It didn't matter much. I was willing to accept either compliment.

The radio was on, and the man was going down a lengthy list of school and business closings. It was eight thirty, and the snow was just now starting to taper off. Fifteen inches had fallen in Apple Valley, a suburb south of the Cities, while eight inches had been recorded in Blaine, north of the Cities. I figured we had about ten inches in Falcon Heights.

"This is so good," Nina said.

"We aim to please," I told her.

By then I was nibbling on the back of her neck.

"This might be the best French toast I've ever had," Nina said.

"Are you saying I'm a better cook than Monica?"

"No. On the other hand, your presentation is fantastic."

She hummed again, and this time I was pretty sure she was reacting to what I was doing with my hands.

A moment later, she rolled off the mattress, placed the empty plate on my nightstand, and climbed back into bed. She sat facing me, straddling my thighs, and kissed me hard on the mouth. After a few minutes of that, her lips found my chin, my cheek, my neck and throat. It was my turn to moan softly.

"I love snow days," I said.

Later, I was lying flat on my back in the bed. Nina had cuddled up next to me, resting her head against my chest. My arm was beneath her, my hand gently caressing her shoulder. My arm had gone numb long ago, but I didn't dare move it.

"I need to get up," she said.

"Why?"

"I have to get dressed; I have to go to Rickie's."

"Why?"

"Some of my staff probably won't be able to make it in for a while. I should be there."

"Snow day, Nina. Snow day."

"C'mon, McKenzie, you know better. By noon, all of the major streets will be plowed. By five, half of the secondary streets will be cleared. By nine, I bet I'm packed."

Instead of arguing with her, I shifted my weight on the bed and started gently moving my fingers across her warm flesh.

"I'll give you twenty minutes to cut that out," she said.

Turned out, that was exactly how much time she gave me before she rolled out of bed and headed for the bathroom.

"I'm really unhappy about this," I said.

"You know, McKenzie, some people like to go to work. They enjoy their jobs. It gives them satisfaction."

"Poor, brainwashed bastards. Wait a minute. Did you come over last night because you thought it would be easier to get to work from here than your place in Mahtomedi?"

Nina didn't answer. Instead, she turned on the shower. She did not get in, though. That was one of her quirks—she had to let the shower run for a good five minutes before actually using it.

"Nuts," I said and got up.

Nina poked her head through the bathroom door. She was holding a toothbrush in her hand.

"You can stay in bed, if you want," she said.

"What's the point?"

For some reason she thought that was funny.

"If you have to go in, I want you to take my Cherokee," I said.

"Why?"

"Four-wheel drive and an eleven-inch ground clearance. It should be able to get up the hill and to Cleveland Avenue, which, you're right, is probably plowed by now. That heap of a Lexus you drive is so low to the ground, you'll never make it."

"Don't say nasty things about Lexi."

"Lexi? You call your car Lexi?"

"Yes. What do you call your car?"

Twenty minutes later I was dressed in a red snowmobile suit that I had inherited from my father and blowing the snow out of my driveway using a two-stage, eight-speed, self-propelled snowblower with a 318 cc 4-cycle engine, 28-inch clearing width, 45-foot throwing distance, electric start, tire chains, and a front headlight. Yes, it was way too big and powerful for my driveway. Hell, I could have cleared the entire street with it. It was also expensive, about $1,500 including tax, which epitomized the schizophrenic relationship I have with my money. Because of my middle-class upbringing, I can't bring myself to spend more than $25 for a pair of jeans or $100 for a pair of shoes, yet I think nothing of spending $71,000 for a car or $750 for a coffeemaker. Nina claims it's because I'm a boy who likes his toys, only I'm not quite sure what that means.

I was nearly finished with the driveway when Nina came out of the house and started the Cherokee. She let it warm up for ten minutes, like the shower, which was another quirk of hers. You don't need to warm up a car even in the coldest weather unless you're planning on going from zero to 3,000 rpms in about six seconds. Yet the more I tell her that, the less she listens. Oh well. I gave her a kiss and she drove off, maneuvering through the snow up to Cleveland with no trouble at all.

I went back to snowblowing, finishing my driveway and then blowing the driveway of my neighbor before starting on the driveway of my neighbor's neighbor. I did it partly because I'm a helluva nice guy. Also because I wanted to build up some goodwill with the folks living in the community who have pointed out to me on more than one occasion that there had been no murders, kidnappings, and running gun battles along Hoyt before I moved in. By that time, the municipal snow-removal guys had plowed the avenue, piling huge heaps of snow at the end of each driveway, so I went up and down the street blowing that out, too. None of this was a burden to me. I love blowing snow. Boys with toys.

Afterward, I packed down the snow in my backyard and poured out some corn for the turkeys that were nowhere in sight. It was early afternoon by the time I returned to my house with thoughts of cleaning up before Mr. Donatucci arrived. The phone was ringing, and I caught it just before it rolled over to voice mail.

"McKenzie," Nina said. She sounded out of breath. "I've been calling. Where were you?"

"What is it?"

"Someone followed me to the club from your house."

"Are you sure?"

"A red SUV. He followed me right into the parking lot."

"Stay there. I'm on my way."

"No, no, it's okay. He left. When I got out of the Cherokee and walked to the door, he saw that it was me and I was alone and he left."

"He followed the Cherokee thinking I was driving."

"That's what I think, too."

"I'm sorry, Nina. I thought I had gotten rid of that sonuvabitch."

"It's okay. I just want you to be careful. When he left, well, he must be going back to your place, right?"

She's not worried about herself, she's worried about you, my inner voice said.

"I love you, Nina," I said.

"I know."

———

Five minutes later I was on the phone with Bobby Dunston.

"Did you check on that license plate number I gave you?" I asked.

"I thought you weren't in a hurry about that," Bobby said.

"The guy in the Acura, he followed Nina right up to the front door of Rickie's."

Bobby paused for a moment and said, "Hang on for a minute."

One minute turned into a couple before Bobby returned to the phone.

"Acura MDX, it's a company car belonging to Minnesota Disposal and Recycling," he said. "It's assigned to Nicholas Garin of Wayzata. We have nothing on this guy, McKenzie. Not even a speeding ticket."

"Thanks, Bobby."

"Is Nina okay?"

"She sure is."

Bobby paused for another moment and then said, "About hockey tonight."

"I might have to blow if off."

I explained about my conversations with the artnappers and Mr. Donatucci.

"In that case, I have only one word to say to you, McKenzie. Are you listening?"

"Sure."

"One word."

"What is it?"

"Kevlar."

Not long ago people were up in arms over the threat the Internet posed to their privacy, and they were right to be upset.

The Internet made it easy to learn just about anything you wanted to know about an individual from their criminal record to the charities they support. I could have easily gained the information Bobby had given me in a day on my own at the cost of just a few bucks. Yet what continued to surprise me was that instead of struggling to protect their privacy, most people were giving it up without a fight. Take Nicholas Garin of Wayzata, for example. He had both a Facebook and LinkedIn page, and between the two of them he revealed just about everything about himself a guy might care to know, including his favorite ice cream—Kemps Raspberry Cow Tracks.

It was from his LinkedIn site that I discovered that he was twenty-nine years old, married to a graphic designer named Alicia, and played Class A softball in a park and rec league in the summer. I also learned that he had an MBA from the University of St. Thomas and worked first as a fund-raising consultant and then as a public relations director for a local nonprofit before becoming a new business development consultant with a small Minneapolis firm. A former client said, "Nick Garin is an innovative thinker with the ability to be resilient in the face of change, responding quickly and efficiently to it."

The firm was purchased eighteen months ago by Minnesota Disposal and Recycling.

"Minnesota Disposal and Recycling." I said it aloud just to prove that I was paying attention. "Jonathan Hemsted and Branko Pozderac are staying in a hotel suite owned by MDR."

The firm was renamed and put to work providing community relations. This included supporting education, arts, and culture groups through the company's nonprofit foundation. It reported directly to MDR's president and CEO, Randolph Fiegen.

That little bit of intel caught me by surprise. What's more, I had no idea what to do with it.

I left my computer and went into the kitchen for a cup of joe. I took the mug, sipping from it every now and then, while I meandered through my mostly empty house, pacing, walking in circles, never sitting down. I did that sometimes when I was thinking, and let's face it, I had a lot to think about. Eventually I decided I needed to get cleaned up. Before I went upstairs, I looked up and down Hoyt Avenue from my front window. Nicholas Garin was nowhere in sight.

It took me about forty minutes to make myself presentable to the outside world, and that was because I lingered in the shower. By the time I had finished, I had devised a plan of action, such as it was. I returned to my PC and started surfing Web sites for information about Bosnia and Herzegovina. I found a government site that dealt with business opportunities for U.S. companies overseas.

DOING BUSINESS IN BOSNIA AND HERZEGOVINA

I read the information several times, making note of those points I considered salient.

Still regarded as a transition economy, Bosnia and Herzegovina is open to foreign investment.

Still-to-come privatization of state-owned entities will offer significant opportunities.

There is no single best way to do business in Bosnia and Herzegovina. New entrants to the market will most likely be displacing/supplanting nearby suppliers, such as Croatia and

Serbia, as well as dominant EU member countries. Sales agents, representatives, and distributors all have important roles to play in this market. Financing is a key factor for a Bosnian company making a decision to take on a U.S. product line.

"Financing is a key factor," I wrote, underlining the word "financing." "Does that mean bribery?"

The U.S. Commercial Service Office at the U.S. Embassy in Sarajevo will provide you with a fresh insight on doing business in Bosnia and Herzegovina.

I wrote: "U.S. Commercial Service Office—isn't that where Jeremy Hemsted works?" I looked it up.

The CSO cooperates extensively with the Foreign Investment Promotion Agency of Bosnia and Herzegovina.

I Googled the organization and discovered a Web site that served as an open invitation to foreign businesses. In fact, there was a personal message welcoming potential investors to the site and thanking them for their interest in Bosnia and Herzegovina. It was signed by the chief administrator of the promotion agency—Branko Pozderac.

Privatization in Bosnia and Herzegovina provides the possibility to both local and foreign physical and legal entities to participate in the purchase of state-run enterprises.

Bosnia and Herzegovina is accelerating the privatization process for companies of strategic importance in order to increase economic growth and enhance the volume of foreign investment.

An estimated 60% of small companies and more than 30% of the large ones are now privately owned or publicly traded. However, a number of strategic enterprises including power companies, telecommunications providers, mines and other public utilities are still not privatized, presenting a choice of opportunities for potential foreign and local investors.

The Foreign Investment Promotion Agency of Bosnia and Herzegovina also provided a list of publicly owned enterprises ripe for privatization, breaking them down by city. As I read the list, it became obvious to me that nearly every city in Bosnia and Herzegovina—Visoko, Kakanj, Zenica, Sarajevo, Banovići, Visočica—required the same thing.

Garbage and wastewater cleaning.

"What the hell?" I said to no one in particular.

After pausing for a couple of minutes to think it through, I looked up the Web site for the U.S. Embassy in Sarajevo and called the number provided. It was 8:00 P.M. when the phone rang there, yet someone answered it just the same.

"United States Embassy," a pretty voice said.

"Good evening," I said. "I would like to speak to Jeremy Hemsted. I believe he is with your Commercial Service Office."

"May I ask who is calling, please?"

I gave the woman my name and location. Why not? The embassy probably had caller ID, anyway.

"I'm sorry, Mr. McKenzie, Mr. Hemsted is unavailable. Is there someone else who might be able to help you?"

"Do you mean Jeremy is unavailable as in he's not in the embassy right now"—I purposely used Hemsted's first name

so the woman would think that he and I were acquainted—
"or he's unavailable as in he's not in the country?"

"Mr. Hemsted is on vacation, sir."

"On vacation or on assignment?"

"On vacation, sir, although he will be calling in to check his messages."

"Will you be kind enough to deliver a message for me?"

"Would you like his voice mail?"

"Oh, no. Just tell him that McKenzie called and that I look forward to seeing him again soon."

After a few moments, I refreshed my coffee mug and started wandering around again. It all made sense in that the pieces seemed to fit. Beyond that . . .

I called Harry. He wasn't in his office at FBI headquarters in Brooklyn Center, so I tried his cell phone. His first question: "Why are you interrupting my lunch?"

"Explain diplomatic immunity to me."

"Have you ever heard of the Internet? Invest in an online encyclopedia, why don't you?"

"I need an official ruling."

"Oh, please. Okay, um, diplomatic immunity—it's an international law agreed upon during the Vienna Convention on Diplomatic Relations that ensures that diplomats are given safe passage across borders and are immune from prosecution under the host nation's laws. It was enacted during the Cold War to keep rival countries from harassing each other's representatives, accusing them of spying, that sort of thing."

"Who gets it?"

"Official representatives of a sovereign nation and their families."

"What if a foreign politician who is not representing his

country—let's say he's on vacation. What if he comes to the United States and commits a crime that is totally unconnected to his diplomatic role?"

"I suppose that depends on where he's from and what he's done. Some countries will waive immunity if the guy's a dirt bag, and some will bring him home and prosecute him there. In this case, I'm not sure if he's covered. We are talking about our friend Branko Pozderac, aren't we?"

"Who has jurisdiction?"

"We do. Is this about Branko?"

"Yep."

"What's he done?"

"I haven't decided yet."

"Geez, McKenzie, you're messing with international law now. Please, please, please, I'm begging you—don't do anything stupid."

"Who? Me?"

After I hung up on Harry, I went to my junk drawer in the kitchen and pulled out the Beretta.

Nicholas Garin had parked his cherry red Acura in the lot of the gymnasium located on the St. Paul campus of the University of Minnesota. From there he had a clear view of Hoyt Avenue where it intersected with Cleveland. Ninety-nine times out of a hundred, when I'm driving somewhere I'll go through that intersection.

Unfortunately for Garin, I wasn't driving. I was on foot. Garin wasn't looking for pedestrians, so he didn't see me walking east on Hoyt dressed in a Timberwolves players jacket and a Vikings hat pulled low. Nor did he pay attention when I headed north on Cleveland past the tennis courts and then crossed the street at Folwell, although I was in plain sight the entire time. I made my way south on Cleveland and then cut through the parking lot until I was standing directly behind him. Even then, Garin didn't see me, never glancing around, never checking his mirrors. He slouched against the driver's door of the SUV, gazing more or less toward the mouth of Hoyt Avenue, oblivious to the world. For all I knew, he was sound asleep. Certainly he jumped as if I had awakened him from a pleasant daydream when I tapped the window with the nose of the Beretta.

Surprise became terror became panic. He grabbed the steering wheel with both hands, and although I couldn't see it, I knew his foot was stomping on the accelerator in an effort to escape. Only the SUV wasn't running. He pounded on the steering wheel with both hands until he realized that the SUV wasn't running and reached for the ignition key.

"C'mon, Nick, don't do that," I said.

I tapped the window again, only I was more forceful than I intended. The safety glass shattered into a hundred tiny shards that rained all over him. Panic became anger.

"What are you doing?" Garin shouted.

The guy is burning through emotions like an acetylene torch, my inner voice said.

"Sorry about that, Nick," I said aloud. "I was just trying to get your attention."

"You broke my window."

"I said I was sorry."

"Have you any idea how expensive it is to fix a window on an SUV these days? On top of what it cost me to replace the tire you shot out?"

"Don't you have insurance?"

"Yes, I have insurance. I also have a high deductible."

"Get your boss to pay for it."

"Like that's going to happen."

For God's sake, McKenzie, my inner voice said. *You're the one with the gun. Take charge.*

"Hey." I rapped the frame of the car door with the barrel of the Beretta, where the window had been, sending more glass shards flying. "I'm the aggrieved party here."

"What did I ever do to you?"

"Among other things, you frightened my girlfriend. On a bad day I'd shoot you just for that alone."

To prove it, I pointed the Beretta at Garin's heart. Anger became anxiety. Garin backed away as far as he could while still remaining in his seat.

"What are you going to do?" he asked.

"Fortunately for you, Nick—do you mind if I call you Nick? Fortunately for you, Nick, this is not a bad day, so I'm willing to negotiate. Here are my terms—you do exactly what I say and I won't shoot you. Take it or leave it."

"How do you know my name?"

"I know everything about you, Nick, including who you work for. What did Fiegen expect to accomplish by sending you out here, anyway?"

Garin hesitated for a moment, his eyes narrowed, and he looked off to his left.

"Who?" he said. "Fiegen?"

"Nick, you have an MBA from the University of St. Thomas. Are you telling me you can't lie any better than that?"

"I'm not lying."

I raised my gun like I was going to hit him with it. He cringed and turned his head.

"What do you want?" he asked.

"Tell me what your job was."

"Just watch. Don't get involved, don't interfere, just watch and report on what you do."

"Were you watching Wednesday night when I threw a man in front of a speeding car? Did you report on that?"

Garin's eyes widened. Anxiety became fear.

"Does Alicia know what you've been up to?" I asked.

Fear became something I couldn't read.

"You're not trained for this, pal," I said. "Fiegen sending you instead of someone with experience, that's amateur night. I expected more from him."

"He didn't want . . ."

"What didn't he want?"

"He didn't want to go outside the company."

"So he sent an MBA to do a punk's job. Risk a dime to save a nickel. And people wonder why our economy is in a shambles. All right, this is what you're going to do. You're going to contact your penny-pinching boss. You're going to tell him that I know everything. Tell Fiegen to call me or I'm going to call the FBI. Tell him if I get bored waiting for his call, I might blow his deal with the Bosnians just for the fun of it. Are we clear on that?"

Garin didn't answer, so I rapped the door frame with my gun again.

"Are we clear?" I asked.

"We're clear."

"One more thing, Nick. I don't want to see you or your cherry red Acura ever again. If you think dealing with auto insurance guys is tough, wait until you have to negotiate with health insurance people. They're sonsabitches. Do we understand each other?"

"This wasn't my idea," he said.

"I never thought it was."

I was so pleased with myself when I arrived back home that I mixed a shot of bourbon into my coffee. A friend of my father's who helped raise me, Mr. Mosley, used to insist that you should never add anything to either coffee or bourbon—"Take 'em both straight, like a man," he'd say—so I doubt he would have approved. You should give it a try, though. It tastes good. I was thinking, in fact, of having a second cup when I heard my front doorbell ring.

Instead of saying hello when I opened the door, Mr. Donatucci asked, "Are you alone?"

"I am," I answered. "Mr. Donatucci, what do you think of mixing coffee with bourbon?"

"I think it's a waste of two good drinks."

Okay, then.

Donatucci waved at the cream-colored van parked in my driveway behind Nina's Lexus. A door opened and an armed guard stepped out. He looked slowly around him, his hand resting on the butt of the handgun holstered to his thigh, which I took as an amateur move. If he didn't already know that the coast was clear, he should never have gotten out of the vehicle.

He rapped on the frame of the van and a side door slid open. Another guard emerged and did a little pirouette, looking for danger in the same places as his partner. He, too, had his hand on his gun. A moment later, they pulled a dolly with three gym bags strapped to it from the vehicle. The two of them slowly rolled it to my front porch, banging the wheels against the wooden steps as they dragged it onto the porch while swiveling their heads in long arcs as if they expected an ambush at any moment.

"I like melodrama as much as the next guy," I said, "but honestly, Mr. Donatucci."

"Quiet, McKenzie," he said.

The two guards pulled the dolly into my house, rolling it across the living room carpet as if they didn't care about the stains it made. Once inside, with the door locked, we stood in a circle, the money in the center of the circle, and stared at each other.

"Now what?" one of the guards asked.

"Now we wait," Donatucci said.

Everyone turned to look at me.

"Have you guys ever mixed bourbon with coffee?" I asked.

A few minutes later, the guards dispersed with mugs of coffee sans bourbon. One went to an empty upstairs bedroom that gave him a clear view of the front of the house as well as both ends of Hoyt Avenue. The other found a perch in my dining room that revealed the whole of my backyard and the houses on my right and left.

"Are those wild turkeys?" he asked.

"Yes," I told him.

"Huh," he said.

Mr. Donatucci and I sat at my kitchen table and reviewed the situation. He was as opposed to paying the ransom as ever.

"Then let's not do it," I said.

He shook his head sadly as if the decision were out of his hands.

"You can tell your boss that I refused to cooperate," I said. "Better yet—we can blame the cops. Put it on Rask. Say that he threatened to arrest us for obstruction of justice."

"They'd probably fire me."

"Let them. How old are you, anyway? You should have retired years ago."

"You know, McKenzie, some people like their jobs. They like going to work in the morning."

"You're the second person to tell me that today, so I guess it must be true."

A moment later my cell phone sang. I answered it without wondering who it might be.

"This is Mr. Fiegen," a voice said.

I had never heard anyone use "mister" as a title in the same way a doctor or governor might, and I said so aloud.

"I do not like your tone," Fiegen said.

"If you had told me that yesterday, I might have cared. Hang on."

I gestured toward Donatucci. "Make yourself comfortable," I said. "I'll be right back."

I descended a flight of stairs just off the kitchen to my basement, which held my hockey equipment, my golf clubs, my camping and fishing equipment, and a treadmill that I hadn't used since I bought it. When I was sure no one could overhear our conversation, I said "Okay," into the cell's microphone.

"The young man delivered your message," Fiegen said. His voice was angry, which made me smile. It was about to get worse.

"You're a sonuvabitch, Fiegen," I said. "A rat, a liar, a hypocrite—I could probably think of a few other insults, but what's the point?"

"What do you want, McKenzie?"

"How much is the garbage business in Bosnia and Herzegovina worth to you?"

"Are you trying to blackmail me?"

"Yes, I am. How much is it worth?"

Fiegen inhaled deeply and answered with the exhale.

"Bosnia and Herzegovina is an emerging country. As its gross national product increases, so will the amount of solid waste it'll produce. We estimate that in ten years it will be generating as much as twenty-five percent more than it does now."

"That's not the answer I was looking for."

"MDR estimates gross profits at between one-point-three and one-point-seven billion euros in the first fiscal year, assuming we acquire all the territories we are bidding on."

"A tidy sum."

"Yes, it is. How much do you want?"

"How big is the bribe you're paying Jonathan Hemsted to steer Pozderac your way?"

Another pause; another sigh.

"Two hundred and fifty thousand dollars if the deal is made," Fiegen said. "Fifty thousand if it goes away."

"That's pretty good money for government work."

"Hemsted is acting as a go-between in much the same way as you are. There is nothing unethical about it."

"I'm not arguing with you. Just making an observation. The bribe to Pozderac, though—how did you expect to deliver the Jade Lily to him?"

"Oh, some legal hocus-pocus involving condemnation via eminent domain."

"Except the federal government isn't actually taking title to the property, is it? Nobody would be compensated for their loss, would they?"

"Your outrage is born of ignorance, McKenzie. This is the

price of doing business, especially in that part of the world. Everyone does it, including our competitors."

"Then why keep it a secret? Why tell the mayor and police department in Minneapolis that Hemsted is acting on behalf of the State Department when he's not?"

"It's the system we live under."

"Sure. It's just business."

"That's right. It's just business."

"You're a thief, Fiegen. Plain and simple. A lousy, second-rate thief. I have more respect for Patrick Tarpley and the crooks that walked the Lily out of the museum. They at least have the balls to do their own dirty work. You? You're just a punk hiding behind a business title. I bet you the boys and girls at the Justice Department that enforce the antibribery provisions of the Foreign Corrupt Practices Act will agree with me, too."

"What do you intend to do, McKenzie? Call Justice? Call the police? And tell them what? Show them what? You have no hard evidence. McKenzie, we both know you are just posturing. Just tell me what you want to go away?"

"I want a letter," I said. "A contract if you prefer, signed by you and notarized. I want it delivered to me by the end of the day. The letter will state clearly that you will pay Midwest Farmers Insurance Group one million two hundred seventy thousand dollars should the ransom be lost to the artnappers in our attempts to recover the Jade Lily. It will state that the City of Lakes Art Museum will make no claim in any way or fashion against the insurance company as a result of the theft. It will state that you—and I mean you personally—will compensate Jeremy Gillard three million eight hundred thousand dollars for the loss of the Lily. It will state that Perrin Stewart will retain her job as executive director of the art museum for five years with a ten percent pay raise each year."

"Why would I give you such a damning document?"

"In exchange, when I recover the Jade Lily, I will give it to Jonathan Hemsted of the United States State Department with the understanding that he will pass it on to Branko Pozderac and the peoples of Bosnia and Herzegovina. You'll get what you want. Everyone else gets what they want. No harm, no foul."

Another pause, this one much longer.

"You surprise me, McKenzie," Fiegen said.

"Sometimes I surprise myself."

"I don't know what to say."

I didn't either, so I hung up.

ELEVEN

My phone rang at exactly 11:00 A.M.

The guards each jumped about three feet when it did, which didn't surprise me—they had been twitchy all morning. They crowded around me in the kitchen when I answered the phone pretty much as they had late Friday when a courier appeared at my front door with an envelope in his hand. One suggested that it might be a letter bomb, and the other actually sighed with relief when it didn't blow up after I opened it. The letter was from Fiegen, and it contained everything that I had demanded, including the stamp and signature of a notary public. I folded it and placed it in my pocket while the guards stared.

"Guys," I said. "Relax."

Only they didn't relax until they were relieved for the night by another pair of security agents with intense dispositions. The original guards returned at about 9:00 A.M. Saturday. I would have offered them coffee, but they already seemed overcaffeinated.

The voice on the phone was very specific about where I was supposed to be and when. It did not threaten; it did not warn me about what would happen to the Lily if I were late.

I hung up the phone and said, "Gentlemen, help me with this."

"This" was high-tenacity Kevlar XP bullet-resistant body armor that I strapped around my torso and camouflaged with an angora sweater. When I finished, I took the Beretta from my junk drawer, checked the load, and slipped it under my belt behind my right hip.

"Are you supposed to be wearing a bulletproof vest, are you supposed to be carrying a gun?" a guard asked. "Isn't that against the rules?"

"What rules?" I said.

He didn't have an answer for that.

I put on my leather coat. The money was still packed in the gym bags, the gym bags strapped to the dolly in the center of my living room. I grabbed the handle and started wheeling it to the back door of my house. I had a remote control hanging from the lock on the window overlooking my unattached garage. I used it to open the garage door.

"There's no reason for you guys to hang around anymore," I said.

The guards followed me out of my back door, across the driveway, and into the garage just the same. They stood by and watched while I loaded the dolly and the gym bags into the trunk of the Audi.

"Nice car," one of them said.

If he had offered me ten bucks, I would have sold the Audi and all of its contents to him right then and there. Because he didn't, I unlocked the driver's door and slid behind the wheel.

"Good luck," the guard said and closed the door for me. He smiled like I was a patient about to be wheeled into surgery; smiled like he felt sorry for me.

I put the key in the ignition, started up the car, depressed the clutch, put the transmission in reverse, and—sat there for five seconds, ten, fifteen . . .

Why are you doing this? my inner voice asked. *Are you crazy?*

The guard watched me through the window, an expression of concern mixed with puzzlement on his face.

"McKenzie, are you okay?" he asked.

"Never better," I said.

I slowly released the clutch and backed the Audi out of my driveway.

The artnappers had chosen the location wisely—a motel overlooking Interstate 694 within minutes of three freeways and three major highways. Make the exchange and boom, the thieves would have quick access to the 2,950 miles of U.S., state, and county thoroughfares that crisscrossed the Twin Cities in a pattern as complicated as a cobweb. If things didn't work out, they'd also have half a dozen shopping malls to hide in as well.

There were two levels to the motel. The doors to the rooms on the bottom level opened onto the asphalt lot—you could park directly in front of them. The doors to the rooms on top opened onto a metal and concrete landing that ran the length of the motel. There was a square window next to each door. Two staircases led to the upper level, one to each side of the motel. A second, smaller structure was separated from the actual motel and contained the office, a bar, a restaurant and several banquet rooms. There was a small swimming pool between the two structures that was surrounded by a tall iron fence. The pool was filled with snow—it was January, after all. The sight of it made me feel a bit sad.

I parked between a pair of white lines painted on the asphalt directly in front of the office and turned off the engine as I had been instructed.

The artnappers could be working it in a number of different ways, I decided. They could have followed me from my house, although that wasn't likely. Since my conversation with Heavenly Petryk, I had become ultra careful about that. Or they could have already checked into the motel and were watching me now. Hell, they could have been sitting on the motel for days watching the traffic, getting a sense when it was normal and when it wasn't. Or they could be somewhere else, across the freeway perhaps, sitting in a car with a pair of binoculars. What else could they do?

I sat in the Audi, my cell phone in my hand, my coat open so I could reach the Beretta in a hurry. I had powered down the driver's window to keep the interior glass from fogging over. It was cold, but not too cold—about twenty-eight degrees. Granted, it was a temperature that would freak out most people. On the other hand, I went to San Antonio in February a couple of years ago to play golf. It was seventy degrees down there, and most of the natives were dressed in coats and sweaters and wore hats and gloves. My buddies and I were dressed in shorts and polo shirts. This old guy looked at us and said, "You boys aren't from around here, are ya?" It's all about what you're used to. Twenty-eight in the middle of January—we'll take that in Minnesota every time.

A good half hour passed, and I was beginning to think that it was another dry run when the cell phone sang to me.

"Park in front of room 122," the voice said. "The room is unlocked. Take the money inside."

I started the Audi and drove from the office through the parking lot, following the room numbers as I went. Room 122 was in the center of the motel. When I found it, I parked backward with my trunk facing the motel room door. The window drapes had been drawn, and I couldn't see inside. As I did at Loring Park, I refrained from using the interior latch and instead waited to open the trunk with my remote once I was sure that there was no one nearby. I muscled the dolly and gym bags out of the trunk and pivoted toward the door. I carefully turned the knob. As promised, it was unlocked. I nudged the door open with the toe of my boot, my left hand holding the handle of the dolly and my right gripping the butt of my Beretta under my leather coat. Nothing bad happened, so I stepped inside. It was like every other motel room you had ever been in. There was a bed, a nightstand, a dresser, a small table, a pair of chairs, a cheap clock radio and telephone on the nightstand, a TV on the dresser, a lamp on the table, and a couple of paintings securely fastened to the walls—nothing anyone would ever want to steal. I closed and locked the door and rolled the dolly next to the bed. It was dark inside the room with the drapes drawn, yet not so dark that I couldn't see. I looked in the bathroom. No one was hiding there. I turned on the overhead light and sat on the edge of the bed and waited. After a few minutes, I stretched out on the bed and waited some more. Time passed slowly. I got off the bed and went to the window. I pulled the drapes open a crack and looked outside. I saw no one. I sat down again, this time on a chair. I slipped the Beretta out from under my coat and set it within easy reach on the table. More time passed. The phone on the nightstand rang. It had a loud ringtone that was so startling I grabbed the Beretta, went into a crouch, and aimed it at the phone—I almost shot it.

Dammit, McKenzie, my inner voice said. *Get a grip.*

I lunged for the phone.

"Yes," I said.

"Empty the bags; put the money on the bed," the voice said before he hung up.

I didn't ask why. I knew why. The thieves wanted to easily check the bundles for ink packs and tracers, just like I had told Mr. Donatucci they would. I did as I was instructed, examining the bundles myself in case someone had tried to pull a fast one. The money was clean. I waited some more.

The phone rang again. I let it ring four times before I answered.

"Bebe's Peanut Shop, Bebe speaking."

There was a long pause before the voice said, "Are you fucking crazy?"

I didn't answer.

"McKenzie?"

"I'm listening."

"The Jade Lily is in the room directly above you—room 222. You will leave your room, take a right outside the door, and walk to the staircase, climb it, go to 222—the door is unlocked."

"All right," I said. "Now you listen. I scattered the money nicely over the bed. It'll take you a few minutes to gather it together, check for tracers and ink packs, and then put it all in bags. That's all the time I'll need to make sure the Lily is in the room as promised. If it's not, you're going to find out just how crazy I am."

"McKenzie, I will be so very glad when our business with you is concluded. Shall we get to it?"

"I'm leaving the room now."

The first step, they say, is the hardest. I went to the door and pulled it open and stood there for what seemed like a very long moment. If someone wanted to pot me with a .30-06, that was as good a moment as any. The fact that I wasn't shot encouraged me to take the next step and then the one after that. I walked the length of the motel until I reached the staircase. Did I say it was twenty-eight degrees? The way the sweat beaded on my forehead and welled up under my arms it could have been ninety-eight. I jogged up the staircase and followed the landing to room 222. It occurred to me then that we were playing out the exact same scenario as when I recovered my friend Jenny's jewels from her Internet lover, and I wondered if there was a handbook that these bastards followed, a template. As with that time, I did not look right or left, only straight ahead until I reached the door. The drapes were closed over the lone window so I couldn't see inside this room, either. I tried the knob. It turned easily. I opened the door and stepped inside, locking it behind me.

The Jade Lily was sitting on the table in front of the window.

I turned on the overhead light. It didn't give me the light that I needed, so I opened the drapes. Sunlight danced over the spinach-colored flowers.

"Wow," I said.

The sculpture was not nearly as fragile as the photographs had made it seem. I rubbed a jade flower petal between my thumb and forefinger. It seemed quite sturdy. It also had the soaplike feel that India Cooper told me to look for. I pulled the magnifying glass she had given me from my pocket and trained it on the stalk where it sprouted from the ground. *"M, M, M,"* I chanted as I looked through the glass. It took a moment before I realized I was looking on the wrong side of the sculpture. I turned it around, surprised by how heavy it was. I searched again. This time I found it, easily. "*M* for McKenzie."

The *M* brought a smile to my face, but it didn't last long. I saw movement outside the window. A red SUV was moving through the parking lot, moving much faster than it should have been. The SUV contained the artnappers and the money—I knew it without knowing it.

The phone rang. It was sitting on the nightstand on the opposite side of the bed. Someone had lain down on the bed before I arrived—the spread was matted, and two pillows were squashed against the headboard. The phone startled me as it had in room 122. I paused for a moment, then circled the bed and answered it.

"Yes," I said.

"Are you satisfied?"

"I am."

"Are you sure?"

"You kept your end of the bargain."

"All right, then. McKenzie?"

"Yes."

"There is a bomb in the room. It will go off in ten seconds. Good luck."

TWELVE

I snapped awake the way you do when you hear a sound that shouldn't be there. The sound was two voices talking, two women. One was a doctor; the other was a nurse. The nurse said, "I don't know if I should go out with him," and the doctor said, "He acts like a jerk sometimes, but he's awfully cute," so I knew they weren't talking about me.

"Keep it down," I said. "There are sick people trying to get some sleep."

"Good morning, Mr. McKenzie," the doctor said. She picked up my hand, careful not to disturb the device clamped to my finger that resembled a white plastic clothespin. The clothespin was attached to a wire. The wire ran to a monitor above my head that the doctor was reading. The lights, except for those that came from the monitors, were dialed down. The blinds were drawn over the window, yet I knew it was dark outside.

"What time is it?" I asked.

Instead of answering, the doctor said, "Do you know where you are?"

"Target Field?"

She sighed with exasperation.

"North Memorial Medical Center in Robbinsdale," I said.

"Do you know why?"

"Because it was closest?"

She sighed again.

"C'mon," I said. "We've gone through all of this before."

"And we're going to go through it again. Tell me who you are."

"Rushmore McKenzie."

"How did you get a name like Rushmore?"

"My parents took a trip to the Badlands of South Dakota. They told me I was conceived in a motel near Mount Rushmore, so that's what they named me. I'm sure they thought it was a good idea at the time. Still, it could have been worse. It could have been Deadwood."

The doctor smiled but did not laugh.

"You thought it was funny the first time I told you the story," I said.

"When did you do that?"

"A couple of hours ago—the last time you woke me."

"You remembered."

"You don't think I'm still demonstrating perseveration, do you?"

"What is perseveration?"

"I don't know the clinical definition, but it manifests itself in the repetition of a particular response and is often associated with head trauma. I'll ask, 'Where am I, how did I get here?' and you'll answer. Fifteen seconds later I'll ask again."

"Who told you that?"

"You did, Doctor—when you woke me up the first time."

The doctor smiled some more. "What happened to you?" she asked.

She already knew—I had explained it twice before, so I gave her the abbreviated version.

"I was in a motel room off I-694. I was examining the Jade Lily. I was looking for an imperfection caused by the carving process that resembled an *M*. And then—"

"What happened next, McKenzie?"

"I don't remember."

"What do you remember?"

"I was in the parking lot of the motel next to my car. I was on the ground, the asphalt. My shoulder . . ." I tried to sit up in the bed, and when I did, the broken ends of my collarbone rubbed together and a pain as excruciating as anything I've ever felt rushed like a tsunami from my shoulder to my brain. "Oh—God!" My hand went to my collarbone. Touching it only made the pain worse. "Dammit." I started laughing because it hurt so much. "I remember that. I remember the pain in my shoulder."

"You fractured your clavicle," the doctor said.

"I know," I said. "I know, I know."

"You also sprained your left ankle and sustained numerous cuts, contusions, and abrasions, mostly on your extremities."

"I forgot about those. Thanks for reminding me."

"You were fortunate to be wearing a Kevlar vest."

"Be prepared—I learned that in the Boy Scouts."

"Somehow I find it hard to believe that you were ever a Boy Scout."

"Truth be told, I wasn't. They tossed me out. Said I had a problem with authority."

"What else do you remember?"

"About the Scouts?"

"McKenzie . . ."

"I remember hearing the sirens while I was lying in the parking lot. Then there's a gap. Then I remember the paramedics were putting a collar around my neck and sliding me onto a backboard and loading me into the ambulance. The rest is all bits and pieces—the ride to the hospital, the ER, a CAT scan—how did that go, by the way?"

"It was negative. No bleeding whatsoever."

"That's good."

The doctor shrugged.

"Isn't it?" I asked.

"A head injury and resultant cognitive impact is not readily measured by any blood test or X-ray."

"What does that mean?"

"It means that people with a normal CT can still have significant issues."

"What kind of issues?"

"Severe headaches, nausea, problems with concentration, with balance, blurred vision, ringing in the ears."

"I've had concussions before."

"I know you have. What you need to know is that the more concussions you have, the more susceptible to concussions you become and the more persistent the symptoms you will experience. Being in motel rooms that blow up—not a wise choice for you, McKenzie."

"Ain't that the truth," I said. And moved my shoulder. And felt the pain. "Oh, God. Shouldn't you be giving me morphine or something?"

"The trouble with pain medicines is that they can mask symptoms that we need to be aware of."

"How 'bout aspirin? How 'bout ibuprofen? How 'bout you just hit me over the head with a two-by-four and get it over with?"

"I'll get you some Tylenol for your headache. You do have a headache, don't you?"

"You've read my mind."

"Afterward, I want you to try to get some sleep."

"So you can wake me up in a couple of hours and do this all over again?"

"It's important that you can be roused to normal consciousness."

"You call this normal?"

The doctor set my hand back on the bed and gave it a gentle pat. "I'll see you soon," she said.

Bright sunlight flooded the hospital room. I was sitting up in bed, my back against the headboard. Lieutenant Rask stood at my side. His eyes were tired, his clothes were rumpled, and his face was in need of a shave. I doubted he'd had a moment of sleep since I was blown up—was it only twenty-four hours ago? It seemed so much longer. Mr. Donatucci was standing next to the window staring out at God knew what. He looked the same as he always did. I had spoken to both of them earlier, giving them bits and pieces of information. Now they were back for more.

The doctor was leaning against the door, her hands behind her back, monitoring the interrogation.

"How did you get out of the motel room, McKenzie?" Rask asked.

"I don't remember."

I winced as I turned my head toward him. It's impossible

to put a cast on a broken collarbone. Instead, the doctor put me in a shoulder immobilizer—a wide elastic belt that wrapped around my chest. An elastic cuff went over my upper arm, another went around my forearm, and both cuffs were firmly pinned to the belt so that I was unable to move either. The immobilizer supported the weight of my arm, keeping it from pulling the fracture out of alignment. It also limited shoulder rotation. All this was supposed to allow the bone to heal itself within six to eight weeks. Unfortunately, it didn't do anything for the pain, which I was assured would remain my constant companion for at least three weeks. I was offered Vicodin and Percocet, but both made me nauseous, so I settled for Tylenol and ibuprofen. Neither seemed particularly helpful.

"We found you in the parking lot outside the room," Rask said. "How did you get there?"

"I don't remember."

"You weren't blown out of the room. The blast was too powerful. You would have been shredded like the bed, like the windows, like everything else."

"Was the bomb in the room?" I asked.

"No. It was a shape charge attached to the ceiling of the room beneath you and detonated by remote control."

"The artnappers set it."

"Obviously. What isn't obvious is how you got out alive."

"I don't remember."

"McKenzie, when we found you, when the paramedics were treating you, glass, plaster from the walls, other debris, it was under your body. You collapsed on top of the debris after the bomb went off."

I kept looking Rask in the eye because it seemed important that I do so regardless of the pain it caused me.

"I don't know what to tell you, LT," I said.

"How is that possible?" Rask turned to look at the doctor. "How is this possible?"

"Amnesia for the events at and preceding a head injury with loss of consciousness is very common," she said. "It's possible memory will return, but probably it won't."

"You said there was no demonstrable injury to his brain."

"That means nothing."

Rask spun around to face me. I lifted my right hand and then let it fall back on the bed because I couldn't lift my left.

"Sorry," I said.

"Yeah," Rask said. "So am I."

"Do you have anything yet?"

"We have the credit card number used to reserve the two rooms," Rask said. "It was stolen. We have security footage of the young man who registered. He made the reservations late Thursday afternoon during the blizzard. We're attempting to match his face to the mug shots in our database. No hits so far, and truth be told, we're not likely to get any. I'll get you a photograph later. You said you never saw any of the artnappers, but who knows? We have video of what we believe to be the SUV that the artnappers drove in and out of the parking lot. It matches the SUV we saw in the footage taken at the museum when the Lily was stolen—I have a car guy who claims it's a Toyota RAV4. Unfortunately, we can't read the plates. What else? Forensics is trying to put the bomb back together, find out where the explosive came from, see if we can read the signature of the bomber—we might get something there, but it'll probably take a while. The thieves just made a big score, and they're likely to celebrate. We have people checking strip joints, casinos—the big-buck clubs. All of our undercover guys have been briefed—they have their ears open, and of course, we're leaning on all of our CIs. The money was marked—the thieves have to know that, so they might try to launder it. We're watching everyone we know who is available to do that sort of thing. We've also alerted Homeland Security in case they try to smuggle the cash out of town by plane or train. Nothing so far."

"I wish I could help," I said.

"McKenzie?" Donatucci stepped away from the window and turned to face me across the length of the bed. "In your earlier statements, you said the Lily was in the motel room . . ."

"No. I said—look, it could have been the Lily, it could have been a fake, I don't know. I remember examining it. I was looking for the *M*. That's the last thing I remember before the paramedics arrived."

"Then you did not authenticate the Lily."

"I don't know."

"Fake or not, you said it was made of jade," Donatucci said.

"It felt like jade."

"McKenzie, we've examined the debris left after the explosion. We sifted through it very carefully and we can't find any jade. Not a shard, not even a sliver."

"Huh?"

"Can you explain that?"

"No, I can't," I said.

"You're absolutely sure it was there, the Lily?"

"Yes. Or at least something resembling the Lily."

"The money . . ."

"It was in room 122 last time I saw it."

"We found your dolly and the three gym bags—the shape charge blew upward, so room 122 was more or less intact. The money was gone."

"Big surprise."

Donatucci threw a hard look at Rask. I don't know what passed between the two, but it was clear that neither of them was satisfied with my answers.

"I presume you won't be paying off a claim on the Jade Lily anytime soon," I said.

"No," Donatucci said. "Not until we have more definitive evidence that it's irretrievably lost."

Good, my inner voice said.

"Have you informed the boys and girls at the museum?" I asked.

Donatucci quickly glanced at his watch. "They're having another one of their emergency meetings in about an hour. I'll tell them then."

"Good." This time I said it aloud.

"I'm also going to tell them that the investigation will continue. This isn't over yet, McKenzie."

"Gentlemen," the doctor said from the door, "if there's nothing else, Mr. McKenzie needs his rest."

To emphasize her point, she pushed herself away from the door and then pulled it open.

The doctor had been very good at protecting me while I was in her care, even refusing to acknowledge to the media that I was in the hospital. Fortunately, if I can use that word, several other people were also injured in the explosion, although none of them seriously—most of them had been staying in rooms adjacent to 222. They were more than happy to provide the news media with all the interviews they wanted, so I was left more or less alone. A TV reporter named Kelly Bressandes, who, to the great pleasure of her male audience, always dressed like a hostess in a gentlemen's club, recognized my name among the injured—I had given her a story a couple of years back in exchange for a few favors. She had managed to sneak into my room the night before, startling the hell out of me. I hadn't been put into an immobilizer then, and flinching the way I did caused pain in my shoulder that brought tears to my eyes.

"McKenzie," she said as she approached the bed, her honey-colored hair reflecting the lights of the monitors. I had no idea why she was whispering.

"Monica?" I said.

"It's Kelly. Kelly Bressandes."

"Monica?"

"No, it's Kelly. McKenzie, what happened at the motel?"

I brought a knuckle to my eye yet did not brush away the tears. I turned my head so she could get a good look at the scratches on my cheek and the bruise on my forehead. I was hoping I looked as pathetic as I felt.

"Motel. Boom," I said.

"Yes, there was an explosion. McKenzie, tell me about the Jade Lily."

"Lily?"

"Yes."

"Lily Bressandes?"

"No, I'm—the Lily, McKenzie. The Jade Lily."

That's when the doctor entered the room. She demanded to know who Bressandes was but clearly didn't care, because in her next breath she told her to get out and never come back. As the reporter was leaving, I called to her.

"Good to see you again, Kelly. I'll talk to you soon."

The doctor told me I was pathetic, so I knew the look I was going for had worked. She then interviewed me as she had just hours earlier. I never did get much sleep, so I really was tired when she told Rask and Donatucci it was time to leave.

Lieutenant Rask was tapping my knee through the bed-sheets.

"We'll talk again," he told me.

"Sure," I said.

Both men moved to the door. Donatucci left the room first. I called to Rask.

"LT?" I said. "What happened to my car?"

"I had it towed to the City of Minneapolis impound lot," he said.

"The one near International Market Square?"

"Yes."

"I suppose that's as secure a place as any."

Rask paused for a moment as if he were trying to decipher a coded message and then gave it up.

"I have your Beretta," he said. "Come see me when you get out of here."

"Sure."

After he left, I closed my eyes and settled against my pillows as best I could without moving my shoulder. I hated like hell to lie to them, especially Rask.

"I'll make it up to you guys first chance I get," I said.

"What did you say?"

I opened my eyes. The doctor was standing inside the door.

"When can I leave?" I asked.

"As far as I can tell, you're neurologically intact—"

"That sounds promising."

"You have a normal CT. I am concerned about the confusion and amnesia you demonstrated earlier, however, especially when you were in the ER and speaking to the investigators from the police department and insurance company for the first time."

"I am not confused any longer."

"If you want to make a big deal out of it, I can let you go right now. Otherwise, I'd like to keep you overnight."

"Are you going to wake me up every two hours?"

"I'll wake you once. How's that?"

I thought about it for a few beats. On one hand, I needed to move and move fast if I was going to get the money back. On the other hand, my broken collarbone meant I would need help, and I wasn't sure who to ask. On the other hand, all hell was going to break loose as soon as Mr. Donatucci met with the museum's executive board. On the other hand, I wanted all hell to break loose. I was counting on it. On the other hand, I wasn't prepared for it yet—all hell breaking loose, I mean. On the other hand, this wasn't rocket surgery. I mean brain science. I mean—Jeezus! How many hands have you got? Focus.

Confusion and an inability to concentrate are symptoms of a concussion, my inner voice said. *That and the ringing in your ears.*

"That could be simple tinnitus," I said aloud.

"What?" the doctor asked.

"Tinnitus—ringing in the ears. Everybody experiences ringing in the ears at one time or another, right? It doesn't need to be a symptom of a concussion, right?"

"You tell me."

"Hey, you're the doctor. I'm the one with the degree in umm, in umm . . . What did I go to college for? Criminology. I have a degree in—Doc, is irritability also symptomatic of a concussion? I bet it is."

"McKenzie . . ."

"You know, it probably wouldn't kill me to spend another night in this fine establishment. The food sucks, but I could always send out for pizza. I know this great Vietnamese place that delivers, too. Yeah, I'll stay. I'm going to need my cell phone, though."

I was sitting up, a plastic plate on top of the hospital's roll-away overbed table and both positioned so that they were tight against my stomach. I had attempted to eat beef lo mein with chopsticks and failed miserably, so I switched to a fork. That didn't work out any better. Most people lean over their plates when they eat, only leaning forward was suddenly a painful practice for me. So I tried to eat while keeping my back straight, tilting my head down, and bringing the fork to my mouth instead of meeting it halfway. I kept spilling food all over the napkin I had tucked into the neckline of the hospital gown they had insisted I wear.

"Need any help?" Nina asked.

"No."

Nina shrugged and continued to consume her kung pao chicken. She was sitting at a table near the window, her feet resting on a chair opposite her, eating directly from the white takeout carton. She didn't have any problem at all working her chopsticks. Every once in a while she'd fish a cheese puff or a bite of egg roll from one of the other cartons arranged on the table.

"This sucks," I said.

"You did say you wanted to lose a few pounds," Nina said. "Here's your chance."

"I said I needed to work out more. I didn't say anything about losing weight."

Nina smiled.

"Do you think I need to lose some weight?' I asked.

She smiled some more.

"This sucks," I said.

"You're the one who insists on visiting the dark side all the time."

I didn't like the tone of her voice, so I asked, "Are you mad at me?"

"No more than usual," she said. "I'm tired of visiting you in hospitals, though."

"When did you visit me in a hospital?"

"There was the time after we first met . . ."

"Oh, yeah, but that doesn't count. We weren't even dating then."

"It counts. And then . . ."

"Yeah?"

"And then there was that time in South Dakota."

"You didn't visit me in the hospital in South Dakota."

"I would have if I had known you were in the hospital in South Dakota. The point is, I'm tired of it. Don't make me do this anymore."

"I promise."

"Okay."

"Are we going to have another one of those conversations?"

"No, I'm tired of that, too. You are who you are and I'm who I am. How the hell we ended up together, God only knows."

"Actually, it was God's doing. Didn't you know that?"

"What do you mean?"

"God said to me, 'McKenzie . . .'"

"He talks to you personally?"

"All the time. He said, 'McKenzie, you get Nina.'"

"Did he tell you why?"

"Because he likes me."

"Obviously."

I tried to eat more beef lo mein, but it fell off the fork as I was about to scoop it into my mouth.

"Are you sure you don't need any help with that?" Nina asked.

"No, but you can come over if you like."

Nina set down her meal and made her way to the bed. She sat on the edge of it and leaned in. Her kiss was as soft as a butterfly's wings.

"Exactly how long did they say you have to wait before you can start working out again?" she asked.

"God knows."

Nina kissed me without putting any pressure on my shoulder at all. I felt her warmth all down my right arm and chest and spreading through the rest of my body. I wanted to shove the tray away and see how far we could take this before I started screaming out in pain, but I didn't get a chance. There was a heavy knock on the door, and a moment later Jeremy Gillard sauntered into the hospital room, stopped, looked at me, looked at Nina, looked back at me, and said, "Boy, do I know when to enter a room."

Nina eased herself off the bed and returned to the table.

"It's okay," I said.

"I am so sorry. I didn't mean to interrupt."

"Don't worry about it."

"I can leave and come back in an hour."

"Jeremy," I said. "What's going on?"

"I was just at the museum." He threw a thumb at the door as if the museum were just on the other side of it. He smiled at Nina. "Ms. Truhler," he said. "It is a pleasure to see you again." He crossed the room and shook Nina's hand, holding it much longer than I was comfortable with. "You're looking as lovely as ever."

Nina thanked him and offered an egg roll.

"Oh, I couldn't," Gillard said.

"Please, help yourself," Nina said.

Gillard said, "Well, if you insist," scooped an egg roll from the carton, and took a bite. "Oh my God, this is amazing," he quickly added. "Where did you get these?"

"There's a Vietnamese restaurant in Northeast Minneapolis called Que Viet Village House."

"These are great. You know, there's this joint in Chinatown in Chicago that I go to that makes egg rolls, but these . . ."

"Hey, guys," I said.

"The difference is the filler," Nina said. "The Chinese use cabbage, and the Vietnamese use noodles. Plus, the Vietnamese wrappers are thinner and crispier."

"Guys?"

They both turned toward me.

"I presume you're here for a reason, Jer," I said.

"Oh, yeah," Gillard said. "I was just at a meeting at the museum. The insurance guy, Donatucci, he told us that you got blown up trying to retrieve the Jade Lily. I just wanted to drop around and see how you were. Donatucci said you were okay, but honestly, McKenzie, you don't look okay. Are you okay?"

"I have a concussion, a broken collarbone, sprained left ankle, my forehead looks and feels like someone hit me with a baseball bat, and I have cuts and bruises all over the place, so to answer your question—yeah, I'm okay."

"Just rub some dirt on it, right? That's what my old football coach would have said."

"I played baseball, and my coach would have said to walk it off. 'Don't baby yourself. Walk it off.' "

"I'm really sorry about this, McKenzie."

"It's not your fault."

"Yes, it is," Nina said.

We both looked at her.

"Not all your fault, but you get your share of blame," she said.

"I'm sorry," Gillard said.

"Have some more egg roll."

He did.

"How did the boys and girls take the news?" I asked. "The boys and girls at the museum."

"Everyone's pretty upset," Gillard said. "What's her name, Perrin Stewart? I thought she was going to break down and cry. That Anderson guy, the one with the big mouth? He went a little crazy; wanted to fire everybody. Said they should get rid of Stewart; said he knew just the woman who should take her place. Stewart claimed that Anderson had wanted to get rid of her ever since he started sleeping with some blond bimbo who knew nothing about art but plenty about, well"—he smiled at Nina—"since there's a lady present I won't complete the quote. But by the reaction around the room, I'm guessing not everyone knew about Anderson's extracurriculars. Accusations really began to fly. It was all very entertaining. I wouldn't be surprised if Bravo made a reality TV series out of it."

"Did you get a name?"

"A name? Oh, for the woman. No, she was always referred to as 'the bimbo.' Why?"

"What about Randolph Fiegen? How did he take all this?"

"The man who's really in charge?"

"You noticed that, too, did you?"

"Yeah, I noticed. Fiegen was very quiet. Didn't say much of anything. You could see the wheels spinning in his head, though. While everyone else was carrying on, I think he was wondering about the same thing I was wondering about—how come there was no sign of the Lily in the debris?"

"Good question," I said.

"You don't know anything about it?"

"Not that I recall."

"That's what Donatucci said. The concussion, because of that you don't remember what happened."

"I don't know what to tell you, Jer."

"Well . . ." Gillard picked up another egg roll, prepared to take a bite, and then put it back in the carton. "Well. The insurance company is going to drag its feet just like you said. I suppose if we knew for sure that the Jade Lily had been destroyed in the explosion . . ."

"Sorry," I said.

"Nothing, huh?"

"Sorry."

"If you were to remember, it would be worth a lot of money." Gillard waved at me then. "If you remember. No worries. That damn Lily—you know what? I think it really is cursed."

"I think you're right."

Gillard might have said more, might have become even more blatant in his bribery attempt, except he was interrupted by another knock on the door, this one much softer. Unlike Gillard, my visitor waited until I called, "Come in," before opening the door.

Heavenly Petryk stepped into the room.

"Speaking of curses," Nina said.

Heavenly paused, glanced from face to face, smiled that incandescent smile of hers, and said, "Hello everyone."

"Look who's here," Gillard said.

He moved toward Heavenly as if he wanted to give her a hug. She rotated her shoulder to block him, patted his arm, and said, "Jeremy, good to see you," as she made her way to my bedside. "McKenzie, are you all right?"

"People keep asking that. I'm in a hospital, for God's sake. Of course I'm not all right."

She nodded as if she expected that answer all along.

"I'm sorry you were hurt," Heavenly said.

"It wasn't your fault."

"We don't know that for sure, do we?" Nina said.

There was a shocked expression on Heavenly's face, but it didn't last. She watched Nina return to the chair next to the table, pick up her carton of kung pao chicken, prop her feet up on the chair opposite hers, and start eating.

"The reason I came is because it's important that you know I had nothing to do with what happened," Heavenly said. She was looking at Nina when she spoke. Nina waved her chopsticks at her.

"It's true," Heavenly said. This time she was talking directly to me.

"Why would you want to blow up McKenzie?" Gillard asked.

"Exactly," Heavenly said.

"I never thought you were involved," I said. "But I am glad you're here."

That caused Nina to raise an eyebrow, although she didn't speak. Heavenly took my hand and gave it a squeeze like we were the best of friends. Nina said nothing about that, either.

"Have you heard what happened to the Lily?" I asked.

"I heard," Heavenly said.

"Looks like nobody gets it now."

"So it would seem."

"Poor Tatjana."

"Yes, poor Tatjana, poor Jeremy, poor Branko Pozderac, poor City of Lakes Art Museum, poor Midwest Farmers Insurance Group, poor who else?"

"Don't say poor me," Gillard said. "I'll get the insurance—eventually, anyway."

"A lot of people are unhappy that the Lily has gone poof," Heavenly said.

"You're going to lose your finder's fee," I said.

"Yes. I'm sure you're all broken up about that."

"You wound me, Heavenly, to think I'd wish you ill. Especially after all the trouble you went through. And poor Tommy, too."

Heavenly released my hand, moved around the bed, and settled near the table. Nina did not remove her feet from the chair so she could sit, nor did she offer up any egg rolls.

"The thing is, though—I'm curious," Heavenly said. "I guess everyone is curious. Why couldn't they find any sign of the Jade Lily when they examined the wreckage after the bomb blast?"

"You know, Heavenly, Jerry, I'm getting awfully tired. Plus my head hurts and . . . It was nice of you to come around. I appreciate it."

Gillard got the hint right away.

"I'm glad you're more or less intact, McKenzie," he said. He gave my leg a gentle tap through the blanket. "You take care of yourself. We'll talk again soon. Don't forget, we're going to paint the town when you're up to it."

"Sounds like fun," I said.

Gillard went to the door and paused, waiting for Heavenly. Heavenly took her time, though, rubbing her beautiful face with both hands before moving back to the bed. Her eyes were hard and glistening, and for the first time I understood why some people use the color blue to describe ice. She leaned in like she was going to kiss my cheek. Instead, she whispered in my ear. "I know you have it." Then, because Nina was watching intently, Heavenly kissed me on the mouth. Afterward, she went through the door that Gillard held open without saying another word.

Nina finished swallowing a mouthful of kung pao chicken before she spoke.

"Glad she was here, were you?" she said.

"It answers a question that has been nagging at me for a couple of days."

"What question?"

Instead of answering, I went back to work on my beef lo mein. It wasn't that I wanted to keep things from her; it was just that I thought it was best to wait until I was out of the hospital before I told Nina the truth. She wasn't pleased, of course, but after four years, three months, and seventeen days, she was starting to get used to me.

"You know before when you said that I liked Heavenly?" Nina said. "It's not true."

THIRTEEN

Looking back, they were perhaps the five hardest words I had ever spoken. There she was, looking as beautiful as ever, standing in my empty living room, one of those rolling suitcases that you see people pulling across airport concourses next to her. She had obviously come to stay, and in case I didn't get the hint, she explained it to me.

"I have to go in every once in a while to check on things—we can have dinner at the club anytime you want," she said. "Jenness and Monica, I spoke to them, and they're more than happy to run things while I take time off so, hey, I can stay with you until you heal."

My first thought was that I could probably arrange it so that I never recovered, keeping her with me more or less forever. Instead of saying that, I looked deep into her silver-blue eyes, brushed her soft cheek with my fingertips, and said, "Nina, you should go home."

"What?"

"You should go home, now."

Nina had picked me up at the hospital and had taken me home in my Jeep Cherokee. That hadn't been the plan. I was going to drive. Unfortunately, opening the driver's door and then pulling it closed, putting the key in the ignition, firing up the SUV, and attempting to back out of the hospital parking lot had been more than enough to tell me this just wasn't going to work out. For the first time in my life I knew how it must feel to get old, my body refusing to behave according to my instructions. Driving the Audi would have been even worse—the S5 had a six-speed manual transmission.

"Who's going to take care of you?" Nina asked.

It was a good question. Getting out of bed that morning—I had slept sitting up—was the start of a long, painful ordeal that turned the simple act of brushing my teeth, shaving, and showering into an exercise in self-torture. By the time I had on underwear, socks, jeans, and shirt, my body was wet with perspiration and shaking. It took ten painful minutes to work myself into the immobilizer—tying my shoes had damn near killed me. I had attempted to put the Kevlar vest on; however, its weight pulled so heavily on my fracture that I almost passed out. It hurt even as I stood there in front of Nina. My right arm was inside the sleeve of my jacket, the back of the jacket draped over my shoulders, my left arm immobilized against my side. I kept pulling in the left side of the jacket to keep it from falling open.

"I talked to Chopper," I said. "It's all been arranged."

"Chopper?" Nina took a step backward and then spoke the name again as if she wanted to make sure she got it right. "Chopper?"

"Yeah."

"Something's going to happen."

"Yeah."

"What? Don't tell me. You're going after them, aren't you—the men who put the bomb in the motel room?"

"The doctor said I should get mild exercise followed by rest."

"Dammit, McKenzie. You have a broken collarbone, you have a concussion—I saw the way you rubbed your temples when we were driving home. You were feeling dizzy, weren't you? Because of the concussion. McKenzie, c'mon. You're in no condition—what if they try to kill you again?"

"That's the thing, Nina. They didn't try to kill me. They called me on the phone. They warned me to get out of the room before the bomb went off."

"You said—I thought you couldn't remember."

"Nina my love, my beating heart—you of all people should know what a terrible liar I am."

Nina stared at me for a few beats and then looked around the room. It would have been more dramatic if there had been a chair or sofa to take possession of, but since there wasn't, Nina sat on top of her suitcase, folded her arms across her chest, and announced, "I'm not going anywhere until you tell me what's going on."

So I did . . .

Ten seconds is a long time. You can win a gold medal in the Olympics in ten seconds. You can go from first to third on a bloop single in ten seconds. You can tie both shoes in ten seconds. If you don't believe me, set a timer and close your eyes while it counts down. Ten seconds can seem like an eternity.

"There is a bomb in the room. It will go off in ten seconds. Good luck."

The moment the caller finished speaking, I heard a soft

mmm that reminded me of the sound a TV makes when you first switch it on with a remote control. Knowing what I know now, it couldn't have been the bomb. The bomb was stuck to the ceiling directly below me. Yet I heard the sound just the same. Perhaps it was an internal clock counting down the seconds I had to live.

The phone was sitting on a nightstand on the far side of the bed, which meant the bed was between the door and me. I did not hang up the phone. Instead, I simply dropped the receiver and dove across the bed, dragging the two pillows that had been propped against the headboard with me. It's funny how the mind works. I remembered instantly what India Cooper had told me about jade—that it was one tough sonuvabitch—so I wasn't gentle at all when I slid the heavy artifact off the table and dropped it on top of one of the pillows. I covered it with the second pillow—a jade sandwich— lifted it off the bed, and pressed it against my left side with one arm. I unlocked the door and pulled it open with my free hand, crossed the landing, grabbed the top of the railing, and leaped over it.

The landing was ten feet above the parking lot surface, which doesn't seem like much unless you try to jump it. Still, I probably would have been fine except that while I was in midair, the bomb went off—in hindsight, I think the artnappers actually gave me an extra second or two. In any case, the force of the blast pushed me sideways, not to mention the glass and other debris that raked my face and torso. Instead of landing on both feet, I hit the ground with the outside of my left foot. My ankle rolled under me. I probably still would have been fine; however, my instincts told me to protect the Lily, so I wrapped my right arm around the pillows as well as my left and twisted my body so that I smacked against the asphalt, shoulder first. I knew my collarbone was broken, knew it even before I felt the pain. I had fractured it once before while playing basketball. It's a feeling you don't forget. I didn't actually feel the pain until I rolled to my knees, still clutching the jade sandwich to my body. Stuff was raining against my back—I have no idea what stuff. I only knew that it was hot and sharp and it hurt despite the Kevlar. I pushed myself up with my right hand. That's how I sliced open my palm. (I held it up for Nina to see.) I must have cut it on broken glass.

I walked to the car; my body hunched over like Igor in the old Frankenstein movies. My Audi was parked in front of the room directly beneath the room that had exploded. I had managed to leap clear of it, although bomb fragments and whatnot had showered it like hail. There were plenty of dents and dings, and I was pretty sure my rear window had been cracked. I dug my key chain out of my jacket pocket and used the remote to pop the trunk. I stuffed the Lily and the pillows and my keys inside and slammed the lid shut.

You need to understand something—I did not think any of this through, did not justify my actions for a moment. I just did it. The thinking part, that came later in the ER.

Afterward, I limped across the parking lot. I have no idea what I was doing. Maybe I just wanted to get a look at what was left of room 222. The romantic in me believed I wanted to see if there was anyone who needed help. In the distance I could hear sirens—cops and ambulances. I stepped on something with my left foot. My sprained ankle gave out and I started to fall. This time I twisted my body to protect my damaged shoulder. I hit my head. (I touched the bruise on my forehead.) That's how I was knocked unconscious; that's how I got the concussion. The next thing I remember, the paramedics were putting a collar around my neck and sliding me onto a backboard before loading me into an ambulance. I remember everything from that moment on quite vividly.

"I don't understand," Nina said. "You're saying—the Lily was not destroyed in the explosion? Is that what you're saying?"

"Yes."

"You have it?"

"Yes."

"Where?"

"It should still be locked in the trunk of my car. By the way, I need your copy of my house key. My keys are in the trunk."

"Where's your car?"

"Rask told me it was towed to the City of Minneapolis impound lot. Believe me, I had a car towed there a few years ago during a snow emergency—the place is like fricking Fort Knox."

"But, but . . ."

"But what?"

"They wanted you to—they asked you to retrieve the Jade Lily. They asked you to trade the insurance money for it, and you did that. I mean, I know the motel room blowing up wasn't part of the deal, but you did what they asked, you have the Lily. Why not give it to the insurance company like you promised and forget the whole thing? The job is over, isn't it?"

"People have been killed for the Jade Lily. I can't let that go."

"Why not?"

"Because I killed one of them."

"Heavenly's friend Tommy?"

"Yes."

"That's on her."

"It's on me, too."

"What are you going to do? Are you going to hide the Lily from the insurance company, from the police?"

"For now."

"Why?"

"There are a few things I need to sort out."

"Such as?"

"Such as who the Lily actually belongs to."

She paused for a few moments and said, "You could get into big trouble over this."

I started to laugh. "Yes," I said and laughed some more. "Yes, I could." I have no idea why I laughed. Mark it down to nervous energy.

"You think this is funny?" Nina asked.

I shook my head yet continued to laugh.

"Dammit, but you make me so mad sometimes," Nina said.

"I'm sorry, I'm sorry. You're right, it isn't funny. You have to admit, though—it's the damnedest thing."

"You can be so terribly immature sometimes, do you know that?"

"Yeah, I guess."

"You also have a secret passion for justice."

"How immature is that?"

"Justice in this case would be for . . . who?"

"I'm still working that out."

"What can I do to help?" she asked, the implication being that I needed all the help I could get.

"I don't want you to get into trouble," I said. "Who would bail me out if I get arrested?"

Nina came off her suitcase and crossed the few steps between us. She grabbed both ends of my leather jacket and pulled it close.

"What are you going to do?" she asked.

"I'm going back to the beginning."

"The beginning?"

"The artnappers requested that I act as go-between without knowing who I was. Someone gave them my name. When I find out who that person was, I'll find out who they are."

"As easy as that, huh?"

"Well, the premise is simple. We'll find out how easy it is."

"Do you know what really frightens me?" Nina said. "The idea that the Jade Lily really is cursed; that something terrible happens to everyone who holds it, because right now you're the one who's holding it."

"The history of the Lily—all that proves is that bad things happen to greedy people."

"That's my point, McKenzie. You're the greediest person I know. You might not want fame or fortune, but you do love the game."

Not long after Nina departed, Herzog arrived. I was glad she didn't see him. He might have frightened her. The way he filled my doorway, dressed in black boots, black jeans, black turtleneck, and black leather jacket, his hands crossed just above his silver belt buckle, and said, "I'm not happy t' be 'ere," Herzog scared the hell out of me, and I was carrying a gun.

As soon as I let him into the house, he made a grasping motion with the fingers of his right hand. I gave him an envelope. The envelope contained $5,000. I took the money from a safe in my basement floor—I had learned long ago to keep a sizable sum of "mad money" on hand for just such an occurrence as this. Fishing the cash out of the safe had been painful, what with all the bending and leaning I had to do. Almost as painful as dropping the envelope in Herzog's hand.

"Half now, half later," I said.

"What if you get killed?"

"I guess you'll just have to sue my estate."

Herzog nodded as if it seemed perfectly reasonable to him. He turned the envelope over in his hand yet did not open it, did not count the money. It wasn't a matter of trust. Only an idiot would short-change the man.

"I ain't doin' nothin' gonna get me sent back t' Stillwater."

"I don't blame you."

"I mean it, McKenzie."

"All I need you to do is drive and maybe run an errand or two. And, oh yeah, keep me from getting shot."

Herzog slipped the envelope into an inside pocket.

"I'm only doin' this cuz Chopper said," he told me.

"I know."

I had called Chopper from the hospital. He asked many questions about my condition that suggested a working knowledge of both emergency medicine and clinical procedures— the man never ceased to amaze. At the same time, he was very apologetic about not wanting to come and visit.

"You know me and hospitals," he said.

I knew. If you had been rolled perfectly healthy into a hospital—well, except for two bullets in your back—and then came out in a wheelchair, you might want to avoid them, too.

I asked Chopper for a couple of favors. The first was to arrange another meeting with El Cid. The second was Herzog.

"I don' like helpin' no cops," the big man informed me yet again.

"I appreciate that. Are you heavy?"

He sniffed like it was the dumbest question he had ever heard. Or maybe it was the way I asked it.

"Are you?" he repeated.

I pulled a Walther PPK out of my jacket pocket and held it up. The butt was firm against the bandage covering the cut in my hand, and it hurt. 'Course, so did my head, my ankle, my shoulder, and my back where the debris from the explosion had rained down on it.

"What th' hell is 'at?" he asked. "A fuckin' toy?"

"Hey, man, it's the same gun that James Bond carries."

"Fuckin' A."

I didn't blame him for being skeptical. I was no more impressed by the Walther's stopping power than Herzog. I chose it because of its size—the automatic fit comfortably inside my jacket pocket—and because of its weight. Twenty-two ounces was easier to wave around with one hand and, God help me, if I had to shoot, it would be with one hand. Hell, the only reason I even bought the .32 was that, well, it *was* the gun James Bond used in the movies. Still, I felt the need to defend myself.

"One-handed, I doubt I could shoot a heavy-caliber gun accurately," I said.

"Fuck," Herzog said, holding the word like the last note of a power ballad. At least he didn't call me a pussy.

"You drive," I said.

I handed him the keys to my Jeep Cherokee. I had switched vehicles with Nina again. She had driven off in her Lexus after giving me her keys to my car and house.

"Where we goin'?" Herzog asked.

"Minneapolis Police Department."

"Say what?"

"Don't worry, Herzy. You can wait in the car."

Lieutenant Rask was waiting for me when I limped into his office in room 108 of Minneapolis City Hall. He was so happy to see me that he left me standing there on my sprained ankle, completely ignoring my presence while he read a file on his desk. When he finished, he leaned back in his chair, propped his feet on the desk, locked the fingers of his hands behind his head, and announced, "I'm this close to throwing your ass in jail."

"What charge?"

"Conspiring to receive stolen property."

"If you arrest me, you'll need to arrest everyone else, including Branko Pozderac and Jonathan Hemsted."

"Don't think I haven't thought about it."

"Tell me why you're really angry, Clay," I said.

"I told you not to call me that."

"Sorry."

"I'm angry because you didn't contact me when the art-nappers set up the exchange like you promised."

"I didn't have time."

"Bullshit. Bullshit, McKenzie. There was plenty of time. You could have made time. Instead, the bastards blow up a fucking motel and we have nothing. Nothing, McKenzie."

"I wouldn't go so far as to say that."

"Oh, you wouldn't?" Rask stared at me for a few beats. "Why wouldn't you say that?"

"May I sit down?"

Rask's eyes went from the empty chair in front of his desk to me, then back to the chair. He waved his hand as if he didn't care if I stood, sat, or went to Wisconsin. I sat, trying hard to keep my back straight. I was actually happier to take the weight off my throbbing ankle than my aching shoulder, but Rask didn't care about that.

"How's your collarbone?" he asked.

"It's broken, LT."

"You're lucky you're not dead."

"I don't feel lucky."

"Talk to me, McKenzie."

"Have you ever heard the phrase 'plausible deniability'?"

"Are you trying to be funny?"

"People keep asking that. No, I'm not trying to be funny. I'm just trying to avoid going to jail while I make your case."

"Oh? You're going to make my case, are you? Which case? Tell me. I have so many."

"Who killed Scott Noehring, that case. Who killed Patrick Tarpley, that case, too."

Rask shook his head slowly and muttered, "Uh-uh, uh-uh, no way. You don't keep things from me."

"I told you last week when you dragged me into this that I was high maintenance."

"You think I'm fucking Bobby Dunston? I'm not going to play this game with you, McKenzie."

"I'm sorry. Aren't you the one who told me to get the Lily back—which I believe is conspiring to receive stolen property? Aren't you the one who told me to get intel on the artnappers in order to help you in the Noehring investigation?"

"Oh, you're helping me, is that what you're doing? You're withholding information because you're helping me."

"Give me a couple of days and then I'll tell you everything."

The way he shook his head, I knew Rask wasn't buying it, so I played my ace.

"Give me a couple of days, LT, and I'll throw in a sweetener."

"What sweetener?"

"Pozderac and Hemsted on a silver platter."

I could see that Rask liked the idea. He rolled the thought over his tongue like a piece of Amedei chocolate but wouldn't swallow it.

"Pozderac has diplomatic immunity," he said.

"Maybe not. Neither Pozderac nor Hemsted, for that matter, is here representing his country. They're both just a couple of punks looking for a payoff."

"I can't touch them."

"You might not be able to, but the FBI . . . That's a different matter."

"Have you spoken to the FBI?"

"Yes, I have."

"What is their position?"

"They would love to arrange a perp walk with these two clowns."

Yeah, I know; I was laying it on pretty thick, but Rask seemed to like it.

"I wouldn't mind seeing that myself," he said. "All right, what do you need from me?"

"You said you had a photo of the man who registered at the motel."

Rask glanced around his cluttered desk, found a large white envelope, and removed a color photograph that looked like it had had been printed on white office stock with a laser printer. I gave the photo a long, hard look. It was a man in his midtwenties; dark-skinned, maybe Hispanic, maybe not, although I was sure the boys in Arizona would pick him up just to be sure. There was something familiar about him, only I couldn't place it.

"Know him?" Rask asked.

"Never saw him before in my life."

He thrust his face at me. There was a hard warning in his eyes. "Are you sure about that?"

I couldn't imagine what I had done to make him so suspicious of me.

"I'm sure," I said.

"If you say so."

I held up the photo. "Can I keep this?" I asked.

"Frame it if you want."

While I carefully folded it and slipped it into my inside jacket pocket, I said, "Last time we spoke you were waiting on a ballistics report."

"Yeah, the gun—the bullets that killed Patrick Tarpley and Lieutenant Noehring were fired from the same piece," he said. "A .25."

"Then it wasn't a professional shooter."

"No. A pro would never have kept the gun. Anyone who watches *CSI* would know not to keep the gun."

"If the shooter didn't dump the weapon after the first killing, odds are he didn't dump it after the second."

"From your lips to God's ear," Rask said. "The question is, where do we look for it?"

It was a long walk down the marble corridor from room 108 to the Fifth Street entrance of the Minneapolis City Hall, and I was feeling light-headed and a little dizzy by the time I reached it, not unlike the way you do when you get up too fast after lying on a couch for a while. Except the feeling didn't go away after a few moments. It stayed with me while I pushed open the door and descended the steps to the street. The tracks for the Hiawatha light rail line ran along Fifth, but I didn't notice them. I walked across the tracks and into Fifth Street, and then two strong arms yanked me forward, pulling me out of the street and pushing me up against an SUV. I felt the jagged ends of my fractured collarbone rubbing together. My blurred vision became a flashing red light.

"What the fuck, McKenzie?" a voice shouted at me.

"Huh?"

"McKenzie?"

My head cleared and the world came into sharp focus.

"McKenzie," Herzog said again and gave me a shake.

"Don't do that," I said. "Shaking a guy with a concussion is not a good thing."

Not to mention a fractured clavicle, my inner voice said.

"Fuckin' A, man. You almos' got hit by a fuckin' train."

It was cold. Herzog's words condensed into clouds that rose up in the air between us. I tilted my head so I could follow the clouds.

"I did?" I said.

"Didn' you see it?"

My body began to tremble. I leaned forward, despite the excruciating pain in my shoulder, and rested my right hand against my thigh. My disorientation had been replaced by a feeling of nausea. Herzog stepped back as if he were afraid of getting splattered by vomit. I didn't throw up, though. Instead, I slowly straightened up and leaned against the SUV. It was mine, by the way, the Jeep Cherokee.

"McKenzie, you look white as a ghost," Herzog said.

"They'd love me over at Rickie's, then," I said. "Goddammit, my shoulder hurts."

"We should git you home, git you to a hospital or somethin'."

"Just give me a second."

I straightened my back as best I could while still leaning against the Cherokee and took long, deep breaths, exhaling slowly.

"McKenzie," a voice called.

It wasn't Herzog's.

My eyes snapped open. Kelly Bressandes was fast approaching. I closed my eyes again.

"Crap," I said. "See if there are cameras, see if she has sound equipment."

"McKenzie, it is you," Bressandes said as soon as she was near. "My God, you look terrible."

I opened my eyes and smiled. The smile took a lot of effort.

"You, on the other hand, look gorgeous," I said. She was wearing a black trench coat that was cinched tightly at the waist so the world would know she had curves even if the world couldn't see them under the coat. Her legs were bare—"the best legs on television," a cop once told me. "What brings you here on such a cold day?"

"The cops are part of my beat," she said. "McKenzie, we spoke in the hospital, remember? What happened to you? I know you were in the explosion at the motel. I was told that you went there to retrieve a stolen art object called the Jade Lily."

"Who told you that?" I asked.

Herzog leaned and whispered in my ear. "We good," he said.

The reporter's eyes went from me to Herzog and back again. "I can't reveal my sources," she said. "You know that."

"You the one that's on TV," Herzog said. "You look better in person."

Bressandes smiled brightly. "Well, thank you, sir," she said.

"I saw that thing you did on them dogs 'at were abused," Herzog said. " 'At was terrible. Not you, not you. I mean about the dogs. Wha' happened about that?"

"The owner is going to jail. Sentencing should be tomorrow."

"Jail is where he belong."

Throughout the exchange, I continued to breathe slowly and deeply. I don't know if my color returned. I was starting to feel better, though.

"McKenzie," Bressandes said, "tell me about the Jade Lily."

"Tell me who your source is."

"I can't."

"That's okay, I'm pretty sure I already know."

"McKenzie, I want to interview you on camera."

"No."

"Off the record, then."

"No."

"I'm going to do the story anyway."

"And say what?"

"That the Jade Lily was stolen from the City of Lakes Art Museum a week ago Sunday night by Patrick Tarpley, who was murdered by his partners. That the thieves demanded a ransom of one-third of the object's value. That you were hired to retrieve it. That you went to the motel Saturday to make the exchange. That a bomb was set in the room where the Lily was kept." Bressandes moved close enough that I could smell her perfume, and she lowered her voice a couple of octaves—she just loved a conspiracy. "I'm going to report that the Lily was removed from the motel room before the bomb went off."

"You seem well informed."

"Is that a confirmation?"

"No."

Her smile suggested that she didn't believe me.

"Tell you what," I said. "Give me a couple of days and I will not only confirm your story, I'll not only give you all the details that you seem to be lacking, I'll identify all the villains—and, Kelly, there are lots of villains, some of them in very high places."

She thought about it, the smile never leaving her face.

"You promise to go on camera?" she asked.

"Broken bones and all."

"Deal."

To seal it, Bressandes shook my hand and then kissed my cheek.

"I love doing business with you," she said.

She skipped down the street, crossed at the light, and entered City Hall. Herzog and I watched her go.

"Are you really goin' on TV?" he asked.

"Hell no."

I brought my hand to my forehead and then my cheek—I probably looked like I was checking my own temperature. The dizziness was gone, and so was the nausea, but now I had a headache.

"We gonna take you back home, what?" Herzog said.

"We're going to ah . . ." I let the words form in my head before I spoke them. "There's a marina on Lake Minnetonka. A yacht club. We're going to meet someone."

"On a boat? You know it's winter, right? That the lakes are frozen?"

"Herzy, let's assume from this moment forward that I am sound of mind."

" 'At's askin' a lot."

FOURTEEN

From City Hall we worked our way to I-94 and then to I-394 heading west toward Lake Minnetonka. There was nothing pretty about the drive. Thick gray clouds blocked the sun, which made the air, the three-day-old snow, and just about everything else, for that matter, look gray, too. I tried to sit straight up in my seat. That was uncomfortable enough, but the bouncing caused by cracked pavement and potholes made it worse. Minnesota Public Radio reported that between them, Minneapolis, St. Paul, Hennepin, and Ramsey counties, and the Minnesota Department of Transportation had as many as twenty-two crews working more or less around the clock to patch the holes and cracks caused by the never-ending freeze/thaw cycle of winter. Yet you couldn't prove it by me that they had made any progress at all, and the winter wasn't half over!

"Pitchers and catchers don't even report for another month," I mumbled.

"Tell me about it," Herzog said.

Herzy's a baseball fan, my inner voice said. *Who would have thunk it?*

As we approached Highway 169 my cell phone rang.

"Is 'at Ella?" Herzog asked. "Fuckin' A, it is Ella."

I answered the phone without checking the caller ID, without thinking at all. It was a mistake.

"This is Jonathan Hemsted of the U.S. State Department," the caller said. "We need to talk."

You really don't want to talk to him, my inner voice said.

"I'm in the middle of something right now, Jon," I said aloud.

"We need to talk immediately."

Ahh, Christ.

"Where are you?"

"The hotel."

"I'll be there in a few minutes."

I turned off my phone.

"Herzy," I said, "there's been a change of plans. We need to see a guy. Turn around at the next exit."

"Is 'at Ella Fitzgerald on your ringtone?"

"Yeah. Her and Louis Armstrong."

"You're not as big a pussy as I thought you were."

"Heady praise, Herzy. Heady praise, indeed."

We met in the same bar located just off the hotel lobby with a good view of the comings and goings of just about everyone. Pozderac was drinking clear liquid from a squat glass—somehow I didn't think it was water. Hemsted was drinking wine. I decided to shake things up a bit. When the waitress arrived, instead of beer, I ordered a Seven and Seven. Pozderac and Hemsted requested a second round of the same.

"What about your friend?" Hemsted asked. Herzog stood

like a sentinel off to the side, his hands crossed over his stomach, a menacing expression on his face. He was pretending not to watch or listen to us at the table, but I knew he was doing both.

"He's driving," I said.

After the waitress departed, Hemsted made some cursory remarks about my damaged shoulder and my bruised and scratched face, although none of them sounded particularly sympathetic. I found it telling that he did not ask how I sustained my injuries. It wasn't until the waitress returned with our drinks that he got down to it.

"I am very upset that you called the embassy," he said.

"Upset that I called or upset that I discovered that you are not here on embassy business?"

"This is very much embassy business."

"Yeah, you're just looking out for the welfare of the good ol' U.S. of A. A quarter-of-a-million-dollar bribe doesn't enter into it."

Hemsted glanced at Pozderac and then back at me. "That's a damnable lie," he said.

Where have you heard that before? my inner voice asked.

"Tell it to Fiegen," I said.

"Fiegen?"

"The man you're working for. I used to think it was the secretary of state. That's why I let you frighten me before. Now I know better."

"Mr. Fiegen is an American citizen wishing to conduct business in Bosnia and Herzegovina," Hemsted said. "I am merely helping to facilitate matters as per my position with the Commercial Service Office of the U.S. Embassy."

"And if you can get a little something for yourself under the table, why not, right?"

From the expression on his face, Hemsted clearly did not like to hear his character impugned. Pozderac, on the other hand, could not have cared less. He slapped the tabletop four or five times and shouted, "Where is Jade Lily?" From the way heads turned and mouths fell open, the hotel's customers probably thought he was demanding to see a stripper.

Hemsted leaned his head toward him and tried to say something, but Pozderac put his hand against his face and shoved him away.

"Where is Jade Lily?" he repeated, only not quite as loudly.

Hemsted was visibly shaken by Pozderac's behavior yet refused to give in to his anger. He turned toward me and spoke between clenched teeth.

"We know that you attempted to retrieve the Lily last Saturday—again without contacting us first," Hemsted said. "We know about the bomb. We also know that there is no evidence that the Lily was destroyed in the subsequent explosion."

"Then where is it?" I asked.

"You have it," Pozderac insisted, his voice loud and clear. "You have Jade Lily."

"A lot of people seem to think so."

Pozderac pounded the table some more. "It is mine," he said. "Give it to me."

"Say please."

"Do not fuck with me"—*if you know what's good for you,* he might have added but didn't.

I paused for a moment before responding.

"I'm sorry," I said. "Was that meant to be threatening? Am I supposed to be chilled to the bone? Tell you what. Try it again, only this time sneer."

Pozderac rose quickly to his feet, knocking over his chair. "I am Branko," he proclaimed.

Just one name, my inner voice said. *Like Elvis, Cher, Madonna, LeBron, Kobe, Fergie, Bono, and Liberace, only not nearly as entertaining.*

"I kill many." He jabbed his finger at me. "Many. You are nothing. I kill you"

I sat straight in my chair, not moving for fear the pain might cause me to wince in front of Pozderac, giving him the wrong impression.

"Are you counting women, children, and old men?" I asked.

Pozderac's face reddened. He started to come around the table. Hemsted moved to block him, and Pozderac pushed him away. He couldn't push Herzog, though. Without a word, the big man stepped between us.

"Get out of way, nigger," Pozderac said.

For a long moment, the world became quiet. The loudest sound was the light shining through the hotel's windows. To Herzog's everlasting credit, he did not lose his temper. He merely glared at the man. Pozderac knew he had made a grievous error in judgment, but he was not one to back down. He placed his hand on Herzog's chest and tried to shove him. Herzog didn't give an inch.

"Nigger," Pozderac hissed.

He said it again? My inner voice was amazed. *What an idiot.*

"Herzy," I said aloud. His head turned imperceptibly toward me. "I'm not paying you enough to put up with this shit."

Herzog closed his hand around Pozderac's throat and squeezed. Pozderac's eyes grew wide with terror. He seized Herzog's wrist with both of his hands, and tried to pull the big man off. It didn't work. Pozderac began gasping for breath. Herzog took hold of Pozderac's shoulder and, with his hand still clasped over his throat, lifted him several feet in the air and then threw him more or less toward the elevators. Pozderac spent a lot of time in the air before crashing and rolling across the floor, colliding with a table and chair, knocking both over. About half of the people in the bar looked amazed. The rest looked away, not wanting to get involved.

"Jesus Christ," Hemsted said. He rushed to Pozderac's side and cradled him in his arms like a fallen comrade. "McKenzie, what have you done?"

"What have I done?" I stood up and looked at Herzog, who wore an almost beatific smile on his face. "What have I done?"

"He's a foreign dignitary assaulted on American soil," Hemsted said.

"That's terrible," I said. "You should call the police. Better yet, call the FBI. We'll be happy to wait."

From the way his expression suddenly changed, I didn't think Herzog liked that idea at all. As it turned out, Pozderac and Hemsted didn't care for it, either.

"Get out of here, McKenzie," Hemsted said. "Just go away."

"Fuck you," Pozderac added for dramatic effect.

"I'll be in touch," I said.

"Fuck you," Pozderac repeated.

Herzog and I moved slowly through the bar and across the lobby while people turned their heads to watch, some blatantly, others furtively. By our leisurely pace, we weren't trying to prove how unconcerned we were. My sprained ankle simply wouldn't let me walk any faster.

Before we reached the door, I rotated my immobilized shoulder so I could glance behind me. Hemsted was helping

Pozderac toward the elevator while the Bosnian shouted at him. I could not hear what he said.

"We're having some fun now, aren't we?" I said.

Herzog moved in front of me and opened the hotel's heavy door. He held it open until I passed through.

"You like Ella, huh?" he said.

Jenny once invited me to a party that she and her husband threw at their palatial estate on Lake Minnetonka not long after they were married. When we met at the door, she warned me about her new friends, warned me before I had even been introduced to them.

"These are people," she said, "who never go to ball games unless they have a luxury suite and who have never, ever been to the Minnesota State Fair. They don't want to be bothered by the riffraff."

"Then why am I here?" I asked.

"So I have someone to talk to," she said.

It was the only time I had been to Jenny's home. Not long after that, she began trading her middle-class pals from Merriam Park for the company of her husband's friends. My impression was that she wasn't happy with the exchange. Still, I had lost track of her until she called a couple of years back and asked that I retrieve the jewels from her blackmailing lover. When I returned them she kissed me and hugged me and said I was the best friend she ever had, yet we didn't speak again until I called her that morning. I asked for a meeting. She seemed reluctant if not downright frightened, yet she agreed. After all, she owed me one.

Lake Minnetonka was actually a collection of sixteen

interconnected lakes and heaven knows how many bays and inlets. It was Jenny who suggested we meet at a yacht club named after one of the bays, "where we would be alone," she said. My guess was that her previous dalliances with infidelity had taught her to be discreet, whether she was cheating or not.

Like most of the properties on and around Lake Minnetonka, the club was designed to be out-of-the-way. To reach it, Herzog had to navigate a series of private roads that were more or less unmarked. Its carefully landscaped grounds and antebellum-style clubhouse reminded me of an exclusive country club, and so did its members-only restaurant and bar. It seated just 105, yet it seemed much larger because of the huge windows that offered a panoramic view of the snow-covered marina with its 117 deepwater slips and the bay beyond. There were no boats in the slips, yet there were plenty of snowmobile tracks, and I could envision Chip and Buffy crossing the frozen lake on their machines—the snowmobile suits they wore, of course, would have designer labels. Still, I wondered if the club did much business in January. A three-season porch that jutted out over the bay was closed, and a sign locked in a glass frame just inside the door announced that complete breakfast, lunch, and dinner menus would resume when the ice left the lake, although a limited lunch menu and dinner menu were available during the winter months.

There were only three people in the restaurant when I arrived. A middle-aged man and woman, who were holding hands and leaning in so close that their foreheads nearly touched, sat at a table in the corner, and my first thought was that they didn't need a bar, they needed a motel. The third person was Jenny. She was sitting alone and staring out the window at the deserted marina, a glass of gold-colored wine in front of her. Herzog and I would have made five, but he elected to remain in the Cherokee.

"You tryin' t' do this on the down low," he said.

"So?"

"A black man in a place like this gonna draw attention."

"Do you think a black man sitting alone in a car outside a place like this will go unnoticed?"

Herzog waved at the nearly empty parking lot.

"Take my chances," he said.

Jenny seemed anxious as I approached, her eyes darting right and left as if she were afraid someone might recognize us. She was tall, with the body of a gym rat, but definitely not young. Her hair was too shiny to be her natural color; over the years her thin face had lost the youthful prettiness that had originally attracted her rich husband, yet it somehow managed to retain its beauty. She was wearing an impeccably tailored blue dress with blue shoes that matched her dress and a blue bag hanging by a blue strap over the back of her chair that matched the blue shoes. I guessed that she bought all three in the same place at the same time off the same mannequin. When I reached the table, I said her name and leaned in to kiss her cheek, grunting at the effort. Her nervousness left her then, replaced by genuine concern.

"McKenzie, are you okay?" she asked.

"I'm fine," I said. I settled into the chair opposite her, slipping my coat off and sitting as straight as possible. "How is it that after all these years you still look like the girl in the yellow bikini?"

Jenny laughed at the reference, laughed as if she suddenly didn't care who saw her. "That was a long time ago," she said.

"I remember it like yesterday. You came home from college

that summer, stretched out on a lounge chair, and never seemed to leave it."

"Yes, and I remember you and Bobby Dunston were forever cutting through our backyard."

"We were hanging out with your brother, Paul."

"You hated Paulie."

"Not that summer we didn't."

"What little perverts you were."

"We were in junior high and you were the most beautiful woman we had ever seen."

"Long time ago."

"Not so long," I told her.

A waiter materialized out of nowhere. Jenny asked for another glass of German Riesling. I ordered a Seven and Seven. After we were served, Jenny said, "What happened to your shoulder? You didn't get shot, did you?"

I didn't want to go into a long explanation, so I said, "Nothing as dramatic as all that. I broke a collarbone playing hockey."

"Oh, McKenzie, you're too old to be playing hockey."

"Gordie Howe was fifty-two when he retired, and I'm nowhere near his age."

"You're not Gordie Howe, either."

She had me there.

"Were you playing without a helmet?" she asked.

"Of course not."

"Then why do you have a bruise on your forehead? Why is your cheek scratched and your hand bandaged?"

"I'm accident-prone."

Jenny drank half of her wine in one gulp before setting the glass in front of her. She held the stem with fingers from both hands, but when her hands began to tremble, she released it and slid them under the table. All of a sudden, she was afraid again.

"What's wrong, Jenny?" I asked.

Her eyes left the glass, met mine, and looked away. "You're lying to me," she said.

"I'm sorry. It's just that it's a very long story and I don't want to go into it."

"Are you sure that's the reason?"

"What do you mean?"

She didn't answer.

"Jen?"

"Why did you call me? Are you worried? You have to know I won't tell anybody."

"Tell anybody what?"

"Nothing. I don't know anything. McKenzie, please."

"Jenny Hackert," I said.

"It's Thomas now, and has been for almost twenty years."

"You'll always be the girl in the yellow bikini to me, Jen. Tell me what's wrong?"

Jenny's hands came out from under the table and took hold of the wineglass again. "Why are you here?" she asked.

"Why do you think I'm here? What's made you so nervous?"

"Don't be like that, McKenzie. You know what's making me nervous."

"I really don't."

"What happened to Patrick Tarpley—I don't know anything about it. Anyone asks, that's what I'll say. You have to know that."

"Tarpley? Sweetie, what makes you think I'm interested in Tarpley?"

Jenny gave me a puzzled look that wandered around the

room before coming back to me. "Wait, wait a minute." She covered her face with both hands. When she uncovered them, she had a thoughtful expression on her face. "Let me think." She turned in her chair to look out the window. While she did that, the waiter reappeared. I ordered another round. He delivered it, and I sucked on the Seven and Seven until Jenny decided to start speaking again. She was excited. I knew because of the way she spoke in short, quick bursts as if she were conserving her breath.

"Patrick Tarpley," she said. "You didn't—you didn't kill him. Did you?"

"No. Of course not. What would make you even think such a thing?"

"Oh God, McKenzie. Oh God. I am so relieved. I thought . . ." She started to chuckle. "I thought you came here—I'm not sure what I thought."

"Jennifer, please, tell me what's going on."

"You're serious now. You're using my full name, so I know. McKenzie, why did you come here? Why did you want to meet me?"

"I needed to ask you a question, although I think I might have part of the answer already."

"What question?"

"I'm sure you remember a couple of years ago I did you a favor."

"I remember."

"Did you ever tell anyone about that? About what happened?"

"No. Well, yes. I mean . . . I'm not stupid, McKenzie. If my husband ever found out . . ."

"But you told someone."

"I did," she said. "You know that. At least I thought you

did. Are you saying she never called you? She never got in touch?"

"Who?"

"Von Tarpley."

"Patrick Tarpley's wife? How do you know her?"

"We met through the City of Lakes Art Museum. We're members of the board of trustees, my husband and I."

"When did you meet?" I asked.

"I don't know. Just before the museum opened."

"You gave her my name?"

"A few weeks ago. She was in trouble," Jenny added. "She needed help. I told her—if it's broken, you can fix it. I said, 'McKenzie can fix anything.' "

"Fix what exactly?"

"That's where it gets a little complicated. You see, I saw Von kissing a man who was not her husband a month or so ago. It was at one of those exhibit openings at the museum. It was an accident. I walked in on her, saw what I saw, turned around, and walked away. Either she or her lover must have seen me, because twenty minutes later Von sidled up to me in the buffet line and said, 'Please.' No explanations, no excuses, no anything, just 'Please.' I never said anything to anyone, McKenzie. I never had any intention of doing so. I'm not a gossip. That's not because I'm virtuous. It's just that I've never been very curious about other people's lives. I have enough problems of my own to keep myself occupied. Anyway, because I never tattled on her, I guess Von decided she could confide in me. A couple of weeks ago she told me she was sure her husband was cheating on her with someone at the museum."

"Her husband was cheating on her?"

"That's the complicated part. I know what you're thinking.

You're thinking about the kiss. You're thinking she was the one stepping out. I'm not going to defend it, McKenzie, but a kiss doesn't mean she was cheating. Some guy flirted with her and she let him. That doesn't mean she stepped over the line. So many men pursued me after I was married, my husband's business associates, employees, competitors. I never could figure that out. It was like they had to possess something that my husband had. But I never crossed the line until the one time I did cross the line, and then I made sure he wasn't connected to my husband in any way. At least I managed that small bit of propriety. I felt sorry for Von. That's what it came down to. She was in a May-December relationship like I was. Her husband moved her to the Cities from Phoenix, so her only friends were his friends, which is pretty much what happened with me. I saw her heading down the same path I had taken, so when she asked if I knew someone who could help, I gave her the name of the only man I trusted completely."

That explains a lot, my inner voice said.

"Did Von tell you what she wanted done?" I asked.

"Not exactly. My impression was that she wanted someone who could get the facts about her husband quietly. At the same time she said the man needed to be capable in case something went wrong. Her husband was a dangerous man, after all. He carried a gun. He knew security. He understood how the police worked. So I told her about you. Told her what you had done for me. Did I screw up, McKenzie? Is that why you're hurt?"

"Indirectly."

"I am so sorry."

"It's okay. It's not your fault. Tell me, have you spoken to Von lately?"

"No. I—I guess you could say I've been avoiding her."

"Why?"

"Because—because of what happened. I read what happened to Patrick."

"You thought I killed him, didn't you? You thought Von hired me to kill her husband."

Jenny nodded.

"Why did you think that? You've known me for so long."

"Von is a very beautiful woman."

"So are you, Jen. I didn't kill for you. In fact, do you remember the first thing I told you when you called about the jewel thief?"

"You said you wouldn't kill anyone."

"Didn't you believe me?"

"I thought maybe Patrick had forced you into it. Oh, I don't know, McKenzie. I don't know what I was thinking."

"I didn't shoot him, sweetie."

"I know that now. I'm sorry I even thought it. Forgive me, McKenzie."

I waved my hand as if I were shooing away a fly. "You're forgiven," I said, "but I don't want you to tell Von or anyone else that we had this conversation, okay?"

"Okay."

"One more thing. The guy Von was kissing in the museum. Do you know him? Did he work for the museum?"

"No. I mean, he didn't actually work for the museum. He was a trustee. A member of the executive board of trustees."

"Who?"

"Derek Anderson."

The Seven and Sevens seemed to be doing a lot more to mask the pain in my shoulder than the over-the-counter drugs I was taking, so I had another. Probably it was a mistake. Afterward, I kissed Jenny good-bye, told her not to be such a stranger, and limped out of the club to where Herzog had parked the Jeep Cherokee. The journey gave me a frightful headache, and when I reached the door of the SUV I had to pause and wait for the fog that invaded my head to clear and the nausea in my stomach to settle. After getting inside and snapping my seat belt into place I said, "Sorry to keep you waiting so long."

"You look tired," Herzog said.

I offered him a smile that felt strange on my mouth.

"Is that a polite way of saying I look like shit?" I asked.

"I didn' want t' insult you until you paid me the rest of my money."

"Fair enough."

"Where to next?"

"Burnsville."

"Fuckin' A."

"You have something against Burnsville?"

"You mean besides it bein' on t'other side of the planet?"

"I'm not in charge of geography."

"What's in Burnsville?"

"A girl. You'll like her. She's a babe."

I had called Mr. Donatucci while I was having my fourth drink in the past ninety minutes, and he gave me Von Tarpley's address. He asked me what I was doing. I told him I had no idea. He didn't seem surprised.

"She tall?" Herzog asked. "I like 'em tall."

"Define tall."

"Big as me."

"Nobody's big as you, Herzy."

Herzog put the SUV in gear and drove out of the parking lot.

"What's 'er name?" he asked.

"Von."

"Von? What kinda name is 'at for a woman?"

"Short for Yvonne, Evonne, something like that. I don't know, man. I didn't name her."

"Gettin' kinda cranky, ain'tcha, McKenzie?"

"I'm tired. My shoulder is killing me. My ankle is killing me. My head is killing me. My hand aches. A childhood friend thinks I might be a murderer. And I've had too much to drink, or not enough, depending on your point of view."

"Hungry?"

"That, too."

"I know a place not too far outta the way, you like Puerto Ricans."

"You're driving, Herzy."

Herzog walked into Tres Hermanas Mexican Restaurant and Grocery and half a dozen voices shouted, "Herzy." A Hispanic gentleman was sitting at the end of the bar with two friends, all of them wearing hats that declared their affiliation with Pipe Fitters Local 539. He raised his beer glass in greeting, and Herzog gave him a wave in reply. An older woman wearing an apron—I guessed she was one of the Three Sisters—met him at the door and gave him a hug. Herzog hugged her back and called her Rosie, which I later learned was a derivation of Rosita. It reminded me of a scene out of the TV show *Cheers*, and it caught me by surprise. I knew Herzog to be an exceedingly dangerous man who's done time for multiple counts of manslaughter, assault, aggravated robbery, and weapons charges. It never occurred to me that he would have friends, that he'd be popular, that he'd like Ella Fitzgerald and baseball and cozy Mexican restaurants that piped mariachi music over invisible speakers and had ESPN Deportes playing on its TVs.

"*Estoy feliz de verte, mi amigo,*" the woman said. "*¿Cómo estás?*"

I was surprised again when Herzog answered, "*Bueno. 'Stoy bueno. ¿Cómo va el negocio?*"

"*No me puedo quejar.*" The woman gestured at me. "*¿Tu amigo?*"

Herzog waggled her hand.

"*Excúseme, señora, señor,*" I said.

Herzog's eyes widened, and Rosie grinned.

"If I may answer your question, *señora,* Herzog and I are business associates." I waved at the restaurant. "I am glad to hear that you're doing well."

"I didn' say that," Rosie said. "I said I can' complain."

"My mistake."

"You didn' tell me you could speak Spanish," Herzog said.

"You didn't tell me that you could speak Spanish."

Rosie clapped her hands and laughed.

"I like ju," she said.

"Thank you," I said.

"I need somethin' t' drink," Herzog said.

Rosie took a step forward and rested a hand on my arm. A concerned expression crossed her plump face. "*¿Estás herido?*"

"*Sí,*" I said, "but I'm getting better."

"*Bueno.*"

The restaurant was divided in two by an iron gate. The

gate was open. The dining area was on one side of the gate. On the other was a short corridor that led to a brightly lit grocery store that I never did get a good look at. The walls of the restaurant were painted and textured to resemble adobe. Woven *tapicería* hung from the walls, and various Mexican artifacts—piñatas, burros, clowns, painted clay figures of Mexican cowboys on horses, and even elephants—were tastefully scattered throughout. The booths and tables were made of dark wood, and suspended above each was a soft light with a shade made up to resemble a sombrero. Along the wall was a battered and scarred bar with taps for Dos Equis, Corona, Tecate, Negra Modelo, Summit Ale, Budweiser, and Miller Genuine Draft. Ads for Jose Cuervo tequilas were plastered to the walls next to clay lizards.

Rosie led us to a vacant booth, and after we sat down, she slipped a pair of laminated menus in front of us featuring tacos, burritos, enchiladas, tostadas, quesadillas . . .

"*¿Señora?*" I asked.

"*Sí.*"

"Herzy told me you were Puerto Rican."

"*¿Sí?*"

"But your restaurant, the furnishings, menu—it's Mexican."

"*Sí.* Jour right. When we come 'ere thirty-five jear ago, the people, they don' know Puerto Rican from Mexican. They t'ink it is the same. We were afraid if we don' give 'em the food they expect, we would lose business. So we give 'em Mexican. But now"—she pointed at a few dishes on the bottom left-hand side of the menu—"we are cooking dishes from my country."

I studied the selection—*plátano frito, pescado frito, mofongo.* I ordered quickly, "*Empanadas de carne y pollo.*"

Rosie nodded her approval.

"I like jour friend," she told Herzog.

Herzog nodded but didn't agree to anything. Instead, he ordered the daily special—Rosie's Cactus Pepper Stew.

The moment after Rosie left the booth, I said, "Nice place."

Herzog said, "Shut up, McKenzie."

So I did.

The food we ordered was served fairly quickly by a waitress Herzog knew as Mayra—she was happy to see him, too. Eating my fried pastry stuffed with beef and chicken was difficult with one hand, yet well worth the effort. Herzog's stew looked so good I might have broken my personal rule about asking for a taste of someone else's meal except, well, it was Herzog. We ate in silence. Herzog washed his meal down with a Mexican beer; I had switched to iced tea. Suddenly Herzog pointed upward at nothing in particular with his fork.

"Shhh," he said.

I tilted my head and listened. Around us were the murmur of voices and the tinkling of silverware. Above, from hidden speakers, came a Latin rock song.

"The music?" I asked.

"The guitar. Listen t' those riffs."

A moment passed. Herzog's smile became gleeful.

"Carlos Santana," he said the way some people might say, "Lord almighty."

We listened some more.

"He the best," Herzog said when the song ended, replaced by something from Marc Anthony that he didn't care for at all.

"You're starting to grow on me, Herzy," I said.

"Don' go thinkin' we be friends or nothin', McKenzie."

"Never."

"You just the man payin' the bills."

To prove it, when Mayra set the tab in the center of the table, Herzog slid it across to me. I didn't mind. Between the iced tea and stuffed pastry, I was starting to feel pretty good about myself and the world in general. So good that I was actually mulling over the suggestion Nina had made that morning—*Why not give the Jade Lily to the insurance company like you promised and forget the whole thing?* Then the damn phone rang, ruining the moment.

"Yeah," I said.

"This is Mr. Fiegen."

There's that "mister" again, my inner voice reminded me.

"Yeah," I said.

"I just spoke to Branko Pozderac and Jon Hemsted."

"Really?" I glanced at my watch. "It took them this long before they started whining?"

"Branko is livid."

"What's he got to complain about? The man's lucky to be alive."

"He's a foreign national."

"He's a racist. He's also a crook. Come to think of it, so are you."

"Do we need to go through this again, McKenzie?"

"Why don't you tell me why you're calling?"

"You have something that belongs to me."

"Are you referring to the letter? I'm going to hang on to that for a while."

"If you think you're going to blackmail me—"

"I just want to make sure that you keep your end of the deal."

"Do we still have a deal?"

"You tell me."

"I was told that the Jade Lily was destroyed."

"No, you weren't."

"Donatucci said—"

"What did he say? Think about it."

Fiegen paused for a long moment.

"What are you up to?" he asked.

"I told Pozderac, although I don't think he was listening, and now I'm telling you—I'll be in touch." I turned off my cell phone and set it in front of me. "I was starting to like it here. I was going to suggest we hang around for a while, have a few more drinks."

"Still could," Herzog said.

I closed my eyes and leaned back as far as I could without disturbing my collarbone. It had already been a long day.

"Sometimes, Herzy . . ."

I didn't finish the thought, so Herzog finished it for me.

"You a cop," he said. "You always be a cop."

"If you say so."

Herzog pointed at the check.

"I always tip twenty percent," he said.

FIFTEEN

The street where Von Tarpley lived in Burnsville rose upward from the Minnesota River valley to a hilltop section of homes that must have looked impressive when they were first built in the decade following World War II. Times have changed. The average American home has doubled in size since the 1950s, and in today's era of McMansions and three-and-a-half baths, Tarpley's yellow two-story colonial with attached garage now seemed small, quaint, and out of place. It still had its Christmas lights up, which wasn't particularly surprising. Minnesotans usually put them up around Thanksgiving when the ground is comparatively snow free and take them down when the snow melts in April. The question was—did Von still turn them on? Some people argue that Christmas lights must be extinguished the day after Christmas. Others hold out for New Year's Day. Still others, in a staggering breach of etiquette, light them up well into February. Those that keep them shining all year 'round—well, they're just plain nuts. My mother had been a big believer in the Twelve Days of Christmas and turned off the lights on January fifth. After she died, my father kept up the tradition, and now I did.

We parked just down the street from the house and sat watching. No other cars approached or left; no one walked by. The street wasn't used by anyone except the people who lived on it, and then just for transportation. It had been skillfully plowed, and most of the sidewalks and driveways abutting it had been cleared of snow. However, only a hole big enough to allow a car to pass had been carved out of the huge mound thrown up onto Tarpley's driveway, and only a narrow path had been shoveled on his sidewalk, allowing room for just one person to pass. I kept thinking "his." I had to remind myself that Tarpley had been dead for over a week now.

I unlatched the door of the Jeep Cherokee and shoved it open with my good arm.

"Want me t' wait?" Herzog asked.

"Come with," I said.

"Why?"

"You're scarier than I am."

"Fuckin' Girl Scouts scarier 'an you."

We made our way down the street and up the driveway. I knocked on the door. Von Tarpley opened it as if she had been expecting someone else. When she saw it was me, her face drained of color. I was mistaken about Herzog. I didn't need him to frighten the woman. She was ready to be afraid of anyone for any reason, even a guy with a bum shoulder and ankle who couldn't run her down if he tried.

"I know you," she said, although by the sound of her voice it seemed she wasn't quite sure.

"Mrs. Tarpley?" I said. "My name is McKenzie. We met in the corridor outside the police department a few days ago."

She nodded her head as if it had all come back to her. "You've been hurt," she said.

"A minor accident, I said. "This is my associate Mr. Herzog. We represent the City of Lakes Art Museum. I hope we're not disturbing you."

"What do you want?"

"We'd like to ask you a few questions about the Jade Lily."

"I already told the police and that insurance investigator everything I know."

"I appreciate that, ma'am." Von raised an eyebrow at the word "ma'am." "Perhaps you'd be kind enough to discuss the matter with us as well?"

She looked past me at Herzog. "Are you the last?" she asked. "I talk to you, will I finally be done with all of this?"

"I suppose," I said.

"Because I'm tired of it. Tired of the whole thing. Patrick was cremated yesterday."

"Sorry I missed the service," I said.

"There was no service."

Von stepped away from the open door and allowed us to enter her living room. It was small and cramped and littered with cardboard boxes, many of them with handwritten labels that corresponded to various rooms—kitchen, bathroom, and bedroom. Most of them were stacked on top of the chairs, sofas, and tables. The furniture was relatively new yet unimpressive. It looked like the kind of stuff a man might buy without consulting his wife. There were two arches. The one in front of me led to the kitchen. The one to my left led to a room I couldn't identify—dining room, probably. A carpeted staircase led to the upstairs bedrooms and bath. I could hear music in the distance, Stacey Kent's crystal-clear voice singing about love in a hotel made of ice, but I couldn't determine which room it came from.

"Excuse the mess," Von said by way of explanation. "I'm getting ready to move. The real estate agent will put the house up for sale and start conducting tours right after I get packed."

"Where are you going?" I asked.

"Phoenix. I have friends there."

"It's warm in Phoenix."

"Warmer than here."

"When are you leaving?"

"End of the week."

I stared at the packing crates and wondered—what if I started opening boxes and looked inside? What would I find?

"Somehow I expected you to be older," Von said.

"Hmm, what?"

"I expected you to be older. I know we met before, and yet I expected you to be an older man. As old as my husband, anyway."

I shot a glance at Herzog. He was standing near the door, an impassive expression on his face, as if he were watching the opening credits of a movie and wondering if it would be worth the ticket price or not. I looked back at Von. Here was a woman who could give Heavenly Petryk a run for her money. She wore little makeup and no jewelry, not even a wedding ring—the pale band of skin at the base of her fourth finger, left hand was already returning to normal. Her long brown hair was tied back, and she was casually, almost sloppily dressed—clothes chosen for the task of packing card-board boxes. Yet there was no question that there was a real woman beneath the loose-fitting clothes. The color had returned to her lovely face, giving her the look of a college girl ten years her junior. Her scent was light and fresh in the stale air of the house. Her voice was unexpectedly husky and deep, with a rich resonance that seemed to vibrate in the silence that followed her words. Certainly she didn't look or behave like a woman whose husband had been murdered a week ago—there was nothing sulky or mournful in her expression or movements.

"You were expecting me?" I asked.

"No, but I recognized the name. McKenzie. Not from when we met, either. You're the one they hired to take the Jade Lily back to the museum after the ransom was paid."

Her candor caught me by surprise. To disguise my reaction, I glanced around the living room looking for a diversion. There was a stack of framed photographs resting on one of the boxes. The top photograph was apparently a wedding photo of Von and her husband standing on a lush green hill. He was wearing a dark suit. She was wearing a simple white sheath that somehow made Kate Middleton's bridal gown look like a dishrag—or maybe it was just the way she wore it. A pond surrounded by birch trees lay below them. I knew where it had been taken—I had been there—but didn't say. I held it up for Von to see.

"That was taken nearly two years ago," she said. "I'm a lot older than I was then."

They were not married when Tarpley was hired by the museum, my inner voice said. *That came later.*

"Where did you meet your husband?" I asked.

"At an art exhibit." She took the photograph from my

hand and set it back on the pile. "I thought he was dashing. Swear to God. When he was offered the job at City of Lakes, I followed him here. I thought it would be an adventure. Became a tearjerker, instead. Three-hanky special. Aren't you going to ask why?"

"Why?"

"I told the police. They didn't want to hear it. I told the insurance investigator. He didn't believe me. You're going to be different somehow?"

Her tone was both assertive and lacking in self-confidence. It was the tone of a woman who was skating on dangerously thin ice and knew it.

"Unlike them, I'm not looking to arrest anyone," I said.

Von caught my eyes and held them, as if she were looking for a crack that would allow her to see inside my brain. She threw a furtive glance at Herzog, then came back to me.

"What exactly do you want?" she asked.

"Like you said, I'm the guy they hired to get the Jade Lily back."

"The Lily was blown up."

"Who says?"

"Maybe it was the insurance guy who said, I don't remember."

"Uh-huh. I was blown up, too. You could say I'm a little bit miffed about that."

Von went to a purse that rested on yet another box. She fumbled for a cigarette and lit it with a plastic lighter, laying down a blue smoke screen between us.

"You guys should probably leave," she said. "I don't mean to be rude. I have a lot on my mind."

I'll bet, my inner voice said.

"You said the police didn't believe your story," I said.

"Oh, they believed it. They just didn't want me to repeat it."

"Try me."

Von blew some more smoke.

"One last time?" she asked.

"Sure."

"Where to begin?"

"Start with the robbery."

"No, the story begins before that."

"Start where you like."

"I suppose it begins with the cop."

"What cop?"

"Lieutenant Scott Noehring of the Minneapolis Police Department. He's a hero, you know. It said so in the newspaper."

Von paused for a moment as if she expected me to respond. When I didn't, she took a long drag of the cigarette and resumed talking with the exhale.

"He appeared one day not long after Patrick started his new job with the museum," Von said. "He explained that he knew all about Patrick's past, and if Patrick didn't cooperate, he would give the information to City of Lakes and every other museum he could think of, effectively blackballing him from his profession."

"What information?"

Von had enough of the cigarette and put it out in a pristine ashtray. I wondered if smoking was a habit or just something she was using as a prop.

"Let me finish," she said. "Patrick gave in to the cop. He started paying the blackmail. A thousand dollars a month. Doesn't sound like much until you start adding up the months. Twelve in a year. Twenty-four over two years. The cop wasn't satisfied with the amount, so he registered Patrick as a confidential informant. I'm not even sure what a confidential informant is, how it works, but whatever, all the money the police paid Patrick went into the cop's pocket. I begged Patrick to tell me what happened. Finally he did. He told me that when he was a senior in high school he was accused of being a child molester. Of being a pedophile. He said the accusations had followed him ever since."

"Was it true?"

"Technically. What happened, at least what Patrick told me happened, when he was a senior in high school he had sex with a freshman . . ."

"I was told the kid was more like nine."

Von flashed her remarkable brown eyes at me. I didn't know if she was annoyed that I asked the question or that I had interrupted her story again.

"High school freshman," she said. "It was backseat-of-a-parked-car stuff. The freshman's parents found out and went ballistic. They called the police, called the prosecutor. They weren't satisfied with a charge of statutory rape. They bullied the prosecutor into also charging Patrick as a child molester. Eventually all the charges were dropped. The sex was consensual, after all. Both parties were kids. Word got out just the same. It always does, doesn't it? Patrick was ostracized in school. His parents pretty much disowned him. This happened thirty-five years ago. The charges followed him, still. Every job application has the same line—'Have you ever been convicted of a felony?' Patrick was never convicted, but investigators looking into his background could see what he was accused of. Some labels you can't shake off."

"Did the City of Lakes Art Museum know this when they hired him?" I asked.

"I think so. That woman, Perrin something, I think she

knew but didn't care. If word got out, though, got out to the public, she'd care one heckuva lot."

"So Patrick allowed Noehring to blackmail him."

"I'm not sure if 'allowed' is the right word, but yes. At least until he decided he had had enough. Or maybe it was I who made that decision."

"You?"

"I told Patrick I was leaving him."

"Because of the blackmail?"

"I didn't want to live like that anymore. A woman wants a man who—ahh, let's just say I made a mistake when I married Patrick."

She didn't strike me as a woman who made wrong decisions about men, and I told her so.

Von laughed at that. "Well, I made a doozy, only I didn't know it until Noehring came around," she said. "That freshman I told you about wasn't a girl. Was a boy. One of the reasons the parents went crazy. Either Patrick was a pedophile or their son was gay, and they couldn't have that. You need to remember—this was thirty-five years ago. A different age. No homosexuals on TV back then. The news, though, it changed everything between us. Patrick was the best friend I ever had. If he had told me he was gay he'd still be my best friend. He held it back, probably because of what happened when he was a kid. My point is—boys who love boys should marry boys. They shouldn't marry girls and pretend to be something they're not. Sucks for everybody. So we decided to go our separate ways, Patrick and I."

"What does this have to do with the Jade Lily?"

"When I told Patrick I wanted a divorce, I also told him that I didn't want a settlement; I didn't need alimony. It was going to be amicable, you know? He said that I should have something for my trouble, and him, too. I asked what he meant, and he said he was nursing an idea and would get back to me. He didn't, though. I didn't know what happened until the insurance man came to question me about the theft."

"Are you saying that you didn't know your husband was going to steal the Lily?"

"That's exactly what I'm saying."

"Did you tell this to the police?"

"When they came around after they found Patrick, yes, I did. Every word. This cop, his name was Lieutenant Rask; he didn't want to hear it. Told me not to repeat it. Especially the part about Lieutenant Noehring being a blackmailer."

"I understand his point of view," I said.

"Do you?"

"I understand yours, too."

"What's that mean?"

"Von, you are the most beautiful liar I have ever met. No, wait"—I gave it a second's thought—"that honor actually belongs to someone else. You are a strong second place, though. In any case, you're lying. You lied to the cops; you're lying to me. I can't blame you for that."

"I am not lying."

"Sure you are. You were in on the theft. You were involved from the very beginning."

Von smirked. "Prove it," she said.

"I'm not interested in proving anything. Like I said, I don't care if anyone goes to jail. If push comes to shove, though, I'd tell the cops to talk to Jenny Thomas."

Now it was Von's turn to act surprised. She moved to a chair and picked up the box that had been resting on the cushion.

"Are you tired?" she asked. "Do you want to sit down?"

"No, I'm good," I said.

Von returned the box to its original position. Her demeanor had shifted in those few seconds. She was still trying to play me, but it was like a tennis player who suddenly discovered that her opponent had a better backhand than she anticipated. She had become less sure of herself.

"So you talked to Jenny," she said. "What a busy little bee you are."

"Should we quit screwing around, then?" I asked.

"What do you want?"

"A hundred and twenty-seven thousand dollars."

"Excuse me?"

"A hundred and twenty-seven thousand dollars. That's what they were going to pay me when I retrieved the Jade Lily. Only there is no Jade Lily to bring back, so guess what? I'm not getting paid."

Both Von and Herzog seemed quite confused by my remark.

"I don't know anything about this, McKenzie," Von said.

"What do you know?"

"Are you a cop? Are you working for the cops? You have to tell me if you are."

It was one of the great urban legends, of course, that the police have to identify themselves to criminals when they ask. It's simply not true and never has been, but who was I to argue with the woman.

"No, I am not a cop," I said. "No, I am not working for the cops or the insurance company or the museum. What about you, Mr. Herzog?"

"Fuckin' cops," he said.

"All I want is my hundred and twenty-seven thousand. Von . . ." I stepped closer and gave her my most menacing look, the one I practice in front of the mirror when I'm alone. "I mean to get what's mine. I may not be in any condition right now to beat it out of you. My friend . . ." I pointed at Herzog. "What do you say, Mr. Herzog?"

"You oughtn' mess wi' a man's money," he said.

"I don't have your money, McKenzie. I don't have any money. You have to believe me."

"What happened to the one-point-three million that was paid for the Lily?"

"I don't know anything about that."

"What do you know?"

"I know . . ." Von hesitated.

"Yeah," I said.

She retreated behind a wall of moving crates, but they didn't seem to give her much comfort.

"It's true," she said. "I admit it. I knew Patrick was going to steal the Lily. He had it all planned out. All he needed was a go-between that he could trust, someone he chose and not the insurance company. Jenny had given me your name. She gave me your name because of something else that had nothing to do with the Lily."

"This other matter—did it have anything to do with Derek Anderson, the man you were having an affair with?"

It was the second time I caught her by surprise.

"Jenny told you a lot, didn't she?" Von said. "Yes, it was Derek. We weren't having an affair, though. I was still upset about Patrick, and I guess you could say I was trying him on for size. Only he started making demands. I thought I might need help—I still cared enough about Patrick that I didn't want him to find out about Derek and me, only this other thing came up."

"You gave Patrick my name?"

"I did. That's all I did."

"What was Patrick's plan?"

"Steal the Lily and then sell it back," Von said. "He told me that if we worked it right—if *he* worked it right—the insurance company would pay for the Lily's return and the police would never be called. He said he knew a man who could launder the money—he said the insurance company would be sure to have it marked—and afterward he would give me a share and that would be the end of it."

"Why steal the Lily? Why not steal something that was worth more?"

"In case we—he got caught."

"Who was in on it with him?" I asked. "Besides you?"

"I don't know."

"Sure you do."

"I don't. After the Lily was stolen, Patrick was killed. I believe it was his accomplices who did it, just like everyone else, but I don't know who they are. I would have told the police if I knew. I loved Patrick. He was my best friend."

"Who was your best friend?"

The question came from a tall, dark man standing in the doorway. He had opened the front door and stepped into the house without Von or me noticing him. Herzog noticed, though. He took a few steps backward. His right hand was hidden under his jacket at the small of his back. He was staring at the intruder while his peripheral vision picked me up. There was a serious question in his eyes. I answered it with a slight shake of my head. His empty hand came out from under his jacket.

"Who are you people?" the man asked.

"Dennis." Von maneuvered around the boxes to the door. "This is McKenzie and Mr. Herzog. They're working for the museum to retrieve the Jade Lily."

"I don't care who they work for," Dennis said.

Von reached his side and took his arm. "It's all right," she said.

"No it isn't. The way the police and the insurance company keep badgering you. Now these guys. No. I won't allow you to answer any more questions."

"Are you an attorney?" I asked.

"I don't need to be a lawyer to know Mrs. Tarpley has rights."

I drifted to the door until I was standing next to Herzog. I recognized Dennis as I drew closer, even though the first time I had seen him he was standing much farther away. Dennis was the man who met Von in the corridor outside room 108.

"How long have you and Mrs. Tarpley known each other?" I asked.

"We were introduced—" Von said.

Dennis broke her sentence. "That's none of your business," he said.

"My associate and I might just make it our business," I said.

Von stepped in front of Dennis. "McKenzie, please," she said. "He has nothing to do with the Lily. I promise you."

"Just so you know, I meant what I said before. I want my money. I'll be in touch."

I reached out and tapped the tip of her nose with my finger. In hindsight, it was a silly gesture. After that, Herzog and I bulled our way past Von and Dennis and stepped onto the barely shoveled sidewalk.

"I'll be in touch," I repeated.

Dennis slammed the door behind us in reply.

I'm pretty sure I was smiling as we made our way back to the Jeep Cherokee.

"How was I?" I asked. "Scary?"

"Girl Scout," Herzog said.

Herzog started the Cherokee once we were safely inside, but I told him to wait before he put it in gear. I pulled the printed photograph out of my inside pocket and unfolded it. The sun was starting to set, and I turned on the dome light so Herzog could get a good look at it.

"Do you recognize this gentleman?" I asked.

"Yeah," he said. "Yeah. This is—ain't this the dude inside the house? Dennis somethin'? One just threw us out?"

"He's also the guy who put the bomb in the motel room."

"Fuckin' A." Herzog stared at the photo and then at Von's house. "He the one try t' blow you up?"

"It gets better." I pointed at the small SUV that had been parked directly in front of the Cherokee while we were in Tarpley's house—a metallic red Toyota RAV4. "The vehicle he's driving was seen both at the motel and at the museum the night the Jade Lily was lifted."

Herzog opened his door.

"Wait, wait," I said. "Where are you going?"

"Don' you want to smoke this fuck?"

"It can keep."

"No time like the present."

"Nah, nah, not yet."

"What we waitin' on? You gonna call the cops?"

"I thought you didn't like cops."

"McKenzie, you gotta know—if'n he's here, 'at proves 'im and the girl are in on it together. The money you lookin' for probably in one of 'em boxes."

"No," I said. "I know where the money is. It's not here.

Not yet, anyway. Otherwise they wouldn't be wasting time packing."

"Where the money at, then?"

Instead of answering, I pulled a pen from my pocket and used it to write down the license plate number of the Toyota. Afterward, I looked at my watch, which was on my right wrist because my left wrist was pinned to my chest.

"We need to get going," I said. "We're running late."

It was a bad time of day to drive with traffic crawling on the freeway like a distracted infant. Fortunately, since there were two of us in the Cherokee, we were able to use the car pool lanes. That helped us to be only ten minutes late when we reached El Cid's joint in the Phillips neighborhood. 'Course, the way Cid behaved you'd think we had delayed a shuttle launch.

"I don't wait ten minutes for anybody," he announced when we stepped inside the bar.

I was tempted to blame Chopper, say he must have confused the time when I asked him to set up the meeting. That would have been cheap, though.

"I misjudged the rush hour traffic," I said. "Sorry."

"That is no excuse," Cid said. "Punctuality is one way we show respect for each other."

He had me there.

"I apologize," I said.

"This had better be worth my while."

Cid had been standing when he called me out. Now he slipped into the same booth where he had sat when I first met him. His bodyguard was sitting at the same table. The same hat was on top of the table; I presumed his gun was beneath it. If there was a difference, it was that he openly watched Herzog intently. I could have been carrying a bazooka in my pocket instead of the Walther PPK and I doubt he would have noticed.

I moved to the booth and waited until El Cid nodded his permission before I sat. Herzog stood at the door, his hands casually folded over his stomach, and stared at the bodyguard. He told me before we entered the bar, "I gots t' say, 'at pussy pulls on you, I'm gonna cap 'is ass."

"I would certainly hope so," I told him.

"I agreed to meet you again as a favor to Chopper," Cid said, the implication being that otherwise I was beneath his notice.

"I appreciate that," I said.

"Well? What's it about?"

"When last we spoke, you suggested that you'd be happy to take the Jade Lily off my hands should I stumble upon it. If memory serves, you also mentioned several ways an enterprising man might dispose of it—selling it to interested parties in Europe or the Pacific Rim; perhaps locking it in a vault for safekeeping until the statute of limitations expired and/or a convincing provenance was established. These possibilities existed, of course, before the cop killing made the Lily too toxic to handle."

Cid spread his hands wide. "Just idle chatter," he said.

"Of course," I said. "We're just talking here. Speculating. For example, I was speculating that if someone were to be arrested for the cop killing, that would remove the curse, if you will, making the Lily more readily marketable."

"I'm sure it would, although, the last I heard, the Lily was blown to smithereens."

"Yeah, I heard the same thing."

"From the look of you, I'd say you were close to the explosion."

"Close enough to know what others don't."

"What would that be?"

"First I have to ask you a question."

Cid spread his hands wide again.

"Are you an enterprising man?" I asked.

Cid smiled the way some people do when they hear a foolish question. "I believe I am," he said.

"I have never doubted it."

"McKenzie, what are we talking about?"

"I have the Jade Lily. I will sell it to you for one-point-three million."

Cid laughed at my remark. "That's ridiculous," he said.

"The price does seem pretty steep, doesn't it?"

"It does."

"If I were you, I'd laugh, too. Especially if the money was coming out of my own pocket." Cid's laughter subsided as he got an inkling of what I meant. "However, if someone else were to pay for it . . ."

This time I spread my own hands wide.

"What do you mean?" Cid asked.

"Let's say, for argument's sake, that a couple of enterprising thieves—not as enterprising as you, of course—had one-point-three million in illegal funds that they wished to make legal. They would naturally seek out the services of a—what's the word—facilitator."

Cid smiled and nodded at the reference.

"This facilitator, in turn, could invest that sum in a more lucrative venture," I said.

"What you're suggesting is a serious breach of business

ethics," Cid said. "A man could be driven into bankruptcy or worse, behaving that way."

"True, if the couple in question were regular customers and if they were connected in some way. They're not. They're just a couple of amateurs looking for the big score. Amateurs, I might add, whose conduct in this matter has not only created undue turmoil in the business community, it has compromised the dealings of serious professionals such as yourself. If they were to lose their investment, who would they complain to? The SEC? The Better Business Bureau? In any case, they won't need the money where they're going."

"Where would that be?"

"Prison, for killing a police officer. Or hell, depending on how things are arranged."

"Ahh, I see."

"My point is—you could acquire the Jade Lily at no out-of-pocket expense."

Cid studied me for a moment.

"It doesn't fit," he said.

"What doesn't fit?"

"This offer of yours. It doesn't fit your profile."

"I have a profile?"

"You're a doer of good deeds."

"You think so?"

"Besides, you don't need one-point-three million."

"Everyone needs one-point-three million," I said. "You're also forgetting that there's a principle involved."

"What principle?"

"The sonsabitches tried to blow me up." I slapped the table-top for emphasis, startling Cid, his bodyguard, and Herzog. "Look at me. You think I'm going to let them get away with this?" I clenched the fist of my right hand. "First I take their money. Afterward . . ." I made a production of unclenching my fist, letting Cid decide what the gesture meant.

Cid grinned at me like he had won a long-odds bet. "Retribution," he said. "Now that is something I can appreciate."

"Good."

"Where is the Lily now?"

"I can deliver it within one hour after you contact me, day or night."

"I'll let you know."

Ten minutes later, Herzog and I were in the Jeep Cherokee driving east. Herzog was silent, but I could sense there was something on his mind.

"What?" I said.

"How'd you know Cid was launderin' the money for 'em?" he asked. "There's plenty of others coulda done it."

"Educated guess. When we spoke the first time, Cid said he never met Tarpley; they didn't travel in the same circles, he said. Yet he knew what Tarpley's wife looked like."

"He was lyin', then, 'bout knowin' Tarpley."

"Not necessarily. Cid could have met his wife without Tarpley being there."

"How, unless—yeah, okay, I get it. The wife, she was the one that hadda set it up. The meeting, I mean. She met Cid way ahead of time, met 'im before 'er and Dennis coulda brought the money to 'im for launderin', before they even heisted the Lily. Wait. No, 'at don' make no sense. Does it?"

"How should I know? I'm suffering from a concussion."

"How she know to meet wit' Cid, girl like that? You ain't gonna find 'is number in no phone book."

"Tarpley was a chess player. He would have had all of his moves worked out far in advance, including this one."

"I gits it. He was the man wit' the plan. She—she was the one took the plan and made it work. Jus' follow the instructions."

Herzog's typically churlish expression became bright and cheerful.

"Are you having fun, Herzy?" I asked. "Are you glad I called you?"

"What a dumb fuck he was, Tarpley," he said. "No wonder he got iced. Once they had the plan, the wife and Dennis, they didn' need 'im no more. Fucker shoulda saw it comin'."

"What makes you think Von and Dennis killed him?"

The question caught him by surprise.

"You sayin' they didn't?" Herzog asked.

"The possibilities are endless."

"How we gonna find out for sure?"

"That's a job for the police, isn't it?"

"Fuck that."

"We can tie them both to the Lily right now. The only thing that connects either Von or Dennis to the murder of Tarpley and the cop, though, is the gun. The fact they didn't toss it after the first killing means they probably kept it after the second one."

"How you gonna git 'em to show us the gun?"

I didn't answer.

"McKenzie?"

Herzog swiveled his head from the street to me to the street and back again.

"You fuckin' kiddin' me?" he said.

"What do you think I'm paying you ten thousand dollars for? My health?"

Well, yes, actually, it is your health you're paying for, my inner voice said.

I pried my cell out of my pocket and started searching through my contact list with my free hand. I've seen kids send elaborate text messages one-handed while playing soccer, yet I could barely make a phone call. Finally I managed to reach my party.

"Major Crimes," Bobby said. "Commander Dunston."

I tried to make my voice sound like a doddering old woman. "Is this the police?"

"McKenzie, your voice sounds kinda funny. Did they blow your brains out?"

"All right, all right."

"Seriously, how are you?"

"I will recover—more or less."

"I'm sorry I didn't get a chance to visit you in the hospital."

"Believe me, you didn't miss much."

"Everybody over here was worried about you, except Victoria, of course. She thinks you're indestructible."

"She's mistaken."

"So, what's going on?"

"I need a favor."

"Let's not start that again."

"It's police business," I said. "Granted it's Minneapolis police business. Still . . ."

"Why not call Minneapolis, then?"

"You know how impetuous Lieutenant Rask can be."

"Oh? Are you afraid he might actually go out and do his job?"

"That's exactly what I'm afraid of."

"I hate this. I hate doing favors for you, and yet I keep doing them. What is wrong with me?"

I changed the sound of my voice again. "Luke, give in to the power of the dark side."

"Is that supposed to be James Earl Jones? You know, I saw James Earl Jones on the stage. He was playing Othello to Christopher Plummer's Iago. It was the best thing I ever saw in the theater, and McKenzie—you're no James Earl Jones."

"Who is?"

"What do you want?"

I recited the license plate of the Toyota RAV4 I saw outside Von Tarpley's house.

"Must I remind you yet again that this information is available to the general public for a small fee through the Driver and Vehicle Services Division of the Minnesota Department of Public Safety?"

"You know how bureaucracies are. I have to provide signatures and written consents and whatnot. Besides, they're closed."

"Hang on."

Five minutes later Bobby gave me the name the SUV was registered to—India Cooper—and an address in South Minneapolis. She had no record of any kind.

I thanked Bobby and said I'd see him soon. I caught Herzog staring at me out of the corner of his eye as I pocketed the cell phone.

"Well?" he said.

"Well what?"

"Wha'd he say?"

"The problem with asking a lot of questions, Herzy, you sometimes get answers you don't want to hear."

SIXTEEN

I bought Herzog a steak at Mancini's on West Seventh Street in St. Paul, not far from the Xcel Energy Center, where the Wild played hockey. It wasn't a game night, so we had no trouble securing a table for two. In retrospect, it probably wasn't the swiftest move I'd made that day. You're not going to find a more tender sirloin anywhere in the Northern Hemisphere than at Mancini's. On the other hand, they're not so tender that you can cut them with a fork. After a few minutes of watching me struggle, Herzog took my plate and cut the meat for me.

"Chew before you swallow," he said when he gave it back.

"Thanks, Mom," I said.

After that, it was two guys talking who didn't know one another very well. As might be expected, we settled into an extended conversation about sports. I told him a few anecdotes about playing baseball and hockey for St. Paul Central, and he reminisced about playing football for North High School in Minneapolis. He was a linebacker—the *Minnea-*

polis Star Tribune once named him Prep Star of the Week for a game he played against Roosevelt. He had a chance to play college ball but didn't have the ACT scores to get in. I told him I was lucky I had the grades for college because I sure as hell wasn't going to make it on an athletic scholarship. And so on and so on. We were nearing the end of the meal when Herzog changed the subject.

"Settin' yourself up as a target such a good idea?" he asked.

"I'm open to alternatives that will put the gun in their hands."

"You could call the cops. I don't like cops . . ."

"You've made your position known."

"You could call 'em, show 'em that picture of Dennis, tell 'em about Von, let 'em scoop 'em both up, search the house, all those boxes, find the gun, problem solved."

"Yeah, they might find the gun. That doesn't mean they'll be able to prove that either of them used it, though. I need at least one of them arrested for shooting the cop."

"Why?"

"It's all part of the plan."

"You got a plan?"

"You'll see."

"Sure they gonna call?"

"They don't know about the photo of Dennis. They think the only thing connecting them to the theft of the Lily is me. Their first thought will be to pay me off. They don't have the money. So they'll call Cid and ask, 'Where's our dough?' Cid will hem and haw and tell them they'll get it at the end of the week as promised—the end of the week is when they're leaving town, remember? They won't wait till then because they'll be afraid that I won't wait. Eventually, they'll decide the only alternative is to kill me. They'll think of a location, a time, and try to set me up like they did Tarpley. Do you believe the bitch shot him in the same place that they were married?"

"How you know 'at?"

"I saw their wedding photo. It was taken at Wedding Hill in Wirth Park, where they found his body."

" 'At's cold, man."

I glanced at my watch.

"They've been debating pros and cons for about two hours," I said. "I expect them to call any moment now."

"Yeah, if they call. I'm just saying, you think they gonna hit you cuz you can tell the cops about your friend Jenny whatsername. Why not just shoot Jenny? Then it's your word against them."

The thought hadn't occurred to me.

What a fucking egomaniac you are, my inner voice shouted. *You think it's always about you.*

My jacket was hanging on the back of my chair. I spun in my seat to reach it, wrenching my shoulder in the process. I didn't care about the pain—I deserved it. I pulled the cell out of my pocket and searched the log for Jenny's number. I stood up even as I hit the CALL button. The waitress saw me and hurried over.

The phone was ringing.

"I need the bill," I told the waitress. "Now."

Jenny answered the phone. She must have had caller ID because she said, "Hey, McKenzie."

"Where are you?" I said. "Are you at home?"

"Yeah, I'm at home. Why—"

"Are you alone?"

"Yes. My husband is at—"

"Trigger your security system. You have one, right?"

"We do. It's a—"

"You should have a panic button. Do you have one?"

"McKenzie, what's going on?"

"Listen to me carefully, Jennifer. People might be coming to your home to hurt you—"

"What? Why?"

"Hit your damn panic button. Do it now."

"Okay."

Only a few brief moments passed, yet it seemed longer. While I waited, the waitress set a black folder on the table in front of me. I opened the folder, saw the bill, and threw some money at it.

"It's done," Jenny said.

"Now I want you to find a safe place to hide. Are you listening?"

"Yes."

"Find a place to hide, and you stay there until your security people arrive. Until the police arrive. Do you understand?"

"Yes."

"You tell them that you saw an intruder. You do not let them leave until I get there. I'm in St. Paul, so it's going to take at least forty-five minutes."

"All right."

"I'm on my way."

It took longer than forty-five minutes, despite some daredevil driving by Herzog that left me breathless, because Jenny's house was located on Cook's Bay on the far western side of Lake Minnetonka and because the roads that led to it were narrow, winding, and indifferently marked. Finally we found Jenny's private road. It wound upward over a low hill. When we crested the hill, we could see the house. It was made of brick and glass and was lit up like Target Field on game night. There were several vehicles parked in front of the six-car garage, including a City of Mound police cruiser. We parked behind them. The house itself was two stories high and built into the side of the hill with a spectacular view of the lake below. It was erected twenty years ago right after Jenny accepted her husband's proposal of marriage, yet it looked like it was built yesterday. We were stopped at the door by a representative of Jenny's security firm. I gave him my name; told him I was expected. He didn't care. Jenny saw me, though.

"McKenzie, thank God," she said.

That was enough for the guard, who quickly stepped back and let us pass.

Jenny was sitting on a sofa that looked like it could sleep three. She was wearing white fluffy slippers that matched her white fluffy robe. She was sitting with her legs drawn up, her knees pressed against her chest, her chin resting on top of her knees. There was a uniformed police officer standing next to her, a notebook and pen in his hands. A couple of security guards lingered nearby, looking as if they wanted to be useful but didn't know how.

I knelt in front of Jenny and took her hand in mine.

"Are you okay, sweetie?" I asked.

"McKenzie, they were here," Jenny said. "They came, just like you said they would."

"What happened?"

One of the security guards stepped forward.

"Our security system frightened off an intruder," he said.

His expression suggested that he was quite pleased with himself. "There is evidence that a car was parked near the top of the hill. The intruder got out of the car and made his way toward the house through the snow, approaching from the far side." He made a gesture with his hand toward his right. "At about sixty yards from the structure the footprints stopped and the intruder retreated the way he came. He must have been scared off by the lights and the siren from our security system."

I glanced up at the cop. He gave me a slight shrug of his shoulders. "Sounds right," he said.

I turned all of my attention back toward Jenny. "I'm sorry," I said.

She wrapped her arms around my neck and hugged me close. "You saved me," she said.

I didn't have the guts to tell her that I was the one who put her in danger.

"Where's your husband?" I asked.

"I called him after I spoke to you, after I pulled the alarm. He was meeting with a business associate and said he would come home as soon as he could."

"Where is he?"

"Orono."

"Orono? Orono is a lousy five miles away. He could have walked here by now."

"I know."

She spoke the words as if they were all she needed to describe the status of her marriage.

I did a quick three-sixty of the house from where I knelt in front of the sofa. Herzog was standing near the door. The guards were still milling about, talking softly to each other. The cop was impatiently tapping his notebook with his pen.

Someone had the presence of mind to build a fire in the fire-place—I knew the place had four of them. When I looked back, I found Jenny staring into the flames.

"Maybe it's time to move back to Merriam Park," I said.

Jenny turned her head so that her cheek was resting against her knees. There was a sad sort of smile on her lips as if she knew the answer to a complicated question but wished she didn't.

"I'm not the one who's going to move," she said.

The cop had other places to be, but the security guards promised to leave a man at Jenny's house until her husband returned. Herzog and I climbed back into the Jeep Cherokee and worked our way to the county road that wound around Cook's Bay.

"Now what?" he said.

"Time to be proactive."

"Wha's 'at mean?"

"Take me to Burnsville."

" 'Bout fuckin' time."

We drove past Von Tarpley's house twice. The Toyota RAV4 was parked in front both times. Lights burned in most of the rooms—apparently Von paid as much attention to the energy conservation flyers the power company sent out each month as I did. The third time we drove past we could see Dennis through the living room window. His head was bowed as if he was speaking to someone sitting below him.

Herzog pulled over and stopped the Jeep Cherokee at the end of the street.

"How you wanna work this?" he asked.

"When I was a kid, a friend of mine threw a party, a kegger, at his place in White Bear Lake," I said. "It was a fairly quiet affair, yet someone called the cops. The cops drove up, and we all moved to the front of the house to see what was going on. That's when whoever called the cops stole the keg off the back porch."

"Nice."

"I'll give you five minutes to work your way into position. When I go to the front of the house, you go to the back door. I'll knock loudly. Give me a minute and then you go in."

" 'Kay. Now you git your piece outta your pocket. Put it in your belt; put it where you can git at it fast."

"I thought you didn't like my Walther PPK."

"Better'n nothin'."

Herzog opened the driver's door while I opened the other side. I moved around the Cherokee and slid into the driver's seat.

"Where's your gun?" Herzog asked. I held it up for him to see. "You'll be able to drive?"

"I'll manage," I said.

" 'Kay. One more thing. McKenzie?"

"What?"

"I was never in White Bear Lake."

"Five minutes," I said.

I watched Herzog disappear behind a house. The skies had cleared, letting the moon and stars work their magic. I would have preferred overcast. In the winter it never gets entirely dark. The snow and ice always find a light source to magnify and reflect—like the moon and the stars—so it often seems like twilight no matter what the hour, and I was afraid that Herzog would be terribly exposed.

Five minutes later, I put the Cherokee into gear and headed down the street. There was no traffic, so I had an easy time of it. I pulled in behind the Toyota and sat for a minute. I wasn't looking to give Herzog more time so much as I wanted the inhabitants of the Tarpleys' house to get a good look at me; I even revved the engine a bit before shutting it down.

I slipped out of the vehicle and headed for the front door, carefully picking my way along the narrow, snow-covered sidewalk. The Walther PPK was wedged under my elbow where the shoulder immobilizer had more or less pinned it to my body; my jacket was draped over it. I ignored the doorbell. Instead, I opened the glass storm door and pounded hard on the wooden door beneath it. I waited five seconds, then pounded some more. The door was yanked open. I started counting down seconds inside my head.

59 - 58 - 57 . . .

"What are you doing here, McKenzie?" Von Tarpley asked.

"I want my money," I said.

I brushed Von aside and stepped past her into the living room. I looked for Dennis and did not find him. He could have been squatting behind the stacked boxes, I decided. He could have been upstairs. He could have been hiding in the kitchen or the darkened room beyond the arch to my left. I turned toward Von. She had moved away from the door without closing it. That should have told me something, but it didn't.

55 - 54 - 53 . . .

"Where's my money?" I asked.

"I told you, I don't have it," Von said. "I know nothing about it."

She moved deeper into the room. I turned with her until my back was to the front door.

"Then why did you try to pay Jenny Thomas a visit earlier this evening?" I said.

48 - 47 - 46 . . .

"I don't know what you're talking about."

"Have it your own way," I said. "I'll just take the reward, then."

"What reward?"

"The police have a photograph of your boyfriend Dennis paying for the rooms at the motel you guys blew up. They also have photos of his SUV at the motel and the museum the night the Jade Lily was stolen. They haven't been able to identify him yet. I bet they'll pay me a few bucks to help."

I heard a noise beyond the arch that sounded like someone shifting his weight on loose floorboards.

35 - 34 - 33 . . .

"Oh, no," Von said.

"Once they have him in custody—the question is, did he shoot the cop in the back or was that you? What do you think he'll say? Think he'll take the blame?"

Von glanced at the open front door. I imagined her trying to make a run for it.

30 - 29 - 28 . . .

"You know what you should be doing, Von? I mean besides coming up with my money? You should be thinking about what kind of deal you can make with the cops."

Von hesitated for a moment.

"Dennis shot him," she said.

I turned my attention toward the darkened room, turned my body to face it.

"Why?" I asked.

"Noehring was going for the ransom money. He was going to kill you to take it. Dennis shot him to protect you."

20 - 19 - 18 . . .

"That works for me, but the cops—they're going to want to know how Dennis knew who Noehring was; how he recognized him in the dark." I thought I heard the floorboards squeak again. "You might be able to make it work, though. You're a smart girl. 'Course, you're still going to have to explain how your husband was murdered in the exact same spot where you two took your wedding vows."

Von glanced down at her wedding photograph, still in the pile on the box with her other framed photos.

"What were you thinking?" I asked.

"I was thinking that he lied to me." Her voice was surprisingly gentle.

10 - 9 - 8 . . .

"Men lie to women all the time," I said, "and vice versa. You don't shoot them for it."

7 - 6 - 5 . . .

"You do if you can get a million dollars out of it."

4 - 3 . . .

"So, it was a crime of passion, then?"

2 - 1 . . .

"I guess."

Zero.

That's when he came through the door. Only it wasn't Herzog, and it wasn't the back door. It was Dennis, and he came through the front door with a gun in his hand. He pushed his gun hand toward me as if throwing a punch and fired. The gun sounded like a surface-to-air missile in the small living room. The shot went wide, but not by much. I dove behind a stack of packing crates, landing on the shoulder that wasn't broken, which, trust me, didn't make the shoulder that was broken feel any better. I heard the Walther slip out from under my elbow and clatter to the floor, yet I didn't realize what it meant until I reached for the gun only to find that it wasn't there.

I heard Von shouting, although I didn't see her because of the boxes.

"No, no, no," she said. "Not in my house. Are you crazy?"

"Get out of the way," Dennis said.

I found the Walther. It was just out of my reach. I rolled toward it. The two ends of my fractured collarbone rubbed together. I cried out in pain as I snatched the gun off the floor. Dennis was moving around the boxes. An experienced shooter would have fired through the boxes—they were made of paper, after all. I wouldn't have had a chance. Dennis wasn't experienced. He had to see his target. He came around the stack. I rolled onto my back, extended my arm, and threw a shot at him. I missed. Dennis fell backward. I heard him bounce against furniture. The photographs Von had stacked on top of the boxes fell; the glass in the frames shattered on the floor. I rolled to my knees. My head—hell, my entire body was throbbing, and lights flashed in front of my eyes like a Fourth of July fireworks display. I tried to ignore them as best I could. I glanced around the boxes. Dennis was on his feet again. Von was standing between him and me, her hands out as if she were trying to hold him back.

"Stop it," she said.

Dennis shoved her out of the line of fire.

He saw me kneeling behind the boxes.

I sighted on the center of his chest.

He brought his gun up.

At the last possible moment, I shifted my aim slightly over and up.

I shot him low in the shoulder.

Dennis flew backward against the wall and slowly slid to the floor as if he were tired and wanted to sit down.

A streak of blood pouring from his back followed him all the way to the floor.

Von screamed, rushed to his side, and cradled his head against her breast. She began weeping, calling his name, and generally making a racket.

"Is he dead?" Herzog asked.

I watched him emerge from the kitchen, his gun in one hand, his other hand pressed against the side of his skull. Blood seeped between his fingers and trickled down his wrist. I knew instantly what had happened. Dennis saw me parking in front of the house. Instead of hiding in one of the rooms as expected, he went through the back door with the idea of rounding the house and ambushing me from behind, which is exactly what he had done. Along the way he met Herzog, whom he must have taken by surprise. I could picture him wiping Herzog across his skull with his gun, knocking him unconscious, giving him a concussion.

"You're late," I said. "I should dock your salary."

"Don't tell Chopper," Herzog said.

I slowly rose to my feet and approached Von and Dennis on unsteady legs. My head was spinning, and it took a lot of effort to keep from vomiting. The gun had slipped from Dennis's grasp. It was a six-shot Iver Johnson pocket pistol—a .25 caliber. I put my foot on it and slid it backward across the floor until it hit a stack of boxes.

"You—you shot me," Dennis said.

His face was pale and his breathing erratic.

"Sorry 'bout that," I said.

I leaned forward, using the wall for support, and gave his wound a quick examination. The bullet had gone through the fleshy part of his shoulder just above his armpit. I didn't think it had hit bone, yet that didn't mean he was going to play quarterback for the Vikings anytime soon, although he couldn't have been any worse than who was playing.

"I think you'll live," I said.

Von looked up at me, a dark, sorrowful expression clouding her lovely face.

"It was a good plan," I told her. "Such a good plan. The plan would have worked. But you got greedy. Wanted it all. It's an old story. As old as time. As old as rhyme."

I realized then that I was feeling light-headed and wasn't exactly sure of what I was saying. I put my gun in my jacket pocket and moved toward Herzog. He was slumped against the wall, still cradling his head.

"How's it going?" I asked.

He looked at me as if I had asked for the Colonel's secret recipe of eleven herbs and spices.

"As much as you hate 'em, Herzy," I said, "I'm calling the police."

"Uh-huh," he said.

I reached into the pocket of my jeans for my cell phone.

I didn't see her until she spoke.

"You're not getting away with this," she said.

When I turned my back, Von had quickly crawled across the floor and retrieved the Iver Johnson. She was standing now, one eye closed, the other sighting down the barrel of the gun. The gun was pointed at me.

"C'mon," I said.

"If you had just done what you were told, none of this would have happened," she said. "You ruined everything."

She stepped toward me, the Iver Johnson leading the way. I glanced at Herzog, but he didn't seem to notice what was happening.

"Stop," I shouted.

"Huh?" Herzog said.

No, wait, I didn't shout it. I was going to, but . . . The voice came from my left. I looked for it and found Heavenly Petryk standing in the front doorway, her body twisted into a serviceable shooting stance, both hands gripping a compact Smith & Wesson 9 mm. She was pointing it at Von.

"Drop the gun, Von," Heavenly said. "I mean it. Drop the gun. I'll blow your brains out. Von. Drop the gun."

Von dropped the gun at my feet. I kicked it away and turned toward Heavenly. She was smiling her luminous smile.

"No," I said.

"Hi, McKenzie," she said. "Glad to see me?"

"Oh, hell no."

"I told you I knew who stole the Lily."

"Sonuvabitch."

Herzog and I stood outside El Cid's tavern. The cold seemed to be affecting him more than it had before, and for the seventh or eighth time that night I said we should get him to a hospital, and for the seventh or eighth time he said, "Fuck no," adding that only a pussy would go to the hospital for a simple bump on the head. I asked if he meant me, and he said he did.

"Are you sure you're up for this?" I asked.

"Are you going to pay the rest of my money when we done?"

"Yes, sir."

"Let's go."

"Yes, sir."

The Burnsville Police Department had kept us answering questions for several hours. We might still be answering them if not for the intervention of Lieutenant Rask. The fact that we had cornered his cop killer seemed to go a long way with him—and the Burnsville cops, too, for that matter—especially after a preliminary ballistic examination confirmed that the Iver Johnson had indeed fired the bullets that killed both Scott Noehring and Patrick Tarpley. Determining whether Dennis or Von was the shooter was a problem to be solved later. In fact, Rask was so thrilled, he even forgave Heavenly for lying to him. He had asked that we refrain from telling anyone what happened until after the press conference the next morning, but you know how the news media is. Somehow Kelly Bressandes learned of the break in the case and broadcast the information during the 10:00 P.M. newscast. The other stations quickly picked it up, and by the time Leno and Letterman came on, everyone who was paying attention knew that the hero cop's killers had been apprehended and had confessed. The confessed part was a fabrication on the part of Kelly's unidentified source, but what the hell. Soon after, I received a call from El Cid. Because of the fortuitous change in circumstances, he told me, he would be delighted to take the Jade Lily off my hands at the earliest opportunity. I asked him if now was a good time, and he said that it was.

"Here we go," I said, and Herzog opened the door to Cid's bar.

We stepped inside, me first. The bar was empty—it was long past closing time. Only Cid and his bodyguard were there. They were both standing in the center of the room.

A table was between them. There were two medium-sized suitcases on top of the table.

"I don't see the Lily," Cid said.

"I don't see the money."

Cid and the bodyguard opened the suitcases and stepped back. Cid watched me as I approached. The bodyguard watched Herzog, who remained at the door looking as menacing as ever, despite the immense headache I knew he was experiencing. I took a bundle of cash out of the suitcase and thumbed through the bills. The cash was still wrapped in the same paper sleeves that the insurance company had used. I carefully set the bundle back into the suitcase.

"Where's the Lily?" Cid asked.

I made a show of patting my pockets like I had forgotten something.

"Well?" Cid said.

"Two minutes."

I walked back to the door. Herzog opened it for me. We stepped outside, closing the door behind us. The clean, clear winter air had made the full moon seem almost near enough to touch. The moonlight reflected off the weapons held by members of the Minneapolis Police Department's Special Weapons and Tactics team that had fanned out on both sides of the door. Lieutenant Rask was standing with them, wearing an MPD windbreaker over his winter coat.

"He's all yours," I said.

Rask spoke into a handheld radio, and the cops rushed inside the bar. Herzog and I crossed the street and jumped into the Jeep Cherokee. We drove off before anyone came out of the bar. I never did learn the name of the place.

SEVENTEEN

The air was awfully warm and stale by the time I limped into the windowless conference room on the second floor of the City of Lakes Art Museum the next morning, heated no doubt by the thirteen bodies I found there. Perrin Stewart was sitting at the head of the long table as she had been the first time we met. Randolph Fiegen, Derek Anderson, and the other four members of the executive board of trustees had arranged themselves on the far side. Mr. Donatucci, Branko Pozderac, and Jonathan Hemsted were on Perrin's right; India Cooper, Jeremy Gillard, and Heavenly Petryk were on her left. Only Heavenly was smiling, but then she had an idea of what was coming.

"Good morning," I said. "Thank you all for being here."

I stepped around the table to the side Heavenly was on. A large aluminum, foam-filled carrying case had been pushed up against the wall behind her chair.

"You should sit down before you fall down," Anderson said.

He had a point. My sprained ankle had not improved much;

nor had my broken collarbone, which was held in place by the shoulder immobilizer again. What's more, I had cut myself shaving—you try it with one hand—and the addition of a bandage to the bruises, cuts, and scrapes made my face look like the "before" photo in an ad for plastic surgery. Still, I was in no mood to listen to his BS.

"Shut up, Derek," I said.

"You don't talk to me that way."

I found Fiegen. His expression was fretful, and when he wasn't fingering the folder in front of him, he was pressing and patting his red-orange hair. I gestured at him with my chin.

"Shut up, Derek," he said.

Derek glared at him with an expression of amazement, like a man who had just learned that his most trusted comrade-in-arms had switched sides. I was less impressed. Fiegen and I had spent a great deal of time talking on the phone. If he was indeed going to keep his end of the bargain as promised, this was going to be a lot of fun. In fact, I said as much out loud.

"This is going to be fun," I said. "Like those old *Thin Man* movies on TCM with William Powell and Myrna Loy."

"Which one are you?" Heavenly asked.

"Who is this woman?" one of the trustees asked. "What is her position here?"

"I'll get to that," I said.

I maneuvered around the room until I was standing beneath the painting of primary colors splashed on the canvas that Donatucci had found so fascinating earlier.

"First of all, Von Tarpley and her accomplice have been arrested for the murder of Patrick Tarpley and Lieutenant Scott Noehring of the Minneapolis Police Department."

I glanced at India while I spoke. She was dressed as if she

had been called from her bed by some dire emergency and hadn't had time to put herself together yet. Her face was pale despite her dark complexion. She was sitting with her hands folded in front of her, her eyes fixed on her hands.

"The one million two hundred seventy thousand dollars designated by the Midwest Farmers Insurance Group to ransom the Jade Lily has been recovered. Mr. Donatucci?"

"The money is being held by the Minneapolis Police Department as evidence," Donatucci said. "Following legal proceedings, it will be returned to us."

"What about the Lily?" Anderson asked. "Your job was to recover the Jade Lily, remember? Not solve some damn crime."

"You know what, screw it," I said. "Let's deal with you first."

I circled the table until I could look Anderson in the eye.

"Everybody, Derek here is your leak," I said. "He's the one who has been feeding information to Kelly Bressandes and other members of the media despite the board's desire to maintain a low profile—"

Anderson rose to his feet. "That's a lie," he said.

"Bressandes is downstairs with a camera crew. We could ask her. No? Where was I? He also had an affair with Von Tarpley and no doubt fed her important information while she was involved with her husband in planning the theft—"

"No, no, no," Anderson chanted.

I pointed at Heavenly. "Mr. Anderson was also actively involved in helping this woman embarrass the museum." I turned to face Perrin Stewart. "Among other things, she's the blond bimbo that Anderson wanted to replace you with. Aren't you, Heavenly?"

"Well, I'm blond," she said.

"Are you an art major?"

"Nope."

"Do you have any background in museum science?"

"Not at all."

"Wait a minute," Anderson said.

"Why were you involved with Mr. Anderson?" I asked.

"He was helping me take possession of the Jade Lily and return it to Tatjana Durakovic, who, by the way, is the object's rightful owner. Isn't that correct, Jeremy?"

Gillard waved his hand slightly. "Eh," he said.

"Wait a minute," Anderson said. "That's crazy."

"He was hoping to use the controversy surrounding the actual ownership of the Lily as grounds for seeking the dismissal of Ms. Stewart," Heavenly said. "Later, after it was stolen, he gave me information concerning Tarpley, your plans for buying back the Lily, and McKenzie's involvement, with the understanding that I would use it to steal the Lily from the thieves." She held her thumb and index finger an inch apart and peered through the opening. "I was this close."

"Do you want Ms. Stewart's position?" I asked.

"I'm hardly qualified."

"But you told me—" Anderson began.

"Exactly what you wanted to hear," Heavenly finished.

"Mr. Fiegen," I said.

Fiegen cleared his throat. "This matter was brought to our attention earlier," he said. "The other members of the board and I met in closed session, and it was agreed that Mr. Anderson should be dismissed immediately from the executive board of trustees and that he no longer be allowed to participate in any activities involving the City of Lakes Art Museum."

"You can't do that," Anderson insisted.

"All in favor?" Perrin said, and five hands were raised. "Opposed?"

"You can't do that," Anderson repeated.

"Get out," Perrin said. She was smiling when she said it. "Don't come back."

"This is bullshit," Anderson said.

"Derek, my advice—leave quietly," I said, "because even in my diminished state I'd be happy as hell to kick your ass."

Anderson paused for a moment, searched the room for an ally, found none, announced, "This isn't over yet," and left the room, slamming the door behind him.

"I thought he'd never leave," I said.

Mr. Donatucci grinned and shook his head.

We're having some fun now, my inner voice said.

Pozderac started beating on the top of the conference room table. His face was red, and the muscles in his neck were strained—I thought I could detect a few small bruises around his throat.

"Where is Lily?" he shouted. "I want Lily."

Hemsted tried to hush him, but Pozderac would not be hushed.

"Give it to me," he said.

"Yeah, yeah, yeah," I said. "Keep it in your pants, willya, pal?"

"I hate you," he said.

Yeah, that'll keep me awake at night, my inner voice said.

I turned toward Fiegen.

"Mr. Fiegen, do you have anything more to say?"

He gave his hair a couple of pats and looked at his fellow trustees, who all were suddenly as attentive as I had seen them.

"We are delighted that the ransom money has been recovered," he said.

"Where is Lily?" Pozderac asked.

Fiegen flashed him a look then that made me take a step

backward. Did I say the room was hot? For a moment, it felt very chilly indeed. Pozderac, that mass-murdering piece of dog crap, actually looked away.

Are you sure you want to mess with this guy? my inner voice asked.

"Your firm no longer has any claims on the City of Lakes Art Museum, Mr. Donatucci, is that not true?" Fiegen asked.

"It is true."

"We no longer have any claims on you, either. This document"—Fiegen opened his folder and lifted the top sheet—"clearly states that the City of Lakes Art Museum will make no claim against the Midwest Farmers Insurance Group involving the Jade Lily now or in the future."

Gillard leaned forward in his chair. "What about me?" he asked.

"Jer," I said.

I put a finger to my lips, the universal sign for silence. He leaned back in his chair. I took the sheet from Fiegen, limped over to Donatucci, and handed it to him.

"Thank you," Donatucci said.

"Next . . ." Fiegen lifted the second sheet on the pile. "Ms. Stewart, the board of trustees has unanimously agreed to tender you a five-year extension on your current contract with the hope that you will remain executive director of the City of Lakes Art Museum. I am sure you will find the salary and benefits to be quite acceptable."

Again, I took the paper from Fiegen and walked it around the table. Perrin's expression flicked back and forth between delight and confusion. India looked at her friend. A smile formed on her lips; then it went away and she returned her gaze to her folded hands. I set the sheet of paper in front of Perrin.

"McKenzie, did you do this?" she asked.

I whispered my reply. "Take the job, do the job, be happy—don't let what happens next ruin it for you."

"What happens next?" she asked.

"Mr. Gillard," Fiegen said.

"Hey, don't mind me," Gillard said. "I love a song and dance as much as the next guy."

I moved behind Gillard. Fiegen gave him a cold stare. Gillard looked from Fiegen back over his shoulder at me.

"What?" he said.

Fiegen picked up a check.

"I will pay you three-point-eight million for the Jade Lily." He said it like he was in no mood to haggle.

Gillard looked at me again. "You got it back?" he asked.

"Take the money," I said.

Gillard returned his gaze to Fiegen. "I don't know," he said.

"What don't you know?" Fiegen asked.

"Three-point-eight million . . ."

I idiot-slapped Gillard above his right ear with a lot more force than was necessary.

"Okay, okay," Gillard said. He massaged the side of his head. "Fine. I'll take it. Geez."

The check was passed to him. Gillard kissed it, folded it, and stuffed it in his shirt pocket. "Drinks are on me," he said.

He started to rise from his chair, but I pushed him back down.

"Stay," I said. "We're not finished yet."

Fiegen closed the folder in front of him. "McKenzie, I believe that concludes my part of the festivities," he said.

"So it does," I told him. "Heavenly?"

Heavenly left her chair, picked up the aluminum case, and brought it around the table. She set it in front of Branko

Pozderac. Pozderac hugged it to his chest like a Christmas gift he wanted to savor before opening. Hemsted's eyes flicked from the case to me to Fiegen and back to the case as if he were sure there was something terribly wrong, only he couldn't figure out what. Pozderac opened the case. The Jade Lily was inside, nestled in the gray foam bed. Even under the indifferent overhead lights it was exquisite. Everyone in the room stood to take a good look at it except for India and Gillard. Pozderac ran his fingers gently over the Lily's flowers and stems. He spoke several words slowly in the Bosnian language. He looked from the Lily to Hemsted. Hemsted nodded. Pozderac abruptly closed the case.

"It is done," he said.

He turned to face Fiegen. He did not offer his hand, and Fiegen did not offer his.

"It is done," the Bosnian repeated.

"Yes," Fiegen said.

"We go."

Pozderac picked up the case, and he and Hemsted left the room.

"There goes one happy mass murderer," Heavenly said.

"I don't understand," Perrin said. "Mr. Fiegen, what did you just do?"

"I did what was best for the museum," he said.

"Actually, he did what was best for Minnesota Disposal and Recycling," I said. "The museum will come out much further ahead than he will, though."

"You know nothing of big business," Fiegen said.

"Very true. I wouldn't be counting those euros just yet, though. See, I do know a little something about human nature, and there's no telling what Branko is going to do once he discovers that the Jade Lily is a phony."

I turned my eyes on India and Gillard when I spoke. They both slumped in their chairs like inflatable dolls that had been pricked with a pin. It occurred to me that up until that exact moment, they thought they had gotten away with it.

"What are you talking about?" Fiegen asked.

"The Jade Lily—it's a fake, a fraud, a forgery."

"That's impossible," Perrin said. "It was authenticated. We had provenance. Cooper? Cooper?"

Perrin was looking directly at her friend, but her friend wouldn't look at her.

"Dennis was driving your car," I said. "I was hoping you didn't know he was in on the theft. That was just wishful thinking on my part, wasn't it?"

India refused to answer.

"Start talking, McKenzie," Fiegen said. "Talk fast."

"The Lily is a fake," I said. "A forgery committed by a Frenchman named Dr. Arnaud Fornier, who is now doing time for art fraud. He sold it to Mr. Leo Gillard, Jeremy's father. Mr. Gillard didn't know it was a forgery, and neither did Jeremy until India Cooper told him—isn't that right, India?"

She didn't say if it was or wasn't.

"Cooper?" Perrin said. "Is it true?"

She didn't answer.

"I don't know why India didn't tell her friend Perrin," I said. "She did tell Jeremy. I know because India said she had never met Gillard before, yet the other day when we were in the workroom together it was clear that he had met her. Gillard could have taken the Lily back once he realized it was a fraud, but because of the lending agreement, he'd have to have a good reason, and he didn't want to give a reason. The Lily represented half of Gillard's net worth. He told me that he could get by on eight million dollars, but four—I'm guessing not so much. What to do? Intact, the Lily was relatively worthless, but if it was stolen or destroyed . . . I'm guessing Gillard offered India a share if she helped him steal the Lily from the museum. 'Course, neither of them had experience in this sort of thing, so they needed help. Does anyone want to explain how you involved Patrick Tarpley in your plan?"

Neither India nor Gillard replied.

"Perhaps you'll tell us someday," I said. "In any case, Tarpley warmed to the idea for reasons involving his wife and a crooked cop. It was an easy decision to make because it happened before, didn't it? That was why the security system was upgraded six months ago, upgraded a lousy eighteen months after it was originally installed." I pointed a finger at Mr. Donatucci. "Something was stolen from the museum and you bought it back, didn't you?"

"I'm not at liberty to say," Donatucci said.

"Sure. Anyway, Tarpley decided to go after the Lily. He was a smart man. He knew that getting the Lily out of the museum was the hard part. He wore the mask so he could pretend he was conducting a security drill in case someone stopped him. If that didn't work or if he was caught later, he knew that since the Lily was not the priceless artifact it was advertised to be, he could plead down to a gross misdemeanor. Once he was out of the building, Tarpley was home free. Offering to sell the Lily back was the key. He knew that the museum—and the insurance company—would not only agree to his terms, which weren't particularly onerous, you would work real hard to keep the theft a secret from both the cops and the public—protecting your reputation, you told me, remember? You claim to be a businessman, Fiegen. How would you rate the risk-reward of Tarpley's enterprise?"

Fiegen didn't say.

"The reason I was involved—they picked me to act as a go-between because I was reliable and because I was known to the insurance company as being reliable. See, Tarpley and his crew had no intention of returning the Lily. Instead, they had planned from the very beginning to destroy it—once I had authenticated it, of course—knowing the insurance company would accept my word that it was real. That way Tarpley would get the ransom money from my hand. Gillard would get the insurance settlement. And their accomplices, specifically India, would be protected from charges of fraud. In fact, just about everyone would be happy once the Lily was blown sky-high except the insurance company, and who was going to cry crocodile tears for you?"

"Not many," Donatucci said.

"It was a good plan," I said. "The plan would have worked. Tarpley's only mistake was in picking his crew. His wife. India's brother. He thought they were trustworthy. They should have been. They were family, for God's sake. 'Course, the way Von wept over Dennis, well, maybe it was a crime of passion when she shot her husband, after all. By the way, I'm sorry I shot him, India—Dennis, I mean. I wouldn't have if he hadn't tried to shoot me first. I hope he's all right."

"He'll never turn against me, you know," India said.

"A brother's love. Touching."

"It's not true," Perrin said. "It can't possibly be true. India? How could you, India?"

She's using India's first name instead of her last, my inner voice said. *I guess they're not friends anymore.*

"I knew how important the exhibit was to you," India said. "Having the Lily stolen was better than having it revealed that you contracted to exhibit a fake."

"That sounds nice," I said. "Still . . ."

"It's true," India insisted.

"You were in for a third of the ransom once Tarpley was killed. You, Dennis, and Von—three bags containing approximately four hundred and thirty thousand dollars each. How much does a curator make in a year working for a small midwestern museum? Listen, Lieutenant Rask of the Minneapolis Police Department is waiting outside. He did me a big favor by letting me pretend to be Philo Vance for a while. Tell him whatever you like."

"The police are outside?" Fiegen asked.

"Yes," I said. "Also, Special Agent Brian Wilson of the Federal Bureau of Investigation. He should be taking Pozderac and Hemsted into custody even as we speak. No doubt Branko will scream diplomatic immunity. We'll see how that works out for him. Hemsted, on the other hand, does not enjoy that privilege. His testimony might be more easily coerced. As for you . . ."

"I will not be arrested."

"No?"

"I have committed no crime."

"Bribing a foreign national isn't a crime?"

"It was not a bribe. The Jade Lily was a gift, a copy of a priceless artifact no more valuable than tickets to the opera."

"I like it," I said. "I'd hang on to that defense if I were you."

The room emptied soon after Fiegen dashed for the door in search of his co-conspirators. I sat down next to Mr. Donatucci. Heavenly sat across the table from us.

"Well, sir, is this what you had in mind when you came to my house last week?" I asked.

"Almost exactly."

"Sure."

Donatucci removed a check from his inside pocket and set it on the table in front of me.

"One hundred and twenty-seven thousand dollars made out to cash as requested," he said.

"Thank you."

"Thank you, Batman."

"I wish you wouldn't call me that."

Donatucci patted my shoulder and left the room. I glanced at the check, set my hand on top of it, and slid it across the table to Heavenly.

"It's not quite the payout you were hoping for," I said.

She took the check and put it in her bag.

"Just as long as we come out ahead, that's the main thing," she said.

"Thank you for saving my life."

"My pleasure. McKenzie?"

"Hmm?"

"How did you know the Jade Lily was a fake?"

"They told me I had ten seconds to live. If they had wanted to kill me, they wouldn't have called. So why did they call? They wanted me out of the room so they could blow up the Lily and I would be around to tell the tale. Why would they want to do that, blow up the Lily? Because they hated it so much? Because they didn't want anyone else to own it? It's kind of obvious once you think about it. After that, everything fell into place."

"But when did you figure it out?"

"While I was holding the telephone in the motel room just before the bomb went off."

"You're the master of intuitive thinking."

"It's a curse."

JUST SO YOU KNOW

In hindsight, it probably would have been better all around if I had allowed them to blow up the Jade Lily in that damn motel room instead of risking my life to save it.

First of all, Von Tarpley and Dennis Cooper both pled guilty to killing Patrick Tarpley and Lieutenant Scott Noehring. Normally, you shoot a cop they drop you in a hole and you never get to see the sun again, but they cut a deal, Von and Dennis did. They gave up their right to a jury trial—during which they would have presented irrefutable evidence of Noehring's many dastardly deeds—in exchange for the possibility of parole hearings after seventeen years. They also managed to swap the bomb charges for the names and whereabouts of the people who sold them the explosives (I guess making a bomb is worse than exploding a bomb).

That was it as far as the courts were concerned. No one—including India Cooper—was ever charged with the theft of the Jade Lily, largely because both the museum and Jeremy Gillard refused to press charges and the insurance company claimed it had not been defrauded. I got a kick out of that—Gillard refusing to press charges against himself. There was plenty of talk about conspiracy to do this and conspiracy to do that, only nothing came of it.

The original Lily, by the way, has yet to resurface despite Tatjana Durakovic's tireless efforts to locate it.

Branko Pozderac was granted diplomatic immunity and sent home, although his government removed him from the Foreign Investment Promotion Agency. Jonathan Hemsted was fired by the State Department in the morning and hired by Minnesota Disposal and Recycling in the afternoon to work as a liaison between the company and the governments of Bosnia and Herzegovina, Croatia, Serbia, and Montenegro—yes, Fiegen got his garbage and wastewater cleaning contracts. Big surprise. Plus, any plans to charge Fiegen under the antibribery provisions of the Foreign Corrupt Practices Act were discarded when India, testifying on Fiegen's behalf, argued that while it was an inspired facsimile of the original, the Jade Lily held little monetary value and therefore could hardly constitute a bribe.

Hell, even El Cid skated. All charges against him were dropped at just about the same time various joint task forces conducted a half-dozen large-scale gun and drug raids across the Twin Cities. Apparently Cid was correct when he said he could always make a deal with the police.

As for Jeremy Gillard—Fiegen never did cancel the check as I thought he would. When the feds were trying to jam him up on the bribery beef, they suggested that paying Gillard $3.8 million for a "worthless knickknack, isn't that what you called it, sir?" was awfully excessive. Fiegen told them that how he spent his own money was none of their damn business.

Months later, long after everything had settled down, I checked out a few exhibits at the City of Lakes Art Museum. Perrin Stewart told me that she'd had no choice but to fire India and had not seen her since, but that a mutual friend told her that Gillard had given India some of Fiegen's money—she didn't know how much—and took her to Las Vegas. Personally, I hope they had a wonderful time.